THE LIGHTS

UNRESOLVED - BOOK 1

MICHELLE D. BAILLARGEON

For Bob, my most favorite person in the world. Thank you for always knowing the right thing to say to me, even when it's not necessarily what I want to hear. You know you love me.

CHAPTER ONE

It was in the late afternoon, deep in the woods, on a trail high on the Mogollon Rim when Aggie paused to rearranged her camera bag. She took the strap from her right shoulder and placed it over her head onto her left shoulder and then pushed the bag behind her. With her quickened pace, it would be more comfortable there and not bang against her hip like it'd been doing.

Before continuing, she took in the scene once more, slowly making a circle as she scanned the forest around her. She was the only one here. That's what her eyes and ears told her. Again. But, the little hairs on the back of her neck and the tiny goosebumps on her arms said differently.

This was not Aggie's first trip into these woods, but this was the first time she'd been so creeped out. She couldn't shake the feeling of being watched. She'd already been up here for quite a while when it began. It hadn't even started until she was halfway across the clearing. When it finally hit her, it hit hard.

This wasn't a figment of her imagination, but that didn't stop her from trying to convince herself that it was. That had worked, but only for a short time. The sensation came back and it stayed. Now, it had a death grip on the pit of her stomach. She didn't like it one bit. She considered that maybe it was an animal, or another hiker. Every time she looked around, she expected to see someone, or something, looking back at her. But, each time, nothing stared back. Her head had been on a swivel ever since.

Finally, Aggie decided to let whatever was out there have the woods to themselves. She told herself she'd been heading home anyway. If her pace quickened as she left the clearing, well there was no one there to tease her about it. Was there?

THE OBSERVER WATCHED THE FALLEN HIKER FROM THE CENTER OF THE trail, she had been hurrying down path and looking behind her at the same time, when she'd lost her footing. Now, the hiker was unconscious in the ditch. This had not been their intent, no harm was meant.

They had been trailing her all day, trying to get her attention. Nobody comes up here anymore, maybe this hiker could help? They had to try, there was no one else. When the hiker turned to leave, it appeared they had only succeeded in driving her away. Their hopes were dashed. There was no recognition, no acknowledgement. Nothing.

But now, something had changed. Something was different. Even though the hiker was passed out, the observer was finally communicating with her. They sure of it, they could feel it. There was hope after all. And hopefully, the hiker would awaken soon.

CHAPTER TWO

IT WAS EVEN LATER IN THE AFTERNOON, ON THAT SAME TRAIL HIGH ON the Mogollon Rim, when Aggie came to. She was sprawled out on her left side and her head had come to rest on a sharp-edged rock. Moving at a slow pace, she reached up and pushed the rock out from under her head. Wincing at the pain from her forehead, she gasped at the sight of her blood on the rock. Not so much from the sight of the blood itself, but because of the sheer amount. Little puddles of her blood had formed in some of the depressions on the surface of the rock and more had dripped over the sides. A wave of dizziness struck her and twinkling stars passed before her eyes, threatening to knock her out again.

She closed her eyes and rested her head on her left arm until she felt better. As the fog started to clear, she tried to recollect how she'd ended up in this ditch. She remembered getting a terrible case of the creeps and deciding to hike home. But beyond that, she couldn't quite remember what had tripped her up. She hated to admit to herself that she'd been spooked and she was a little embarrassed by it. Maybe, in her haste to leave, she stepped in a hole she didn't see or caught her foot on a branch? She must have lost her balance and gone ass over tea kettle on the edge of the trail. She shrugged, no great mystery there.

She didn't consider herself a clumsy person overall. She would admit that she tended to stumble or catch a foot on things other people seemed to miss. Her friend Rider joked that she could trip on a pocket of air. Usually, if she did fall, she was able to bounce right back up, brush herself off and keep going.

This time was different and it concerned her. She'd never knocked herself out before. Her head was killing her. She must have done quite number on it to have passed out. Another thought worried her: she hadn't been paying attention to the time, so there was no way of telling how long she'd been out.

Aggie lifted her head slowly and gently. *OK, good. No more stars.* She used her right hand to explore her forehead, looking for the source of the pain. She felt a jagged cut above the corner of her left eye. When she pulled her hand away, it was damp and sticky with blood. *Great.* Resting her head on her arm had created pressure on the wound, which had almost stopped the bleeding. But now, the cut was again producing a pretty good trickle of blood and it was beginning to drip into her eye. She pressed the back of her hand against the cut. It was wet, sticky and it hurt. *I guess I'm lucky, I could've put my eye out.*

Aggie gave herself a quick smile and continued to evaluate herself. She found that her hands and arms seemed to be OK, just a few scratches and bruises. However, her left ankle was throbbing and she had a headache that wouldn't quit.

After her brief self-exam, she rolled over and was overcome by another wave of dizziness. And more shooting stars. *Yikes! Slower. Must. Move. Slower.* She returned to her original position, shut her eyes and took deep, calming breaths until the wave passed. Finally, she was able to sit up without too much trouble or any more twinkling stars. *Whew.*

Without thinking, Aggie had let go of her forehead to get into a sitting position. The cut started bleeding once more. A slow, steady drip was making a relentless path to her eye. She realized she had to get serious about stopping it before she did anything else. She searched her camera bag and was able to produce a few ratty old tissues. Luckily, the bag and her camera had escaped any harm. The bag was still strapped cross-body over her shoulders and slung behind her, keeping it out of harm's way.

She pressed the tissues gingerly but firmly against her cut. It soon became clear that the meager tissues were not the right tool for the job. Too old and thin, they became saturated and useless in no time. *God only knows how long they've been in there.* Aggie stopped for moment and looked around at her limited resources. There was nothing of use left in the camera bag and she was sitting in a ditch in the woods.

"Got it."

She pulled her T-shirt off and brushed off the dirt and leaves as best as she could. She looked it over for any clean spots and couldn't find any that passed inspection. This wouldn't work after all. She had to stop the bleeding, but she didn't want an infection.

After a few moments, with her T-shirt in her lap and wheels turning in her mind, she came up with an odd, but even better idea. She reached into the left hand side of her bra to remove her cell phone and put it away (she'd stuck it there out of habit). She could hear the ring better there than if it was in the pocket of her shorts. Her heart sank at the sight of it.

"Crap!"

If she ended up needing to call someone for help, that option was gone now. There was a large crack in the case and it wouldn't power up. It was a gonner. Big time.

"So much for that." She stuffed the broken phone into one of the camera bag's pockets, and continued on with her original idea.

Aggie took off her bra and put her T-Shirt back on. The T-shirt had protected her bra from the dirt and leaves and was, for the most part, pretty clean. *And bonus, DD cups meant there was plenty of material to sop up the blood. Thank you very much.* She folded it up and pressed one of the cups against her cut, patiently waiting for the bleeding to stop.

Finally, when the bleeding seemed to be under control, she set the sad, bloodied bra in her lap. There were no Band-Aids up here, so she'd have to remember not to keep poking at her cut. With luck, it wouldn't start bleeding again. If it did, she was going to have to tie her bra around her head like a bandage. *That would be attractive.*

By the time she finished, specs of dried blood covered everything: her arm, forehead, the side of her face, T-shirt and bra, and hands. She imagined that between the bruises and the blood, she was quite a sight.

Now that she had taken care of her forehead, she turned her attention to her left ankle. It was throbbing and was beginning to swell. Any movement was painful enough to keep her from trying to stand, so she tried her best not to move it.

She could wiggle her toes and bend her knee. *So that's good, anyway.* She smiled and remembered what her Dad told her as a kid anytime she'd hurt herself. He'd say, "if you can wiggle it, it's not broken." The ankle wasn't broken then, because she could wiggle it; but wiggling it hurt. A lot. She wasn't going anywhere if her ankle had anything to say about it.

It seemed like the only thing that made it through the fall in one piece was her camera.

The afternoon continued to pass, as it does, and the sun was now low in the sky. Aggie made several attempts to put weight on her left foot but her ankle wasn't having any part of it. She finally had to resign herself to the fact that she wasn't going anywhere tonight. There was no way for her to hike down the trail through the woods and all the way back to her house. Not with her ankle in this condition and with daylight fading fast.

As she sat there, a memory from earlier unexpectedly returned to her. It unnerved her and she quickly looked around. She waited, listened, and breathed a sigh of relief. *Nothing there.* Her earlier case of the creeps was gone, but not forgotten. *Great. Especially if I have to stay here all night.* Luckily, she had stuffed a few protein bars into her camera bag and she still had a bit of water.

The water! She had been holding a half empty bottle of water when she went down. *Where did it go?* It took her a few minutes to locate it, but it was close. It had landed several feet away from her off the trail, partly hidden by a low bush. She grabbed a nearby downed branch and, after a few tries, was able to retrieve it.

"Ok. Good." She had a few supplies with her. She would be fine in the woods overnight. There's nothing out here. She'd be fine. She repeated it a few times as she tried to convince herself.

Aggie took a small sip of water then wet a small, clean section of her bra. She used the damp material to clean away some of the patches of dried blood from her face, avoiding the cut area. After that, she tried to clean the dirtiest patches the best she could with the damp bra. There was still a few traces of grime and dried blood here and there, but she had gotten the bulk of it. She saved the rest of her water to drink.

She folded up her bra and wedged it into one of the pockets in the camera bag. She was never going to be able to get all the blood out of it, but she didn't want to leave it behind, either. She never considered littering, but, it was funny to imagine a random hiker finding it among the bushes.

Aggie finally decided that, one way or another, she had to at least get up out of the ditch. It was awkward, and she was at an uncomfortable angle. She discovered that crawling didn't hurt too much, as long as she didn't drag her foot. She picked out a large tree with a clearing at its base that was also close to the trail and worked her way over to it.

Aggie shook her head. *What a sight I must be, I'm beat up, bloody and crawling like a baby.*

Slightly winded from her trip up and out of the ditch, she leaned back against the tree and caught her breath. Then, she gently propped her ankle up on her camera bag. *Not bad at all.* Before she knew it, and almost against her will, she'd fallen asleep. She'd only meant to rest a bit and then she would try to come up with a plan to get out of the woods. Her body had other ideas.

CHAPTER THREE

AGGIE AWOKE FROM HER NAP WITH A START AND A GASP. HER HEART beat rapidly in her chest, blood pounded in her ears, her left hand clenched into a fist. Something in her dream had upset her, but she couldn't remember what it was. It took a second or two to calm herself down. She took a few deep breaths and unclenched her left hand, shaking it until the pins and needles were gone.

Now fully awake, the fragments of the dream were dissolving into the night air; but they disappeared much slower than they usually did. Excited, she realized that she could still remember parts of the dream, which wasn't normally the case. She never remembered her dreams. She'd been doing exercises designed to help her remember her dreams, but 'til now they hadn't been very helpful.

Aggie smiled to herself for remembering her exercises. She focused on the fading memory of the dream and was able to make out an impression of a woman reaching out to her. The woman had been cold and wet and standing in darkness.

Well, that's not very scary. She wondered what else had happened in the dream to cause her to awaken so upset. She tried to remember more of the dream but couldn't. Her mind reached out for more details, fragments, anything. They were there - somewhere in the back of her mind, tickling her subconscious, but she couldn't quite make them out. At least it was something, way more than she usually was able to remember - which was nothing.

That train of thought became derailed as she noticed her surroundings; she was still in the woods. Her heart sank a little as the realization set in. She looked around and up at the sky, guessing it had been dark for about an hour. The moon was low in the sky yet so the branches and leaves overhead obscured most of the moonlight.

A small trickle of moonlight had made its way through the canopy and it glinted off the trees and the fallen leaves carpeting the forest floor. She admired the quality of the soft light among the dark shapes and wondered if she could do it justice in a photograph. The wheels in her mind began to turn, if she could fashion a poor man's tripod from something in here in the woods, and if she could keep the camera steady enough for a long exposure, it might come out OK.

As Aggie looked left down the trail (towards home) she felt a few drops of rain on her exposed skin. *Great, now it's going to rain?* She turned and looked to her right, the poor man's tripod was immediately forgotten. There, the trail was lit with a soft red glow.

The source of the glow was a red light hovering above the trail. *No, wait, there are two lights.* They were side by side and moved together. Aggie's breath caught in her throat and she shrunk back against the tree. Goosebumps cropped up on her arms and she tracked the translucent red orbs the way a mouse watches an owl. The lights moved silently away from her. *Good, keep going.*

She pushed herself back with her good leg, aiming to put even more distance between her and them. The tree she was leaning against stopped her. Thwarted in her pitiful and hasty attempt at hiding, she held her breath and froze instead. Aggie shivered at the icy chill running through her veins and tried her best to remain unseen. She was sure that, at any moment, they would notice her and then double-time it back to her. *Then what?* She didn't know. She was pretty sure she didn't want to find out either. As she watched, the lights travelled uneventfully out of sight, the red glow dimmed and then disappeared completely.

When she felt they were truly gone, Aggie exhaled and her breath appeared as a small wispy cloud. She clutched her arms around herself to banish any remaining goosebumps. Her mind and heart were both racing. *Now would be a great time to head home, dark or not, rain or not.* She tested her ankle to see if it was possible. Pain shot up her leg to her hip and out to her toes. *Nope.* She held her hand out in front of her. *No more drizzle, that's one good thing anyway.*

Her brain tried on one idea after another to see which one would best describe what she had just seen. Nothing logical came to mind. Could UFOs be that small? And really, what was so scary about a couple of small lights? *Except for the fact that they were moving on their own, above the ground (not on it), with no apparent means of propulsion? On top of that, without making a sound?*

If she was being honest, Aggie felt a little conflicted. On one hand, she was not at all happy about spending the night in the woods with those lights. In fact, she was a bit freaked out. *What are they? What do I do if they come back?* But, on the other hand, that being said, the whole thing had been kind of uneventful, if you didn't count the goosebumps, and the chill that still ran through her.

When she went to tell the story, she was sure that it would fall flat. At least to Rider, anyway. She could picture it, "and they just glided past me and disappeared." She envisioned Rider's famous eye roll. She shook her head. *I can't believe I'm annoyed that nothing more happened. That should be enough for anyone.* She laughed at herself. *Be careful what you wish for Aggie, the night is young, more could still happen. It's got to be the bump on my head.*

She only now realized that the woods had become completely silent when the lights passed through, purely for the fact that the forest's night sounds were just now starting back up. There were a few cricket chirps here and there, an owl off in the distance, the wind rustling through the trees. She wondered for a moment about that and what it might mean.

Earlier, her biggest fear had been that her case of the creeps would return. That sure would make it tough to stick it out for the whole night. That and the thought of bugs and small animals crawling around while she waited for morning to arrive. *This was a whole other ball of wax now, wasn't it?* She certainly wasn't going to be able to sleep now, that's for sure. There was only one thing left to do. Maybe it was a bit childish, but she didn't care. Anyone else in her place would do the same. Aggie crossed the fingers on both hands, shut her eyes tight, and made a quiet wish: *please keep the spiders, small animals, and most of all, the red lights away for the rest of the night.* She said it twice, just in case.

CHAPTER FOUR

AGGIE SAT BELOW THE TREE WITH A THROBBING HEAD, WISHING FOR some acetaminophen and waiting for morning when it would be bright enough to make it down the trail. Something suddenly occurred to her: What if she had a concussion? *Crap.* She punched herself on her thigh. She fell asleep last night, before the lights appeared. For quite a while. *Crap.* She'd heard somewhere that you weren't supposed to let yourself sleep for a while if you'd had a concussion. Now what? Was the damage already done? She didn't know. Rider would know. *Where are you when I need you?*

Two or three more hours had to have passed, Aggie estimated the time by tracking the moon across the night sky. The lights hadn't returned and her goosebumps had finally vanished. She was still leaning up against the tree, her leg was still resting on the camera bag and she was quite bored. She was sleepier than she thought she'd be, given the nap she'd accidentally had, but she seemed to be managing. Everything still hurt and her tummy had been growling for a while now. She patted her soft rounded belly, *it's not like you're gonna starve to death overnight.* She chuckled at the joke she made at her own expense, but then bent down and pulled one of the two protein bars out of her camera bag. She ate it slowly, to make it last.

She waited about twenty minutes before deciding that she was still hungry. After a quick debate with herself, she ate the second protein bar and washed it down with just a few sips of the water she had left. She made a bargain with herself; she'd consider that the bars had been "supper" and she would save the rest of the water for "breakfast." It was going to have to do.

To keep from falling asleep, and hopefully distract herself, she took out her camera and used the digital panel on the back to review the photos she had taken earlier that day. This would occupy her for a while. She'd taken a bunch of photos figuring she could always edit out the not so good ones later, that was the beauty of digital. There was still plenty of life in the battery, plus she had a backup in the bag.

She smiled to herself thinking about her hike and making it to the end of the trail on top of Western Hill, the photographs she'd taken, and the beautiful journaling spot she'd found overlooking the lake. Not a bad day overall, except for a case of the creeps and the fall. And the lights.

Aggie had discovered a trail in the woods near her house that led to an old cart road in the woods. She'd been out there several times already, hiking and taking photographs. She had been wanting to hike further up the cart road again to confirm a theory she had about where it went.

Previous, shorter hikes had piqued her curiosity and built up her stamina. This morning, she decided to go for it. She grabbed her camera, a few snacks and some water and off she went. It was early afternoon when she came out of the woods into a clearing at the top of the hill. The same hill she could see from her deck. A thought pushed its way in between the memories: *that was where the lights were headed.* The hike had confirmed her guess, if you kept going, eventually the cart road led up and on to the top of Western Hill.

Although less obvious than in the woods, she could see that the cart road had, at one time, continued in a straight line for several hundred yards to the edge of the top of Western Hill. At that point, where the hill dropped off sharply, there was no more evidence of the cart road. There were, however, a few wooden posts sticking up out of the far side of the hill. They were very old and quite decayed. But, if you closed your eyes and used your imagination, you could just make out that an old wooden bridge (now at the bottom of her lake, she was sure of it) could have spanned the distance between Western and Eastern Hills, allowing the cart road to continue down the other side into the next town.

This was where Aggie had taken the bulk of her photographs, snapping away as she soaked in the surroundings. The view from the top of the hill was spectacular. She could see that it was longer than it was wide. From a center point on the path at the top of the hill she could see almost a full 360 degrees around and below her if not for the chunk of woods directly behind her.

To her left, which was west, sat the larger section of the lake not visible from her house because it was blocked by the two hills. It was a beautiful sight. Tiny diamond points of sunlight bobbed on each wave as tourists and fishermen sped across the lake in their boats. She could almost hear the sound of their engines, but most of the noise was carried off towards the Superstition Mountains by the cool lake breezes.

In the opposite direction, she could see her part of the lake as well as her house. It looked so small from up here. Photos of either direction would definitely look like post cards, so she snapped a few more. Directly in front of her, of course, was the gap where the old wooden bridge used to be and beyond that was what she had nicknamed Eastern Hill.

Aggie walked over to the edge of the hill and looked at the remains of the wooden posts that were left behind. She lifted her foot up and kicked at one. Trusting that it seemed strong enough not to crumble under her weight, she sat down after checking for spiders and ants. She sat for a bit to rest and enjoy the scenery.

Eventually, she pulled her camera bag around to her front and sifted through the pockets until she came upon a small pocket sized notebook and pen that she had tucked in there. She'd placed them in there when she began hiking, knowing at some point she'd feel the need to jot something down. Waiting until she got home and trusting her memory didn't usually work, sometimes she needed to write down what she was thinking while she was thinking it. As she rested, she did a bit of journaling, tucking the notebook back into her camera bag only after she felt like she'd gotten all her thoughts down.

Looking up from her camera bag, Aggie realized she'd journaled away a good chunk of time. It was now late afternoon and it had arrived when she wasn't looking. Feeling completely rested, Aggie got off the post and stretched to work out the kinks that had settled in her bones while she was journaling. When she could no longer feel the imprint from the post on her butt, she headed back into the woods. It was at this point when she began to feel someone watching her. She was less than a quarter of a mile into her hike when she fell. The rest was history, as they say.

Eventually, in the late hours of the night, she could no longer fight off sleep. The accommodations really hadn't been that bad, considering she was in the woods (without any camping supplies, mind you). The spot underneath the tree was padded with a pretty good layer of fallen leaves and pine needles and she had put her camera bag into service as a pillow. She ended up sleeping on her right side which seemed to be the best position for her injured ankle and the cut on her forehead. She had expected, but hadn't seen or felt any creepy-crawlies during the night, so that was a bonus. Either that, or they had waited until she was asleep to do their thing. It would've been nice if the red lights had been as considerate.

Although she had been cursing the unseasonably warm temperatures during her hike, her attitude changed once it sank in that she'd be spending the night out here. Without a sweater, she was grateful for the warmish night. Still, sometime during the night she pulled her arms inside of her T-shirt for the extra bit of warmth it offered. The early morning air had a damp chill to it, and that was what finally woke Aggie. She quickly registered her surroundings and remembered the predicament in which she had found herself.

Dawn broke ever so slowly, much like the watched pot that doesn't boil. The sun taunted her as it rose; begrudgingly, bit by bit, it lit the forest around her. Shivering against the morning chill, Aggie searched for a better spot. She should get up off the ground, at least. She spotted a large, flat topped boulder that was about six feet back from the edge of the old cart road and about 20 yards from the tree she'd spent the night under. That's when she had crawled (like a baby, again) over to the boulder and to the warmth of the sunbeam shining down on it. Aggie warmed herself in morning sun like a cat on a window sill.

Once the chill was gone, she tested her bad ankle for the umpteenth time by holding it out in front of her, slowly flexing it around and up and down. Sharp, stabbing pains shot up her leg. *Ow! Crap! Ok.* She gingerly touched the swollen egg shaped bruise and cut on her forehead and winced. *Yup, that still hurts, too.* At least she wasn't woozy anymore, she did still have a bit of a headache, though.

This is ridiculous. I can't sit here all day. Aggie swirled the last bit of water in the bottle absentmindedly and once again took stock of herself and her situation. One more sip and her water would be gone, she had eaten the last of her snacks last night, her tummy was growling again, her left ankle hurt too much to walk on, and the Arizona heat would be coming on soon enough. Now that daylight was here, she had to figure out how she was going to make it all the way home on her injured ankle.

She had stuck to hiking the main trail, the old cart road, but she was still pretty deep into the woods. She had yet to see any other people out here during any of her hikes, so she didn't think her chances of being discovered by passers-by were very good. Crawling out of the woods, all that way (part of it down hill), didn't seem like a very good option. Maybe she could fashion a crutch out of a branch? It would be slow going, but at least she'd be going. She liked that idea better.

CHAPTER FIVE

RIDER PULLED INTO AGGIE'S DRIVEWAY AND FOLLOWED IT TO THE END where it met her garage. He parked his car next to hers and turned it off, glad to see that there was a bit of shade from the few trees that stood nearby. Even though it was still morning, it was already warm out and it was only going to get warmer. He left all the windows open, hoping the shade would last and that it wouldn't feel like an oven when he got back in the car later.

He hustled around to the back of Aggie's house and glanced at the backyard and dock area to see if Aggie was there. He was a bit surprised that she wasn't already outside. They had a standing "not-really-a-date" date for Saturday mornings. They had been getting together on the weekends for a brunch of sorts, alternating between his place and hers. This was Aggie's weekend.

He usually found her sitting on the dock, her feet dangling in the lake, waiting for him to join her. She'd have two beverages with her: a cold drink for herself (sometimes milk, but it was usually a diet cola, even though it was morning) and a strong, hot coffee for him. Aggie didn't drink coffee herself, didn't like the taste or smell of it. She'd told him once that just the smell of it brewing on an empty stomach grossed her out and sometimes made her nauseas. Knowing that made him appreciate the extra effort she took, he didn't have the heart to tell her that sometimes he'd prefer an ice coffee. He'd just thank her and drink it hot.

As he approached her back door, Rider thought it was a little bit curious and unlike her to not be outside already. They'd met for brunch a bunch of times since she moved and she'd always been either at the dock or sitting in a lounge chair on the deck. He figured she was just moving a little slow today. Aggie hadn't responded to either of the texts he had sent yesterday. She was pretty OCD about responding to people, and they spoke pretty often, so when he hadn't heard back from her within a normal timeframe, he'd decided to keep their regular brunch date (maybe get there a bit early, even) and see what was up.

Maybe something was wrong? He tried to convince himself that he was letting his imagination run away with him. *She's starting to rub off on me.* He chuckled to himself. *Between the two of us, she's the worrier.* He was always giving her a hard time about it. He'd tell her that there was no sense in worrying about something she had no control over.

I'm sure that there's nothing to worry about, it's probably just the cell coverage out here. Obviously, they were both expecting to meet this morning, of course she would be expecting him. She probably didn't even realize that he couldn't get ahold of her.

Rider knocked on the back door as he opened it and stepped into the kitchen. She lived so far out in the "boonies" (as she called it) that she never really locked up. And, they'd known each other for so long that knocking was really just a left over formality at this point anyway. It was the same when she came to his place.

He called out her name and listened for a reply. When there was no answer, he worked his way further into the house and tried a few more times. Still no answer. Rider ran one hand through his hair while he waited and listened. Silence. He hesitated at the bottom of the stairs, calling out to her as he climbed to the second floor. Heading upstairs uninvited was pushing the boundaries of familiarity a bit, as close as they were after two decades-plus years of friendship, he still was very careful about respecting her privacy and personal boundaries. He had to be sure she was OK, though, and worry overcame his manners. He was probably more uncomfortable than she would be anyway. Aggie was always giving him a hard time about the strictness of his manners about certain things. "We go way back," she'd say, "it's fine." He remembered a time recently when Aggie had asked him to get something out of her purse. Instead of looking for the item, he'd brought the whole purse to her. He'd given her the purse and she'd told him something along the lines of "Good grief, there's nothing in there you can't see. I wouldn't have asked you, otherwise." Rider just responded that he didn't feel comfortable.

This, however, seemed to be turning into a situation and he was going to have to get over it. He needed to make sure that she hadn't smacked her head in the tub or something like that. He worked his way through the rooms on the second floor. No Aggie. Her bed was made, the bathroom was empty, the second bedroom was vacant. Aggie was nowhere on the second floor.

Making his way back downstairs, Rider wondered where Aggie could have gotten to. He looked around and tried to process it all; her car was here, she wasn't in the house, in the back yard or on the dock. There weren't any dishes left on the table, counter or in the sink, so that didn't help. He ran back upstairs and checked the bathroom. The towels and the shower were dry, she hadn't showered his morning. She might be in the garage, but he remembered it being closed up with the lights off when he pulled into the driveway. After double checking the garage and realizing that he'd been right - no Aggie - he found himself standing at the edge of the backyard, unsure about what to do next.

I'll call her again. The call went directly to voicemail and even though he disliked leaving messages, this situation was beginning to warrant one. He left a brief message asking her to call him as soon as she could. Rider put the phone back in his pocket and ran his fingers through his hair again. He was back to square one and out of ideas. Pretty soon, he'd have to admit to himself that he was worried.

After a few minutes, an idea began to form. He went back inside and looked in the kitchen closet. There was a sweater and a wind breaker, a broom and dustpan, but nothing else. The hook on the inside of the door was empty. He looked around the kitchen, Aggie's journal was on the table along with her laptop and a few pens. He scanned the rest of the room. No camera. This was good news. He quickly checked the other rooms, although he didn't expect to find it if it wasn't in the kitchen. As far as he knew, she had taken to keeping her camera in the kitchen closet so she could grab it quickly.

Not being able to locate the camera bag actually gave his idea more credence. He bet she was out in the woods hiking and taking photos. The longer he thought about it, the more it felt right. He knew she had done just that a few times since moving in and that she'd felt pretty comfortable hiking through the woods alone. Aggie called it familiarizing herself with the area, and she always took her camera "just in case."

For just a moment, he was pleased with himself for figuring out what had happened. That was the good news. Then the reality of the situation began to wash over him. *She's been out there since yesterday sometime.* That was the bad news. A small lump lodged in his stomach at the thought of her being in the woods overnight; something, anything, could have happened. He was officially worried.

CHAPTER SIX

RIDER PUSHED AWAY ALL THE THOUGHTS OF WHAT MIGHT HAVE happened to his friend. *Nothing's happened.* He tried to reassure himself while ignoring the growing lump in his gut. He would take his own advice. Focus on what he had control over and not let his imagination go crazy. He had to go look for her, of course, but how was he going to locate her? The woods seemed to cover a pretty sizable area and he had yet go on any kind of lengthy hike out there with her. He definitely wasn't as familiar with them she was. Both of them lost or stuck in the woods, that's all he needed.

He wanted to act quickly, but he also wanted to act smart. The last thing he wanted was for both of them to be stuck out in the woods - he'd seen the movie 127 Hours - and although he wasn't planning on being pinned down by a giant boulder, the tragedy that unfolded in the movie and in real life was due to the hiker not informing anyone of his whereabouts (he made a mental note to give Aggie heck once he found her). So, to prevent any further problems, and to not do to anyone else what Aggie seemed to be doing to him now, he made a plan. He'd leave a note for Aggie telling her where he was in case she came back before he did, he'd also send a text to a friend/co-worker in the event they both got stuck out there, lastly, he'd grab a few bottles of water and a few packs of peanut butter crackers he'd seen on the countertop. The rest, well, he'd just have to wing it and hope luck was on their side.

After leaving a note and sending the text, he grabbed the water and crackers and headed back to his car. He grabbed a backpack from the trunk, threw the water and crackers inside and slung the pack over his shoulder. Rider paused for a moment and, unable to come up with anything else, he shrugged his shoulders and then headed back around the garage and into the woods. He was anxious to get going now that he had a plan and felt good about it.

Rider approached the edge of the woods and noticed there wasn't really a trail, as far as normal trails go. But, he could tell by the trampled grasses and weeds that Aggie had entered the woods at roughly the same spot each time. It was a faint path at best; but, if you tilted your head and squinted, it was still a path. It seemed as good a place as any to begin. He took a deep breath and entered the woods, choosing the same location that he imagined Aggie using yesterday.

He stuck to the trail as best as he could. It wasn't as hard to follow as he thought it was going to be when he started out. He soon realized that the path was leading him deeper and deeper into the woods. If he'd been able to see it from the air, he would have noticed that it pointed away from the road at about a 90 degree angle. In no time at all, he was completely surrounded by trees and shrubs and saplings and all the various plants that made up the woods. He could no longer see her house or garage and as quiet as it was there, it was twice as quiet out here (even with the occasional buzzing of insects and chirping of birds). The forest had a way of absorbing, or softening, the sounds within. A hushed, reverent atmosphere surrounded him. Every so often, he would stop and call out her name, disturbing the hushed silence. It was necessary, but it felt wrong, almost sacrilegious, to disturb the peaceful surroundings. Even so, as his voice travelled clearly through the trees, there was no response.

After he'd been hiking for about twenty minutes, the path Rider was on intersected with another trail. This was a much wider and clearer trail than the one he'd been using and was much easier to follow. He decided it must be the old cart road Aggie had told him about. It had become overgrown, but he could see that at one time it had been pretty well traveled. It had been carved into the woods long ago by people who must have known their way through and he could see no reason why he shouldn't follow it. Surely, that's what Aggie had done? He reasoned that to go left would eventually bring him out to the main road. He went to the right, figuring that Aggie probably hadn't planned on going into town. Not by way of the woods anyhow. He couldn't imagine that she'd taken to blazing her own trail, so she must have gone along on the cart road. She had plenty of issues on flat ground as it was. He recalled teasing her many times about tripping over air pockets and he smiled to himself. *Maybe finding her won't be so hard after all.*

The old cart road wound through the pines and some other large trees (he realized he didn't know their names and, also, that he was OK with it). Eventually, the trail turned uphill. It was uncharacteristically lush in here, Rider noticed, and if he hadn't been so worried about finding Aggie in one piece, he would have tried to appreciate it a bit more. He was beginning to understand why she'd want to photograph out here.

It was a lot cooler in the woods, he could definitely appreciate that as well. The canopy of tree branches prevented the sun from really beating down on him and he was grateful for the cooler temperature while he searched for Aggie. As he climbed the hill, which had gotten steeper, he scanned the woods on both sides of the cart road and continued shouting her name every few minutes. There was still no answer.

Rider paused on the trail to catch his breath, silently cursing his recent bout of inactivity. He wasn't overweight, but he was apparently a bit out of shape. He was definitely not used to hiking like this. He pulled one of the bottles of water from his back pack and took a few sips. As he caught his breath and quenched his thirst, he listened intently to the forest around him. Aside from a few birds singing their morning songs, it was pretty quiet. He had been hoping for a sound, any sound, that would tell him he was getting closer to finding Aggie. But again, he was met with a hushed atmosphere.

He returned the bottle to his pack and continued up the trail. He was going to keep going. On the surface, it seemed like he was searching for the proverbial needle in a haystack. He should feel like he was in a losing battle, but he didn't. He'd thought it through and felt good about his decision to come out here looking for his best friend. It all made sense. He'd been out here for over an hour, surely she was going to be just around the next corner.

CHAPTER SEVEN

"AGGIE?... AGGIE?" THE WOODS ECHOED HER NAME.

"What?" came the reply.

Surprised but excited, Rider breathed a sigh of relief and turned his head towards the sound. Ever so slowly, hobbling down the trail with a branch for a crutch under one arm, was his friend Aggie.

"Brunch!" she shouted.

"What are you talking about?" he laughed, partly from relief and partly from the vision before him. In addition to the obviously injured leg, her T-shirt was covered in blood, she was dirty all over, and her arms and legs were bruised and scraped up. She had a nasty looking goose egg on her forehead with a jagged, angry looking cut slicing it in half. The nurse in him counted the number of stitches she'd need. He was grateful, though; she appeared to be in one piece. He quickly closed the gap between them. When he got close enough, Aggie gave him a bear hug which made him chuckle. She dropped her branch-crutch during the hug and had to hold on to him for balance while he retrieved it for her.

"You came for brunch this morning, right? My phone is broken, how did you know I was up here?" Aggie asked, breathing heavily.

"You are a mess." He shook his head and laughed at her again.

Rider could tell his friend was out of breath and in pain, so he looked around and helped her over to a fallen log so she could sit. As they rested, they compared notes.

He told Aggie about not being able to reach her last night and how he put it all together this morning with the missing camera being his final clue. She told Rider about her hike, her fall and then her decision to spend the night in the woods.

"Oh yeah," Rider fished the peanut butter crackers and a bottle of water out of his back pack for her. He presented it to her with a flourish, "Brunch is served."

"Thank you, sir," Aggie chuckled. She was starving, "the protein bars I had for supper last night wore off a long time ago."

They continued to chat and compare stories; Aggie filled him in with more details about her hike and reaching the top of Western Hill, Rider teased Aggie about her clumsiness and Aggie protested that it could have happened to anyone. Rider countered with a "not really," and a laugh. She punched him good-naturedly on the shoulder.

After Aggie finished her breakfast, he helped her up and they began to make their way back to her house together. She put the branch-crutch under one arm and she put the other around Rider's shoulder for support, glad they were almost the same height. Going downhill with a bum ankle was a little dicey, but Aggie held on to Rider and focused on each step so she wouldn't slip. They made pretty good time that way.

"Aggie, I can carry your camera bag if you want," Rider offered.

"Thanks, but I've got it. I - oh my God. Wait. I have to tell you what else happened last night."

Wide eyed and eyebrows raised, Aggie stopped mid-trail and smiled at Rider. "Wait until you hear this!"

Aggie told him her experience with the lights as they continued descending. Rider listened intently, but kept an eye out for bench-worthy logs and boulders on the side of the trail. When they came across a good one, he made her take a break. Soon they came to the bottom of the hill where the trail leveled out and although her ankle was still pretty tender, the going was much easier.

They headed for a tree that had fallen beside the trail in the woods. It was probably their fourth break since they had begun.

"Oof!" Aggie groaned involuntarily as she sat down. "Holy cow, hiking is so much more exhausting when you're injured. Good thing it was downhill."

Aggie was grateful for the break. She knew she was out of shape and overweight. She had been for a long time. But, when she moved here she had decided that being on the lake and having all the hiking trails right there was too good of an opportunity to pass up. It was like her new home was giving her a chance for a new, healthier start. A chance to start over in more ways than one; now she could do more outdoor stuff and perhaps lose a few pounds at the same time.

Aggie felt annoyed at her present state and fought back against tears that threatened to well up in her eyes. She could feel her heart beating out of her chest and she was still out of breath. It upset her because she felt like she had been getting better, stronger, with each hike. She was proud of the progress she had made and was able to go for longer and longer hikes before becoming tired. The ankle injury was going to be a setback, hopefully she'd heal quickly so she could get back out here.

As she tried to find a comfortable spot on the log, she angled herself so that she could prop her foot up on one of the fallen tree's branches. She took a few sips from her water bottle and soon her breathing and heart beat returned to normal. She decided right then and there, made a silent promise to herself; she would make sure she healed quickly and she wouldn't let this small setback deter her from her goal to become more active and healthy.

When she first began hiking, she was embarrassed to admit (even to herself), that she could barely get as far as the woods before losing her breath. But she had stuck with it and had made a lot of progress. Side benefits included seeing and experiencing some really beautiful places, which would have gone unseen from the lounge chair in her back yard. She had some pretty good photographs to show for it, too. Even if she did say so herself. She wasn't willing to give all that up because of her ankle. Of course, she'd also had her 'night with the lights'. Aggie smiled to herself, with the benefit of time and daylight, the experience now seemed more exciting than frightening.

Rider leaned over and bumped Aggie with his shoulder, "You OK? You got a little quiet there."

"Yeah, I'm good. Just thinking," she replied.

"Do you feel like going for little bit more?"

"Yup, ready as ever. Let's go." She held out her hand so he could help her to her feet. Well, to her one good foot. Rider passed her the branch-crutch, she propped herself up on it and nodded to her friend, "OK, ready." He moved closer to her so she could lean on him and they set off for her house once more.

CHAPTER EIGHT

"RIDE, SEE THAT TREE UP AHEAD WITH THE WEIRD SCAR ON ITS trunk?" It had been about 20 minutes since their last break; she was tired, winded and in pain. Aggie had been watching the trail expectantly and when they rounded a small bend in the trail, the tree popped into view. The scarred pine tree was a signpost of sorts and it meant they were almost home.

"Yeah, up on the left?" He pointed to the very tree she had indicated. It had a long, blackish scar that ran down the length of its trunk. He thought it had probably suffered a lightning strike long age. "Funny, I don't remember seeing that tree this morning, guess I wasn't paying attention."

"Yeah, that's my landmark. It's where the trail back to my house starts."

"Great," he replied, "how are you holding up?"

She paused on the trail, which forced him to stop. "Ok, I guess. Better now that I know we're closing in on it. "Once we get on that trail," she pointed to it with the end of her branch-crutch, "it should only be another twenty minutes to a half hour." She paused, looked at her left foot, and corrected herself, "Well, that's at a normal pace." She shrugged, "Sorry." They had been making pretty good time, as it was, but nowhere near the speed that two hikers with four good ankles between them could make.

"Aggie, it's fine. We'll get there, no rush. It's not like I have anything else to do today."

"Thanks, I appreciate that. I'm so glad you're here. Who knows how long it would've taken me to get home by myself?"

Aggie and Rider were about 15 minutes into the homestretch when they came to a small bend in the trail. "Hey, stop for a sec," something was bothering Aggie, "this trail doesn't bend." They both stopped walking and faced each other.

"What do you mean?" Rider replied.

"I mean, there's a bend in the trail right here and I've never come across a bend on this stretch. All of the other hikes I've been on, once I leave the old cart road, it's a straight shot to my backyard. Straight. No bends." Confused about what that could mean, Aggie looked at the woods around them trying to orient herself. He did the same, not that he knew what he was look at, or for.

"Aggie, what the Hell?" Rider said, using his free hand to point into the woods. She looked to where he was pointing and fell silent, confused. Up ahead, on the right this time, was a pine tree with a long blackish scar running down the length of the trunk.

Yeah, what the Hell? It was the same exact tree with the same exact lightening scar running down its trunk. And they had passed it no more than 15 minutes ago. There couldn't possibly be two of them. Goosebumps appeared on Aggie's arms, but she was too curious about this development in their hike to pay them any mind.

"We should be almost to my house by now. What are we doing back here?" It was an obvious, rhetorical question; but, still Aggie asked it. She looked at Rider for an explanation, but realized he was just as confused as she was. Besides, these were her woods, not his. It was up to her to get them on the proper trail.

"Maybe we veered off the path somehow and circled back around?" he suggested.

"I don't know, it seems unlikely," Aggie said. "I've been on this trail quite a few times and nothing like this has ever happened." They both stood on the trail, silent and staring at the tree for several more minutes.

"Ok," Aggie allowed, "I suppose it's possible that we veered off course a little. Unlikely, but possible." She thought for a moment, then continued. "If so, we must have circled off to the right somehow in order for us to come upon the tree from this angle."

"That makes sense," Rider nodded in agreement. Then, he offered, "what if we get back on the trail to your house and then make a conscious effort to walk in a straight line, if not veer to the left a little," he gestured with his free hand, making a sweeping motion to the left. "The worst that could happen is that we pop out of the woods further back in your yard, nearer to the lake, instead of right behind your garage. Maybe we just weren't paying attention."

"That sounds as good as anything. Let's give it a shot," Aggie took a deep breath, "I've got to get off my ankle soon."

"Do you want to have a break before we continue?"

"No, thanks, I'd rather just keep going. Besides, I'm going to have to go potty soon and I'd really prefer not to have to do it out here." Aggie chuckled, imagining herself trying to take care of that in the woods with only one good ankle and dried leaves for cleanup. She'd probably end up falling over or peeing on herself. Or both. Better to wait if she could. *If we don't get there soon, I won't have any other options.*

They started forward again, taking a right at the scarred pine tree. They watched the ground for signs of the trail that Aggie, and now Rider, had made on previous hikes through the woods. They followed it as closely as they could, making a mindful effort to keep going straight. Whenever the signs of the trail seemed to vanish, Rider would pick out a tree ahead of them and they would pass it on the left. They kept plodding down the trail, passing big trees on the left side, encouraged by the amount of trail they were putting behind them.

"You've got to be kidding me!" Aggie stopped abruptly, forcing Rider to stop also.

"What?" Startled, he looked up at her and then followed her gaze down the trail.

CHAPTER NINE

THE FRIENDS STOOD SILENT AND DUMBSTRUCK IN THE MIDDLE OF THE trail. About twenty-five yards ahead of them on the right was a pine tree with a long blackish scar running down the length of its trunk. Neither of them spoke for a few minutes; each one trying to come up with some kind of rational explanation. This time they had definitely kept to hiking a straight line - actually, a straight line with a tendency to the left. They had come back to the tree twice. Twice! It was mind-boggling. And frustrating.

Rider looked around at the woods and found a spot with a few good sized, almost-flat-on-top boulders. He helped Aggie over to them and they both sat down.

Aggie blinked back an unwanted tear; she was frustrated, tired, her ankle and her head hurt like crazy, and she really had to pee. Soon. "I don't get it," she said, shaking her head left and right and gesturing with her hands at the tree, "I just don't get it."

Rider ran his hand through his hair, "let's just sit here for a few minutes. You can rest your ankle and we can use the time to figure out our way out of here. You wouldn't think it'd be that hard." He paused, "you would think the hardest part would have been finding you, not getting you home."

"Right?" Aggie laughed and he joined her. It helped to lighten the dark mood that had briefly settled over both of them. "Ok, so let's figure something out. If we don't get back soon, I'm going have another accident."

Aggie thought about their location in the woods and what she knew from her earlier hikes and a solution presented itself. "I know what we can do," she said. She pointed to the main trail in front of them, "this is the old cart road, right? It goes all the way out to the main road, which has to be that way." She pointed to their right.

"Are you sure?" Ride asked.

"Yes." she answered, and pointed to their left. "That way will eventually take us uphill, where we were earlier this morning, right?"

"Well, I'm a bit turned around right now, but OK."

"Trust me, to the left is up the hill. The cart road used to go from out there," Aggie pointed to the right, "which is the main road and then through the woods and up and over the hill. That scarred tree marks the turning point to the trail back to my house. Normally." She pointed to the woods in front of them. "My house should be that way. We just can't get there using that trail for some reason. You with me so far?"

"I guess so." Rider shrugged and laughed, "You know navigating and directions haven't ever really been my strong point."

"That's true," she laughed with him. "OK. I think we should forget about the trail back to my house for now. Something obviously doesn't want us going that way today," Aggie waved her hand at the trail giving them so much trouble. "We'll follow the cart road out to the main road," Aggie said, swinging her arm around and pointing once more to the right. "Then, we'll just walk up the main road back to my house. It's not that far."

"Alright. But, I think we should wait here for a few more minutes and give your ankle a break."

"I really have to go, if you know what I mean. I can't wait very much longer," Aggie replied, raising her eyebrows at him for emphasis.

Rider laughed, "why don't you just go behind a tree? You'll feel much better."

Aggie thought about it for a minute and realized he was probably right. She probably wouldn't be able to hold it much longer, anyway.

"Fine. Here, hold my camera bag, please." She handed Rider her camera bag and scooted forward off the boulder until she could stand up. A thought quickly occurred to her and she paused for a moment, weighing the pros and cons of putting her bra into service once more. But, she quickly dismissed the notion right away.

"What's so funny?" Rider asked, seeing a weird look on his friends face.

"Well, you know how I used my bra to stop the bleeding from the cut on my forehead…"

Rider laughed as a picture formed in his head, "Oh, I can see it now. But then what do you do with it after?"

"I know, right? That's what stopped me." Aggie and Rider continued to laugh while she made her way deeper into the woods and off the trail.

She looked around and found a spot not too far away that had a few low, but thick, bushes. She worked her way over to the grouping of bushes and made her way around back, trying to figure out how she was going to keep her balance and her dignity. She could step out of her shorts and underwear altogether and put them on the top of one of the bushes. Up there, they'd be out of harm's way and she'd have one less thing to hold on to while she was trying to keep her balance.

It wasn't as easy to do as she thought; stepping out of her clothes with her left leg went ok, but trying to step out with the other leg presented a problem because she still couldn't put much (any) weight on her left ankle. Eventually, she let her clothing drop to the ground while she managed a combination of leaning on the branch-crutch and grabbing a one of the bushes with her free hand while she hopped out of them. *Whew.*

She placed her clothes on top of the bushes, and set about the task at hand. It wasn't easy, or pretty, but she was able to accomplish her task.

Aggie managed to get her clothes back on with less trouble than it took to get them off and made her way back to Rider. "Well, that was quite a production," she said as she got closer.

Rider turned around as she approached and looked at her, chuckling. "Get any on ya'?" he said, laughing at the old joke.

"Very funny," she replied, "how long have you been waiting to say that?" She could see her breath. As she spoke, her words came out in a foggy little cloud. Rider looked at her, his eyebrows raised, and exhaled. His breath was visible, too.

Aggie extended her free hand and felt a drizzle of rain for the second time in less than 24 hours. *Great, that's all we need.* The woods were darker, now, too. She looked up expecting to see rain clouds above the tree tops, but there were none. Just blue skies. *Weird.*

She noticed Rider following her gaze and was about to ask him about it when something moved behind him on the trail. Aggie looked past Rider to see what had caught her attention. Rider turned to look at the trail, also, realizing he'd lost her focus.

He turned back to Aggie, "What?"

Aggie's attention went from the trail to her friend and back to the trail. She saw his question come out in little puffs, as if it was a cold, fall day. She had a serious case of goosebumps that went unnoticed. Aggie froze in place, still several feet from the boulder and her friend. She leaned on the branch-crutch, taking the weight off her bad ankle. She held her breath and felt her pulse quicken to the point where she could feel the blood rushing through the veins in her ears. She could actually hear her pulse. Rider watched his friend and tried to follow her stare. Seeing nothing of concern, he turned back to her.

As Aggie looked out on to the old cart road, two red lights, transparent and about the size of a softball, floated by. The lights were low to the ground and, she guessed, about four feet apart. They drifted along silently, seeming to follow the old cart road, traveling from her right to the left in tandem. They lights flickered once or twice and then disappeared once they had travelled about twenty yards. As soon as the lights were gone, the darkness lifted and the woods around them brightened. Only then did Aggie close the distance between her and Rider.

"Aggie," Rider called to her, concern in his voice. "Aggie."

Aggie reached out for Rider's shoulder, "you saw that, didn't you? That was them." She noticed that she couldn't see her breath anymore.

"Them, who?" Rider shook his head, "where?"

Aggie moved around to the front of the boulder and sat down next to Rider to regroup and take some weight off her ankle. "The lights from last night." She looked her friend right in the eye, "the red lights." Her voice trailed off and Rider looked back to the trail and back to Aggie, shaking his head no. She closed her eyes for a moment; all of a sudden her headache was hitting her full force.

"Where?"

His friend stayed silent, but pointed to the trail.

"Aggie, there's nothing there."

"Yes, there was." Aggie looked at her friend defiantly, "two red lights, above the trail, just like last night." A small shiver passed through her and she crossed her arms against a few of the goosebumps that remained. "And then they vanished. Also like last night. Please tell me that you saw them."

"I don't know," it came out as all one word 'dunno'. "Aggie," he tried to suppress a smile that was forming because it felt like a joke, but her eyes said that it wasn't. He chose his words with care, "you did hit your head last night and you have a pretty big goose egg and cut to show for it."

Aggie counted to three silently, took a breath, and looked Rider straight in the eye again. "I saw them. They were right there." She gestured to the trail again and noticed that her hand had begun to tremble. She pulled it back quickly, before he could notice. She didn't want to admit that she was beginning to think the same thing. "Can't believe you didn't see them." She shook her head side to side and crossed her arms.

He searched for something to say that would soften the mood. He really hadn't seen the lights, and she had hit her head pretty badly, but he wasn't here to get her all riled up. Finally, a strange thought occurred to him. "I did see my breath for a second or two, which is not what you'd expect on a warm spring morning in Arizona."

Aggie, who had started to calm down became excited again. "OK." She turned to Rider with hope in her eyes, "I saw that too, so that has to count for something, right?"

Rider sat quietly by, deep in thought. He looked at her, raising his eyebrows for emphasis this time, and nodded 'yes' to his friend. He admitted that it did, indeed, count for something.

Aggie's adrenaline was returning to normal, but now she felt like the all her little hairs were standing on end. "You know what, let's go. I want to get out of these woods."

"Alright."

Rider helped her off the boulder, handed her the branch-crutch and together they turned to the right, down the old cart road. They began walking in the direction they had decided on earlier. The same way, supposedly, from which the lights had appeared.

"The whole thing is so strange. I can't believe how close they were." Rider could still hear a little fear underneath her excitement as she spoke, "they went by right in front of us!" She closed her eyes for a few moments, trusting Rider to guide her while they walked. Her headache was back in full force.

They both fell silent and as they walked, the rest of their trip through the woods was uneventful. They made it to the main road in about fifteen minutes. The number of trees dwindled and turned to bushes. The bushes soon gave way to weeds and wildflowers and finally the old cart road spit them out on to a dirt and pebble filled ditch that ran beside the main road. Rider helped her climb out of the small ditch and they were finally able to put the woods and the old cart road behind them.

Aggie let go of Rider just long enough to raise a fist above her head in victory and give a quick, but hearty, "Woo hoo!" Grateful and relieved to finally have pavement below their feet, they smiled at each other. Overcome by the moment, Aggie surprised Rider with a bear hug which caused him to stumble back a half step. He laughed, like he always did when she forced a hug on him; and then after a moment, like he always did, he hugged her back. Exhausted but determined, they turned to face the final stretch and headed for Aggie's house.

CHAPTER TEN

A QUIET MAN SAT IN A BOOTH BY HIMSELF IN THE BACK OF THE DINER. He was not a local, but he was not a stranger, either; this was his third visit this week. The attraction was not the food or the atmosphere, it was her.

He brought the morning paper with him in the event there was small talk. The paper was beside his plate, opened to and folded around one of the most popular news stories of the week. He glanced at the article every so often and shook his head. He made sure to keep the headline and the photo visible on the table. The now famous photo showed a CIA helicopter evacuating South Vietnamese civilians from the roof of the US Embassy in Saigon that Tuesday. Anyone nearby would assume he was as concerned as the next guy about the end of the US involvement in Vietnam. To be honest, his concern began and ended with the paper's ability to distract from his real motivation. Being near her.

He watched her from his booth as she waited on a few regulars. She was pretty enough, longish light brown hair that she kept pulled back and a giant 'how can I help you' smile. But that wasn't the attraction either. It was what happened on his second visit that did it for him.

He'd noticed her on his first visit, but only because there were only two waitresses. And, he happened to sit in her section. She did not attract his attention any more than the other waitress on that first visit. The food was good (not necessarily spectacular, in his opinion), it was served to him hot and they managed to get his order correct. One didn't always get three out of three on the road.

He came back the second time because he believed 'if it ain't broke, don't fix it'. Why go somewhere else and risk disappointment with your next meal? This time, he was in the other waitress's section, which was fine for now. Everything about this one was short: she was barely over five feet tall, had a short dark hairdo, even her delivery time was short. His experience was quite similar to his first. No complaints.

He thought back to yesterday. He'd stopped in well after mid-day, so business was slow. A few regulars (the familiarity between the staff and the diners gave it away) were spread across the front of the diner. With nothing to do but people watch between bites of his burger, he did just that. And by the time the check came for his three-out-of-three meal, he was in love.

A school-age boy came in and sat down at a booth by himself. He ordered a soda, sipped it slowly, and waited. Soon, the short waitress and her co-worker with the big smile, the object of his affection, sat down with the boy. His face lit up and the small group chatted for a few minutes. Smiley checked the floor to make sure none of the customers wanted for anything and then pulled something out of her pocket and handed it to the boy. The short one, Itsy Bitsy, pulled out her order pad and her pen, jotted something down on it and set it aside.

The man was intrigued and began to listen instead of just watch. He was just within hearing range but, up to now, had tuned out the noise. The boy smiled at the small box in his hand, it was a deck of cards. "C-can we p-p-play Rummy today?"

He felt a twinge in his gut.

"Of course, whatever you want honey" the waitress with the big smile answered him, raising her eyebrows, "I just hope you brought your A Game today. Otherwise…"

The boy shook his head and laughed, "Yup, n-n-o j-jukebox."

"That's right. Better deal those cards, then." The cards were dealt quickly and matter-of-factly, the kid was no slouch.

The man swallowed against a dry throat and almost looked away from the happy group. Memories and feelings from long ago were nipping at him, threatening to resurface. He took a sip of his coffee and fought off his childhood for the thousandth time. It never got easier.

The friends chatted as they played, giving each other a good natured hard time when one or the other played a particularly high scoring set or run, groaning at their own bad luck, and so forth. It appeared to him that the young boy held his own against the wait-resses. Either that, or they were taking it easy on him.

The man reached into his pants pocket and pulled out his source of comfort. He always carried it with him. Just having it in his pocket was reassuring most of the time, but right now, he needed to touch it. He needed to hold it in his hand. It made him feel in control, strong, masculine. Grown up.

Before long, the first hand was over. The boy discarded all his cards first, and when Bitsy tallied everything up, it showed that he had the highest score as well. The waitresses clapped for him and there were high fives all around. The young boy pumped his fist in the air calling out, "yes!"

The two waitresses slid out of the booth, Bitsy patted him on the shoulder and gave him a "be right back."

Smiley dug into the pocket of her apron and handed the boy some change, "what's it gonna be today, Ronny?"

The boy continued to smile and showed her the coin, "y-you know. Are you r-ready?"

"Ready when you are, honey." Smiley signaled her co-worker, who came back to the table, and nodded to the regulars, who nodded back.

He dropped the coin into a small box on the wall of his booth and then pushed two of the buttons on the front of it. Seconds passed and a familiar tune wafted out over the diner. The boy closed his eyes and bobbed his head to the music, waiting for the first verse to begin.

The man recognized the music right away, it was The Band. Just as he was trying to remember the name of the song, the first verse kicked in and the boy, the waitresses and the regulars all joined in singing The Night They Drove Old Dixie Down.

The boy opened his eyes and began to sing. He knew every word and he sang loud and strong and his eyes sparkled with pride. His voice was smooth and flawless, not one stutter. The waitresses and the regulars joined him, but as if by some prior arrangement (and maybe it was) no one (individually, or the crowd as a whole) sang loud enough to drown out the boy's voice.

Everyone sang enthusiastically until the song ended. When it did, there was a hearty round of applause and not a few damp eyes, the quiet man included. The man held his knife tight in his fist, occasionally stroking the side of it with his thumb. He watched as the smiley waitress showered the boy with praise.

"That was your best one yet! You're doing so great!" She kissed the boy on the cheek and he blushed.

"Thank you." His eyes lit up as he heard himself. It was only two words. Spoken, not sung. But they came out easy.

She noticed immediately, "I'm so proud of you." She held the boys stare, "let me check on the others and we'll play another hand, OK?"

She took the time to check on each of the regulars and quietly thanked each one. They all nodded as she thanked them. They were all quite happy to be a part of it.

Even though it wasn't her table, she checked on the lone man in the back. He touched the corner of his eye as inconspicuously as he could as she approached and cleared the frog out of his throat. He nodded towards the boy's booth, "that was great, really great." He smiled at her, "you're doing, I'm guessing?"

She shrugged, "it's nothing. If he wins, he gets to pick the music. When he sings, he doesn't stutter. That gives him confidence." She topped off his coffee, "when he's confident, his stutter improves." She treated him to one of her giant smiles, "he's come a long way."

"What if he doesn't win?" He raised his eyebrows at the waitress.

"Then, the winner gets to choose." She started to laugh, "and then, it's usually The Band. Or Marshall Tucker, his other favorite."

He finally took note of her name tag, he couldn't keep calling her Smiley, could he? He pointed to it, "Darlin'?"

"Yup," she nodded with a straight face and then pointed to Bitsy, "that's Honey."

"You're kidding me, right?" he raised his eyebrows and laughed.

Darlin' joined him in laughing, "it's just a little fun we're having. No one calls us by our real names, anyway."

She headed back to the Rummy game, but not before they exchanged one more smile. As he watched them play, he let a select few of his childhood memories out of their lockbox. He knew exactly what the boy was going through from his own experience. He'd had many frustrating years of teasing and school yard tussles. Many years struggling, trying to force his voice to cooperate. She was a hero to that boy. She was just like the hero who'd finally helped him. They had the same big heart and generous, loving spirit. The two heroes were very much alike.

Darlin' was the one he'd been looking for. He was in love and he didn't even know her name. Yet.

CHAPTER ELEVEN

RIDER WAS SITTING ACROSS THE KITCHEN TABLE FROM AGGIE SURFING the internet on his cell phone. He noticed the time and realized that they had been back for about a half an hour. He was waiting for Aggie to wake up.

The first thing Aggie did when she got inside was to take the camera bag off and place it on the floor just inside the door (she had already ditched the branch-crutch outside). The second thing she did was to hop over to one of the kitchen chairs, the one she now occupied, and sit down. To Rider, though, it seemed more like she had collapsed into the chair, having used the last bit of energy she had to climb up the driveway.

These things could only happen to her, he thought to himself. He smiled remembering other adventures they had been on together which had ended in similar circumstances. For him, part of Aggie's charm was her readiness for adventure. She always managed to remember the fun and exciting parts and forget the bad. No injury or crazy incident was ever a big enough deal to keep her from the next adventure. Talking about it later was always a good source of entertainment for him, and most times Aggie saw the humor in it, too. The key to joking about it was the timing, if the timing was right they could usually joke about most anything.

He pulled a bag of frozen corn out of the freezer, wrapped it in a dish towel and placed it on her injured ankle, which was propped up on a second, nearby kitchen chair.

"Thanks." She said, nodding to the frozen veggies. "I'm just going to sit here for a few minutes to rest. Then, I'm going to shower." Aggie pulled at her T-shirt a few times raising a small dust cloud reminiscent of Pigpen, "gotta get the woods off of me."

Rider paused and gave her the once over; she was covered all over with dirt, hair tangled and messy, and there was blood from her cut on her forehead, face, neck and T-shirt. He shook his head, chuckled, and echoed an earlier statement, "Yeah, you're a mess."

"I know." Aggie grimaced as she agreed with him, then joined him in laughing at the state she was in.

He patted her on the shoulder and headed to the downstairs bathroom. He had worked as a nurse for many years and now he was going to draw upon his medical background, "I'll be right back, I'm gonna see what you have in the medicine cabinet." He silently chastised himself, several thoughts ran through his head: why didn't he bring first aid supplies with him? where had his head been at? and, hopefully Aggie's cut won't get infected.

After rummaging around in the medicine cabinet for a few moments, Rider located a bottle of Ibuprofen. If felt almost empty, so he shook it and then pried it open. Peering inside, he saw that there was probably a few dozen tablets left. "Well, that's something," he gave the bottle one last shake while mentally calculating how long it would last. He put the bottle in his pocket and kept looking; first under the sink and then moving to the closet. He finally located some items that he could use to clean up the cut on her head and headed back to the kitchen juggling soap, hydrogen peroxide, a facecloth, cotton balls, Q-Tips, and Band-Aids. He had also found an old ace bandage, which he could put on her ankle after she showered.

He began to call Aggie as he left the bathroom but paused as he approached the doorway that separated the hallway from the kitchen -

she was out cold. Her head was resting against the chair rail, her eyes were closed and her mouth was slightly open, hands in her lap. *What a sight.*

Rider continued on into the kitchen shaking his head and smiling, taking care this time to be quiet. He set the first aid items down on the table gently and then sat down in a chair across from Aggie. He figured that she'd wouldn't be out for very long and when she woke up he'd give her the pills and fix up her cut.

While he sat there, he tried to figure out a quiet way to occupy his time. He pulled out his phone and as he did, he remembered the message he had sent earlier that morning. He sent a follow up message to that same person letting them know that he had found Aggie and they had made it back to her house, pausing before adding the phrase 'safe and sound'. He grinned and looked over at Aggie for a second. *Guess that depends on your definition.*

Rider switched screens and sorted through his email, after that he did some surfing. He searched some of his favorite conspiracy sites for any reported sightings of lights. He began by trying to narrow it down to the circumstances that fit Aggie's first sighting of the lights in the woods and the second sighting earlier today in the woods. The first several items to pop up were reports of UFO sightings. He checked out a few of the reports, but none of them appeared close enough to her description to be worth noting. Not having seen them himself, he had even less to go on.

With nothing else to do for the time being, he continued scrolling through the links. Hunching over his cell had put a strain on his neck. He glanced around and located her laptop on one of the counters. The research would be a little easier (on his neck) on a bigger piece of equipment. He checked on Aggie, who was still asleep, with her mouth still open. *At least she's not drooling.* Rider turned back to his phone. He wouldn't even consider using it without her permission, even though she had shared her password long ago and even though he was positive Aggie wouldn't mind. This was another one of those boundaries he wouldn't cross. There was no emergency this time to force him past his comfort zone. He'd just have to wait until after she woke up.

CHAPTER TWELVE

"Bee." The sound had come from Aggie, whispered and blurted at the same time. The word had come out quietly but had a sense of urgency about it.

"What?" Rider looked over to at Aggie, slightly startled because he didn't realize she had woken up yet. A chuckle at his own expense died in his throat. Her eyes were open and she was staring straight ahead, but she wasn't looking at him. She wasn't looking at anything.

"Bee-ee," she whisper-shouted the same word again, then, louder "Bee-yee." At the same time, she thrust her left hand out in front of her as if reaching for something. Or someone.

"Aggie?" Rider leaned forward and called to her softly, the small hairs on the back of his neck began tingling and standing on end.

"Beeeyyy!" This time it came out as a scream, full of longing and sadness. Rider winced and jumped back against his chair. He watched as Aggie continued to grasp at the air in front of her. Her eyes were wide open, but he could easily tell that her eyes were unfocused and unseeing. A tear formed in the corner of one eye and spilled out onto her cheek.

Rider jumped out of his chair and circled the table to get to her. What the Hell was going on? He'd never seen her like this before.

Ever. His heart and mind raced; was she having a nightmare? Was this happening because she hit her head? But her eyes were open and she wasn't prone to nightmares, as far as he knew. He reached out and gently shook her by the shoulder while calling out her name.

"Aggie." Nothing. Then louder, "Aggie, wake up!" No response. "Crap!" He silently noted to himself that was one of her expressions, but it fit the situation. Now she had him talking like her, which would have been funny if he wasn't so worried. He ran one hand through his hair while gently shaking her with the other.

She needs to snap out of it. That though triggered his memory and a scene from Moonstruck popped into his head. He tried to keep his attention focused on Aggie, but the remembered scene nipped at his memory. He smiled in spite of himself, knowing Aggie would get the humor in it. Cher's character yells "Snap out of it!" at Nicolas Cage's character while slapping him across the face. Well, he wasn't going to slap her. Yet. He might continue to shake her, though. Or a glass of water to the face? That might work, too. He was only half serious.

"Bee," once more, at a whisper. Aggie left arm fell back into her lap. Her unseeing and unfocused eyes closed slowly while the lone teardrop made its way to her chin.

"Aggie!" Rider shook her shoulder again, a bit more forcefully this time. Her eyes snapped opened again. This time he could tell she was 'awake' because she was looking at him, not through him.

"Ride?" she blinked and as she did a second teardrop was released. She raised a hand and absent-mindedly brushed the tears away. She looked up at her friend, questioning him.

"Holy crap, Aggie!" he used her expression, again, but it was appropriate none-the-less. A small chuckle, borne of both shaken nerves and relief, escaped. "What the Hell was that?" he looked deep into her eyes. He was looking for recognition, for Aggie. She returned his look, it was clear and lucid. She was back.

"What?" Aggie looked around her as she wiped her damp hand on her blood speckled and dirt covered shorts, "what's the matter, Rider?"

CHAPTER THIRTEEN

"AHH," AGGIE SHUT HER EYES TIGHT AND COVERED THEM WITH HER hands. She moved her hands to her temples, while trying to avoid her cut, and rubbed them lightly while she kept her eyes closed. Slowly, the pain in her head began to ease and she opened her eyes to see Rider staring at her from across the table.

"Are you OK?" his eyebrows raised, not quite positive that she was back to herself yet. He searched for any indication that she wasn't all there, but whatever had had happened was over now. He was seeing Aggie, and she was seeing him.

"Yeah, I guess. I think my biggest problem right now is the corn thawing out," Aggie laughed and pointed to her bruised ankle.

"Is it feeling any better?" Rider got up and switched the thawing bag of corn for a bag of frozen broccoli, wrapping it in a dry dish towel and placing it back on her ankle, like he had done with the corn.

"Maybe a little. Thanks."

Rider handed her three of the Ibuprofen and a glass of water, then sat back down across from her at the kitchen table. "So, it looked like you were having a nightmare? Do you remember?"

"Yeah, I guess. But it didn't seem like a nightmare. Maybe it was, I don't know."

Rider stayed quiet while Aggie gathered her thoughts. His questions could wait.

"What I remember of the dream - I guess we'll call it a dream - is that it was really dark and wet, like a rainy night." Aggie closed her eyes to more clearly recall the dream.

"Then out of the darkness, and I know how this is going to sound," she glanced at Rider and raised her eyebrows, "I could see a hand reaching out to me. As the hand got closer, more of the person appeared out of the darkness. Pretty soon I could see a woman. She was in a white, flowing dress,"

Rider chuckled, mirroring her expression with his own raised eyebrows.

Aggie paused and let out a small laugh, in spite of herself. She held up her hand to Rider and his raised his eyebrows. "I told you, I know how it sounds. Just let me finish."

"Go ahead," he lowered his eyebrows but he couldn't help grinning. "Sorry."

"Well, the woman was crying and calling out. She looked cold and drenched and her dress clung to her. The whole time she was reaching out."

"Could you tell what she was saying?"

"No. I could tell she was saying something but I couldn't make it out."

Rider was starting to see a connection, "Which arm was she reaching out to you with?"

Aggie closed her eyes again and thought for a moment, then opened them again when she was sure. Gesturing to confirm her recall, she thrust out her left arm and grasped at the air. "It was her left arm, she went just like this."

Rider sat silent for a moment. Aggie had made the same exact gesture when she was experiencing her nightmare. Her dream? Was it really just a dream?

"Ags, do you realize that your eyes were open and you kept repeating something the whole time you were having this dream?"

"Really? I don't remember that part at all. That's kind of creepy. Really?"

"And you made that same motion with your left arm, too. Several times."

"Huh. I just remember what I told you."

"Well, you were doing all of that. And you were saying 'be'. You said it a couple times, softly; then, the last time, it came out as a wail. A loud wail."

Aggie thought for a moment and shook her head, "what the heck is going on?" Then, in an effort to lighten the mood, which was getting heavy, "do you realize how many pages all of this is going to take up in my journal?"

"I can imagine," Rider chuckled and rolled his eyes, following her lead.

After a few moments of reflection, a thought occurred to Aggie. "Ride? I think there might be something else."

Rider waited for her to continue.

"This is the second time I've had that so-called dream. And you know I don't ever remember my dreams." Aggie shook her head yes to Rider when he raised his eyebrows questioningly a second time.

"The first time was last night in the woods. After I wiped out, I crawled over to a tree to lean against it and I accidentally fell asleep. When I finally woke up, I was upset. I figured I must have been having a bad dream. You know I don't usually remember my dreams. And even still, I could only remember a few fragments. Now I realize it was the same - the fragments that I do remember match up to today's dream."

Aggie crossed her arms and hugged herself as goosebumps appeared. Now that the conversation had paused and everything started to sink in, she could feel her heart beating all the way up in her ears again. She could feel the excitement of these events building inside her (perhaps excitement was the wrong word); she could also feel a cold, clammy hand beginning to grip her heart; what was going on? She looked at Rider, he had a faraway look in his eyes; he was trying to make sense of it all, too.

Aggie supposed that all this could go either way if she let it; it unnerved her a bit, but she was also curious. She could easily dismiss the recent events as coincidences, blame her dreams and the lights she saw on the bump on her head. She was tempted to do just that. It would be easy enough. Or, she could look at the whole of it and take it all in. Things out of the ordinary, weird things, were happening all of a sudden. Things that couldn't easily be explained away. But she, correction 'they', had both been through weird before.

For the moment, she was much too curious to dismiss anything. She was a bit creeped out, sure, but this was her lake and her woods, her house; she wouldn't be kept from them.

So, that's what she told herself in her best "non-mantra-I'm-not-really-trying-to-convince-myself" way. She would focus her thoughts and then journal about everything that had happened. And she'd talk about it with Rider. Then, maybe a different kind of picture would start to form. Perhaps something would stick out, some sort of pattern or clue.

She didn't kid herself that there wouldn't be something else happening at some point, there was obviously something going on. They would make sense of it all together. Hopefully. There. Now she felt better and uncrossed her arms. The goosebumps on her arms had vanished, but there was still a little bit of a cold, clammy handprint on her heart. She told herself that it, too, would fade.

Rider looked up from his thoughts at the same time she did, so she gave him a reassuring smile, "what 'cha thinking about?"

He smiled back, "everything."

"Yeah, me too."

CHAPTER FOURTEEN

AGGIE NEEDED HER JOURNAL. SHE HAD AN ACTUAL, PHYSICAL NEED TO get all of the day's (and yesterday's) happenings down in her journal; the same way a person needs to eat when they're hungry or sleep when they're tired. There was no making sense out of any of this until she did just that. As strong as that need was, though, she tried to push it aside for the moment. *You're just going to have to hold your horses.* There was no way that she could think straight until she got cleaned up.

Aggie rose from the table, barely finished that thought, when she was already making mental notes for her journal. Unbidden, memories of each event from the last 24 hours or so pushed and shoved their way, one at a time, sometimes several at a time, overlapping and crowding each other, into the forefront of her brain. They swirled around randomly in her thoughts, taunting her and daring her to make sense of them. Finally, she shook her head back and forth, trying to clear her thoughts like they were lines on an Etch-a-sketch, but all that did was aggravate her headache.

Leaning against the kitchen table for support, and keeping her weight on her right foot, Aggie closed her eyes and rubbed her temples for a minute. When the pain from the headache eased up a little, she opened her eyes again, took a deep breath and then let it out slowly.

"You gonna make it?" Rider was staring at Aggie with a look that was both half serious and half sarcastic; this time, just one eyebrow raised for effect.

"Probably." Aggie flashed a quick smile at Rider, it was both half reassuring and half sarcastic. They both laughed quickly and softly at each other. Aggie soaked up the warmth of their connection for a moment, smiling. They understood each other so well and Rider always had the perfect sense of when to help her "take it down a notch." It was usually when she didn't even know she needed it and it only took a few words said in the right tone. She read between the lines; he was concerned for her, of course, but he was also trying to convey that 'the situation wasn't life or death, lighten up'.

These few words from Rider had set her on the right frame of mind. She was now able to push all of the nagging thoughts to the back of her brain for the time being, where they belonged. Aggie's smile stayed on her lips as she prepared to let go of the table and hop/hobble over to the downstairs bathroom for her shower. Her hand brushed against the pocket of her shorts which caused a tinkling noise from the disturbed contents. That jogged her memory and she remembered that she had found a few treasures on her hike yesterday; she reached in to her pocket and emptied the contents into a small glass bowl that was sitting on the table.

"With everything else going on, I forgot to tell you," Aggie pushed the bowl over to Rider's side of the table, "I found these crystals on the trail yesterday. Kind of reminded me of when we found those quartz crystals in Payson; these were just sitting on the surface, too."

Rider eyes lit up as he pulled the bowl closer, "I didn't realize there were crystals in this area."

"I wasn't really looking for them, but the sun hit a few of them just right and I followed the flash of light until I realized what was there. I found six of them without really looking, thanks to the sun. A couple of them have pretty good points on them."

Aggie and Rider had been to Payson many times and they had each amassed a small collection of "Payson Diamonds" which were just quartz crystals, and definitely not diamonds. Somehow, though, the crystals were just as enjoyable to collect. She picked up and kept whatever she found, regardless of the size or if they were "terminated" (which she learned meant that the crystal had a nice pointed/pyramid like end to it). She had quite a few and kept them in small glass display jars on her window sills. Maybe someday she'd wire wrap one for a necklace or make a pendulum out of one if it was balanced just right. But for now, she didn't have any specific plans for them, except just to "have" them. She already had a spot on the kitchen window sill picked out for the new ones.

"Aggie, what's this?" Rider held out his hand so that she could see; he was holding a small, decidedly non-crystal, object in his palm.

"What is that?" She leaned over to look, then put her hand out to receive it.

She examined the item carefully; it was about the size of a quarter, chunky, covered in dirt with a small loop sticking out of it. Aggie poked at it gently with one finger trying to clean of some of the dirt, then blew on it as she loosened a few tiny chunks. Unfortunately, she could tell that below the dirt was a layer of tarnish, which she couldn't do anything about at the moment. She could tell that it had been a piece of jewelry at one time, the loop gave it away as a pendant. She wouldn't be able to make out the design or what type of material it was made of until it was cleaned, maybe not even then.

She handed the piece back to Rider, "I think it used to be a piece of jewelry. Where'd you get it?"

"What do you mean, where'd I get it?' He laughed at her, "You just took it out of your pocket. Where'd you get it?" Rider closed his fist around the old, dirty piece of jewelry and tested the weight of it.

"No. The only things I picked up yesterday were crystals. Six of 'em."

"Are you sure?" Rider resisted smirking at her, but he couldn't keep the humor out of his voice completely, "you did get quite a goose egg on your forehead. Maybe you just don't remember?" A small bit of laughter gave him away.

"Rider, I'm sure," She tried to sound indignant, but a smile gave her away, "I can count."

He looked in the bowl once more, pushed the crystals around with his finger and then glanced back at Aggie, "well, there are only five crystals in here."

"I found six, I'm sure of it. I remember thinking I was half way to a cool dozen." Aggie checked her pocket to see if the stray, sixth crystal was in there but came up empty. For the heck of it, she checked her other pocket. It was empty, also. She shrugged and looked back at Rider, who was giving her a look that all but said "OK, if you say so."

She stifled a laugh, she could see his point. If the roles had been reversed, she would be saying the same thing. "I didn't pick it up, I would have remembered. I have no idea where it came from or how it got in my pocket." Aggie raised her eyebrows as she spoke to emphasize the seriousness of her statement. Now she was even beginning to doubt what she was saying.

Finally a nervous laugh escaped, "look, I know how it must sound, but really..." Aggie sighed and sat back down in her chair. Was she losing it? Was her mind playing tricks on her? On top of everything else that had happened, now she was losing her mind?

"Ok. But really now, what the Hell is going on?" She'd asked this question for what seemed to be the hundredth time this weekend. She looked her friend in the eye, searching for a hint that this was some weird joke he was playing on her. But there was no glint of trickery in his eyes or that it had it been a practical joke (perhaps slipping the piece of jewelry into the bowl when she wasn't looking), he wouldn't have been able to hold back his laughter this long. He would have cracked by now.

Rider held her gaze but had no answer for her. In her eyes, he thought he could see a mixture of confusion, curiosity, and a hint of fear.

CHAPTER FIFTEEN

AGGIE WORKED HER WAY TO THE DOWNSTAIRS BATHROOM BY HOLDING on to the wall and hopping on her good foot. She was looking forward to the shower and letting the hot water beat down on her aches and pains. Rider had put a bandage on her forehead, then covered it with a piece of plastic wrap and medical tape. It wasn't pretty, but it would keep the water off of it and hopefully keep it from opening up again. The rest of her bruises and scratches could handle a good hot shower, matter of fact it would do them some good.

Rider told Aggie that he would take charge of Brunch, which by this time, was a late lunch. He looked through her cabinets and fridge for supplies and settled on a brunch menu anyway. He prepared eggs (over medium for him, scrambled for her), sliced ham, a side of fruit which included cantaloupe and seedless grapes. He went back and forth on whether to make toast or not, knowing she was trying to cut back on certain foods. In the end, he made the toast. He decided her diet could handle it after what she'd been through.

Even though he had tried to focus on the cooking, he found himself distracted by some news he was anxious to share with Aggie. He had tried to tuck these thoughts away when he discovered Aggie missing.

First things first, as she would say. But, now was the time. He was slightly anxious because he wasn't quite sure how she'd take the news about this new opportunity. She'd be happy for him, at first. Until it sunk in. Then, she might not be so thrilled. He did have an idea that might soften the blow, for both of them. But, she had a lot going on recently with the loss of her friend and boss, Judith, and all that entailed; if there was going to be a monkey wrench in his plan, that would be it.

By sheer luck, and not by any skill on his part, his train of thought and brunch both finished at the same moment Aggie re-entered the kitchen fresh from her shower, both hands spread above her in a 'Ta-Da' pose.

"Almost good as new."

Aggie had brushed her damp hair back from her face and she had peeled the plastic wrap off of her forehead. Rider's waterproofing idea had worked, the bandage still looked dry and clean. She had on a fresh pair of shorts and a T-shirt that had, luckily, been in the laundry she had been too lazy to bring up to her bedroom. She was still not wearing a bra. The one from the trail, beat up and bloodied, had served its purpose and then some. It was now resigned to the trash. Clean ones were upstairs, and she wasn't climbing stairs yet. Aggie was more comfortable without one and she knew Rider didn't care. He was not a boob-man, or a leg-man for that matter. One of the benefits of having a gay best friend: no sexual tension. She had always been able to relax around him.

"You look like you've gotten a second wind." Rider placed brunch on the table and gestured for her to sit. He got them drinks to go with their brunch, handed her another bag of frozen veggies for her bad ankle, then finally sat down across from her.

"Thanks, I think it's feeling a little better." Aggie put her leg up on the closest chair and applied the bag of veggies. Rider smiled at her and then pushed his egg around while he waited for the best moment to speak. Finally, they both gave into their hunger and ate in silence for several minutes.

Rider rolled a grape between his fingers, looking to it for the words he needed. The grape was of no help to him in this matter, and he realized he was on his own. He swallowed the grape, took a deep breath and started to speak. "I have some good news."

Aggie looked up from her brunch and smiled at him, "oh yeah?"

CHAPTER SIXTEEN

RIDER TOOK A QUICK BREATH AND HIS EYES LIT UP AS HE SPOKE, "I finally have an opportunity I've been hoping for." He met her eyes again, "for work, I mean." He hesitated, looking for her reaction and realized dragging it out wasn't the best idea. He took another breath and began, looking her in the eyes, "I have an offer to work as a traveling nurse."

"Really? Wow." Aggie gave him a big smile and waited to hear the rest. She felt a pang in her chest and immediately felt bad about it, "that's awesome." Hoping it didn't show on her face, she added, "where? when? Give me all the details." She focused on being sincere and sounding happy for him. This was something he had wanted for a long time and she wasn't going to take that away from him.

He shook his head yes, "It's a pretty good sized company, they are all over…"

"All over the state? The country?" Aggie prompted him, eyebrows raised again, waiting for his answer.

"Well, remember I applied to a few international nursing programs a while ago? I hadn't really expected anything to come of it because it had been so long, but they just contacted me to find out if I was available." Rider took a sip of his drink, maybe to settle his nerves or maybe to pause for effect, "they have an unexpected opening…in Italy." A smile he'd been holding back burst out on his face.

"Italy? Holy cow." She smiled back at him as it sunk in. The smile on her lips stayed, but the one in her eyes faded as she realized what this meant. Her brunch started to swirl in her stomach. *He's going to leave.* She waited for the rest of the story, trying not to let it show on her face, but realizing it was probably too late for that.

"Italy," she repeated it, testing it out, her expression the same. She hoped her smile looked natural, but he'd probably seen through it already.

"There's a family just outside of Tuscany that lost their caregiver to a family emergency and they need a replacement within the next few weeks."

"Tuscany," Aggie tried that word on for size, too. Images of green fields, sloping hills and old world architecture flooded her thoughts. "That's awesome," she was smiling again and it was genuine, if not tinged with a bit of jealousy and a hint of sadness, "for how long, do you think?"

"I don't know," Rider shrugged and sat back in his chair; he'd gotten the hard part out. "It just doesn't seem real yet, you know?"

Rider went on to explain the family lived in a remote area and help was hard to find. The patient was an 82 year old matriarch of a large goat farm and she needed general hospice care. They were willing, and able, to pay for a full-time nurse. The company that he had applied to was experiencing a shortage of qualified nurses, and then they came across his application. The pay would be enough to match his current salary, but there were added travel incentives and reimbursement for some expenses. On top of all that, the family had an in-law cottage on the property that he could stay in. The nature of the matriarch's illness made the length of the job unknown; however, if he took the assignment, when this one was over they promised to find him another if he was interested.

Aggie took it all in and as he spoke she imagined what their farm land looked like, she imagined Rider watching the sun set over the Italian countryside and sightseeing on his days off. Not only was being a traveling nurse his dream, but he'd always hoped for an assignment in Europe. Italy was almost too good to be true. It was an amazing opportunity for her friend. While he was explaining everything to her, she interjected appropriate combinations of 'oh my God' and 'holy cow'. Her head was swimming, she could only imagine how he was feeling.

"Well, obviously, you have to go." She gave him the best smile she could muster while blinking back a tear; she was already imagining the giant hole in her life with him so far away. She took a deep breath to hold off the water works, "this is such a great opportunity for you."

Rider held his held out his hand, "you haven't let me finish." It was Aggie's turn to sit back in her chair, she nodded, encouraging him to continue.

Rider looked his friend in the eye, "I had an idea - they are very hospitable and have plenty of room. Come with me."

"Really, to Italy?" Aggie was stunned. First she faced the prospect of her best friend being half way around the world indefinitely; now she was being given an opportunity to join him on a trip of a lifetime. Her stomach flipped again and for one fantastic moment she pictured herself sightseeing with Rider on his days off. In the next moment her heart sank. She had to say no.

Aggie broke away from Rider's gaze. She smiled and shook her head gently from side to side.

"Italy would be amazing," Aggie began.

"Good. That was easier than I thought it was going to be."

"I can't go," she stared down at the table, avoiding his stare. A single tear spilled down her cheek before she could catch it.

"Aggie."

Rider tapped the table in front of her so she'd look at him, "Ags," he spoke softly, "Yes, you can." His eyes pleaded with her to make the trip with him, "you've always wanted to go there, now's your chance."

"How can I?"

He chuckled, "easy, you just get a plane ticket, pack a bag and grab your camera." He was always able to boil a situation down to the simplest solution.

"It's not that easy, though."

"Yes it is, Aggie. You are making it harder." He sighed and ticked off the reasons with his fingers. The first finger went up, "you're not really working anymore so you have the time." The second finger went up, "you can afford it." Third finger, "and, with all that's happened with Judith, I think it would be good for you to get away." He waved the three fingers at her, "What's the problem?"

She chuckled and wiped the corner of her eyes. She looked her friend for a moment, searching for the right words. "I am so happy for you, this is a perfect opportunity. Of course, I would love to go with you."

"Well?"

"It's a few things. First of all, yes, I have the money; but you know that I'm not prepared to spend it like that yet. I still have to figure out the best way to handle it, I can't be traipsing around Europe like I don't have a care in the world." The first statement produced a smirk from Rider, which she returned. "Second, I don't think I can leave with everything going on. They do need me from time to time at work and Judith's estate still needs handling. Then there's the lights, the visions. My ankle." Aggie shook her head, "I can't."

CHAPTER SEVENTEEN

"I KNEW YOU WERE GOING TO SAY THAT," RIDER CHUCKLED AT HIS friend to lighten the mood. "You could come if you want to, you didn't even think about it."

Aggie wiped away the tear with her hand, "what's to think about? I can't just up and leave. What about everything going on here?"

"Like what? Judith's estate? The boxes of stuff will keep and most of the paperwork can be handled digitally. The rest can be mailed or expressed to you. You told me she left people to manage her businesses, so there's that; and, you can afford it now." He waited for her to come up with more excuses, for all of her fun loving and easy going ways, there were always more excuses.

"Having the money and feeling like I can spend it are two different things." She looked away, her thoughts were spinning. First, she lost Judith; her good friend and boss. A mentor and mother figure to her, as well. The pain of the loss was still fresh and sharp. Thinking about her now teased more tears.

Now, Rider. She felt like she was losing him, too; her best-ever friend. It all swept over her like a wave, she felt sea-sick. *He's leaving, going overseas for God knows how long. I would never ask him to stay.*

I want to go, but how can I? It wouldn't be responsible. I'd be letting Judith down. I don't even know how much money there is, how can I think of spending any more than I have to? He doesn't get it.

"Look, Aggie," Rider caught her attention, "I know there is a lot going on right now for you. That's probably exactly why you should consider it. You could put a bit of distance between all this and yourself, take some personal time, relax. Come back to it rested and ready for it."

She looked at him and thought deeply about what he was telling her, running the scenario through her mind. The more she thought about it, the more her sea-sick stomach turned on itself. There was so much to deal with from Judith's estate, and that was on top of all the crazy stuff from the last 24 hours. She felt like she was losing a battle to keep her head above water. On top of that, she still hadn't had a chance to journal anything, to re-center herself.

"I'd love to go with you, I'm going to miss you like crazy; but, I don't even have a passport. Who knew I'd need one of those, right?" She attempted a chuckle, but it came out strangled which made her cough and loosed another tear. She fought the urge to just give in and cry, release it all. After a deep breath and a sip of her drink, she continued, "I should stay. I need to stay. Maybe one of these days, once I've got all this under control here, I can meet up with you."

"What if 'one of these days' never comes, Ag?" He looked her in the eye again, he was serious this time. No chuckle, no smile. "These obligations of yours are self-imposed."

Aggie tried to think of something to counter his statement but couldn't. He was right, she always had excuses when she was caught off guard or overwhelmed.

Rider tried again, "I'm worried about you, you could use a break. Besides, you should be around people right now. You're all alone in the boonies out here, that can't be good for you." He let that linger in the air for a moment, then pleaded with her again, "come."

It was her turn to try to lighten the mood. She wiped her face of any stray tears and smiled her best happy smile. "Tuscany is going to be great, you're going to love it. I am really excited for you."

"Aggie…" He tried pleading to her with his bright blue, dark-lashed eyes. A last resort that usually won her over.

"One of these days, Rider, I promise."

CHAPTER EIGHTEEN

THERE WAS NO MOON AND THE DARK SHADOWS BEHIND THE LARGE boulders at the edge of the sand dune provided perfect cover. The man was standing on a remote section of the beach. Not taking any chances, he'd donned a pair of dark pants and a dark shirt. He was invisible.

Twenty yards in front of him, lit by a small campfire, a young couple was celebrating. They had been tangled up in each other for the whole of the time he'd been watching them, which was about a half hour. There had been laughter, then moaning, then finally, silence. They made no indication that they knew they were being watched.

He was both excited and distraught. She was the one, he would have her and they would be together. But, someone was in the way. Someone was keeping her from him. And that someone was doing indecent things to her.

A shameful memory teased at him and stoked his distress at the scene before him. His mother's voice rang in his head as loud and clear as if she were standing right beside him, "get your hands out of there!" She'd opened his bedroom door to say goodnight and caught him, "that's disgusting and dirty!" He was paralyzed and mortified. From then on it was open season for his mother. His early teens were filled with disapproving looks from his mother and biting comments about how gentlemen should behave, and where they would end up if they didn't. He always knew what she was referring to and he was always embarrassed, even though he often had no reason to be.

He mustn't watch, shouldn't watch. It was dirty and disgusting. But, he couldn't look away. His mother's voice still rang in his ears; but, when he held his knife, his source of strength and comfort, it helped to quiet it.

For the past week, he had been waiting and watching for an opportunity to be alone with her. He'd struck out so far, but he was patient. Tonight wasn't looking good so far, but he was also optimistic. He believed in luck, but only to the extent that you had to be ready for it, meet it halfway. This is how he found himself standing in the shadows, in dark clothing, trying not to be spotted.

The couple finally untangled itself and one figure became two. The smaller figure stood up, *her*, and walked towards the water. The larger figure stayed by the fire and stretched out on a beach blanket.

It had to be now. His heart raced as adrenalin began to flow through is body. He gave his knife one last stroke with his thumb and then opened it. He licked his dry lips and took a deep breath to slow his breathing. He had to act now, there was no telling how long he'd have.

He looked past the campfire for her. She was beyond light shed by the campfire. *Now. Now.* He was going to run out of time if he didn't act. He stroked his pant leg with the side of the blade. Once. Twice. He took a deep breath and crept toward the campfire.

CHAPTER NINETEEN

AGGIE WAS GOING THROUGH WHAT HAD TURNED INTO A DAILY RITUAL. Each afternoon about this time she set about adjusting and wrestling with her lounge chair on the deck by the house. Her struggle was compounded by her injured ankle. She was trying to change its orientation to the setting sun so that it was no longer blinding her. It was that pesky time of day when, although the sun was beginning to set, it was still high enough in the sky to be distracting (if not blinding). A few times each afternoon, she would get up and struggle with her lounge chair; she had to get it to the proper angle so she could do her journaling without being blinded by the sun, and still be able to see the lake. *What I really need is a giant Lazy Susan under my lounge chair,* she chuckled to herself, *that would solve the problem.*

She wore an old baseball cap to help in her ongoing battle against the glare of the setting sun. It never seemed to keep the sun out of her eyes completely, and tonight, the glare seemed to be to blame for the onset of a headache. Of course, it also could have come from the bump on her head, but she didn't want to admit it seeing as how she'd never gone to the doctor about it. She was not going to entertain thoughts about a concussion.

The sun continued to do its thing, dipping lower and lower in the sky on its way to setting for the day. Until then, though, it always seemed to be at the perfect angle to shine in just below the visor of her cap. She was either adjusting the visor or adjusting the chair. It was a losing battle, but she continued the fight. Of course, the easy solution would be to turn her chair so that her back was to the sun. But then she'd be facing her house and not the lake, and that defeated the purpose of journaling (or reading, or just sitting) by the lake.

The view was beautiful and inspiring, especially at this time of day; the setting sun turned the gentle waves a soft golden color, and the lake seemed to sparkle and shimmer just for her. It magnified the peaceful feeling that she got whenever she was near the lake. And she needed that more than anything right now.

Aggie glanced at the sky. Judging from the position of the sun, she guessed that there was still a good chunk of good light left. She'd better hustle, though. She was working in a journal that she had bound by hand and it was filled with good quality, unlined paper that had just the right feel to it and didn't bleed through no matter what type of ink or marker she used. On her small side table, she set out a nice selection of fine point Sharpies (in multiple colors, of course) and gel pens. She used different ones depending on the type of journaling she was doing; sometimes it was notes or plans or lists for a project she was working on, sometimes it was traditional journaling, sometimes just doodling. Tonight, though, she was going over her journaling from the last few days to see if there was anything she had missed. In addition to all the weird stuff that had happened, she had journaled about Rider's new job and all of her conflicting emotions on the subject. It was therapeutic.

She paused for a moment as she sat back down in her chair, her right hand hung in the air over the side table. As she was reaching for a blue marker, something caught her eye. Out in front of her, quite high above the golden, but rapidly darkening water, a light where there shouldn't have been any light flickered. Aggie quickly reasoned that it was probably a reflection. She discarded that thought because the sun was setting faster than she expected and the lake, and the hills behind the flickering light, were darkening fast. As she watched, the light fell towards the lake.

She had unconsciously adopted the familiar 'stance' that near sighted people used to help them see farther: she leaned forward in her chair while squinting and straining her eyes in an effort to focus on the light. The stance came to her naturally and mostly out of habit due to years of nearsightedness. Even though her new contact lens prescription had her seeing better than ever, years and years of habit had her squinting at the lake. She didn't even realize when she was doing it.

Aggie felt lucky to be one of the few, if not the only residence, on this section of the lake. Her home was on the Eastern side of the lake and her property backed up on to some mountains that lead to and eventually became the Mogollon Rim. She guessed that the slight changes in elevation, which also made for a slight change in climate, could explain the appearance of larger trees and lack of Saguaro Cactus around her house. Opposite from her, on the Western side of the lake, the terrain dropped down and became desert. That led over to the Superstition Mountains where it was the more typical desert landscape of Saguaro Cactus and mesquite trees, etc. Somehow, once you crossed over to this side of the lake, the trees got taller and the cacti got smaller and were fewer and farther between.

In the short time she had lived here, this quiet spot had come to be her paradise, her calming, refreshing, get back-to-herself spot that she would come to in the evenings to wind down from the day and its stressors. Some days, she would just sit and relax with a cold drink, sometimes she'd read, and sometimes like tonight, she'd do some journaling. Having the lake for her backyard made everything better.

Aggie's meager outdoor furniture sat on a deck attached to her house, it was met by a somewhat grassy lawn that stretched from behind her house, out on both sides to the woods and then ran down to the shore line of the big lake behind her house. She had her very own little dock off to one side and she could be found there frequently, sitting and sipping on a cold drink while she dangled her feet in the calm, cool water. Her house was located at the very end of the road, so she didn't have to put up with any drive by traffic.

There was an occasional lost tourist who had gotten turned around while searching for the more popular side of the lake, but they were few and far between. In addition, there was about a half mile of country road between her and her next door neighbors (if you could call them that). Her spot on the lake was pretty secluded and it became heavily wooded at the boundaries of her property. The location was perfect for someone looking for privacy, peace and quiet – which she was!

The section of the lake that she selfishly considered hers was just a small piece compared to the overall size of the lake. Her still sizable chunk of the lake seemed to be all but pinched off from the rest by two pieces of land that rose up over the lake and almost, but didn't quite, meet. Aggie had heard that long ago, there was supposed to have been a bridge that had connected the two pieces of land.

There were probably 150 to 200 yards of open water between the two small hills which led from her part of the lake out to the rest of the larger lake. She'd come to think of the hills as the Western Hill (on her left, obviously) and the Eastern Hill (on her right); not very creative she thought, but since they were probably too inconsequential to have actual names this was how she referred to them for herself. She wasn't sure, either, if they were truly oriented westerly and easterly. They probably weren't, but she wasn't going to lose any sleep over it. She could've just as easily nicknamed them Left Hill and Right Hill.

The effect made by the hills and the smallness of the open waterway between them was that her piece of the lake was very calm and many of the ducks and other water fowl joined her for the peace and quiet most nights. Because it was so secluded and separated from the rest of the lake, boaters didn't usually make it back this far; if there were any boaters out there they had most likely cast off from her dock.

A few work friends had already made a few trips around this part of the lake while she watched from the dock - she stayed back hoping to avoid a bout of motion sickness. Aggie was too susceptible to motion sickness to take a chance. She'd suffered from it terribly since she was a child and really had to plan ahead if she was going to be in a situation that could trigger it. She loved the water, though, and promised herself that she'd get out on the lake one of these days. The phrase echoed in her mind and triggered thoughts of her recent talk with Rider.

Aggie pushed these stray thoughts away and observed the lights. Their orientation to her had changed slightly and she could now tell that there were two of them, again. They flickered out in front of her on the lake and they were moving in tandem just as the other lights had.

Her adrenalin kicked in, causing her pulse to quicken. She stole a quick glance around the lake, then turned her attention back to the lights. They didn't appear to be coming from any reflection; there were no boats on the water and there didn't seem to be anything shiny floating in the water which would cause such a reflection. In fact, it seemed that as they got closer to the surface, they danced above it, not on it. Perhaps it was a bird or a duck? She tried all these thoughts on for size but rejected them in the end. Her mind raced to make sense of what she was seeing before they disappeared again.

Aggie continued to watch and concluded that the lights were independent of anything else. They appeared translucent and she could now make out that these, too, were reddish in color. Small hairs on the back of her neck stood on end. She watched as both lights touched down on the surface of the lake, they appeared to bob for a few moments, and then they disappeared below the surface. As they did, the sky brightened and the surface of the lake was golden again.

The whole sighting had taken all of about ten to fifteen seconds, at the most, and there was no trace of the lights once they had gone below the surface. Small goosebumps had appeared on both of her arms and she rubbed them away absent-mindedly. Aggie spent several minutes scanning the surface of the lake hoping for the lights to reappear. They did not. But, she was sure of one thing, the lights had been there tonight and she had seen them before. Twice. They weren't a figment of her imagination or the result of the bump on her head.

The rest of the day's good light faded as Aggie sat there, unmoving, staring at the lake and the woods and hills beyond.

WHAM! WHAM!

A loud crashing noise startled Aggie out of deep thought and caused her to heart to skip a beat. A small squeak, not the kind of scream she could be proud of had she been in a horror movie, or even on an amusement park ride, escaped her. Aggie kept a death grip on the arms of the chair as she waited for something else to happen.

CHAPTER TWENTY

AGGIE DROPPED HER CLENCHED HANDS FROM THE ARM RESTS AND shook them out in front of her while she laughed at herself. *You're a bit jumpy, aren't you girl?* She agreed with herself, but then reasoned that she had a right to be. *I mean, really, after everything that has been going on? Who wouldn't be jumpy?* She took a deep breath and let it out. *Ok, Aggie, time to put on your big girl pants and check on that noise; something just fell over. Maybe.* She couldn't think of what, though. The goose bumps that had made another appearance on her arms hadn't diminished yet. She rubbed her arms for a few moments in a show of defiance against the rising panic in her gut.

She rose gingerly from the lounge chair, slowly testing her weight on her injured ankle. She tried to imagine what could have made that noise. It sounded like the crash had come from behind and above her. Her bedroom. There wasn't really anything up there that could have tipped over. A lot of her stuff was still in boxes; she was waiting to put up some bookshelves and hadn't gotten to it yet. She made a mental note to add that to her 'To Do List'.

Deciding that her ankle wasn't that bad, if she took it slow and held onto the wall for support, Aggie headed inside. Rider's voice rang in her head reminding her to stay off her ankle. She brushed it aside as she made her way slowly to the stairs. She paused at the bottom and gripped the handrail but made no attempt to climb the stairs. Small butterflies fluttered in her chest as she looked up to the top of the stairs. She tried to convince herself she was resting her ankle, but she wasn't buying it; the truth was she was genuinely creeped out. She knew no one was upstairs but at the same time, how could she be sure these days? The butterflies got a little more rowdy and her grip tightened on the rail.

This was one of the parts about living alone that she didn't like very much (having to do the scary stuff alone, stuff like checking on strange noises and dealing with spiders) and she felt a small pang of sadness and regret that she and Rider were no longer roommates. If Rider were here, he'd at least go upstairs with her. He'd tease her, but he'd go with her.

Aggie debated with herself at the bottom of the stairs, pitting reason against fear; logically she knew she was alone in the house. *This is the boonies, who else could be here without me knowing about it?* And then, *anyone could have snuck in the front when I wasn't paying attention.* She turned around to check the front door and was reassured to see the deadbolt locked in place.

Finally, feeling pins and needles in the hand gripping the rail, she let logic win out over fear. She was being ridiculous. Aggie took another deep breath and started up the stairs, ears and eyes peeled, though. *I'll go, but I'm not going to be caught off guard.* She chuckled at herself for feeling so chicken, but at least she was going.

Realizing that she hadn't heard any more noises as she climbed the stairs, she started to relax. The butterflies were almost gone and her mind was back to trying to figure out what could have fallen over and made that noise. *It's probably one of her boxes of books.* She tried not to let herself think about what could have caused the thing to fall over. *Or what could have pushed it.* The boxes of books were pretty heavy, no stray wind was going to topple them. The crash sounded pretty loud, it wasn't something falling off her nightstand or bureau either. She just couldn't imagine what had made that sound.

Aggie finally reached the second floor landing and congratulated herself for making it this far. As she rounded the corner to her bedroom, she was sure of one thing: the noise had come from there. She had left the windows open and she was sitting almost directly below them on the porch.

WHAM!

Aggie froze, her heart pounded against her breast bone. And the butterflies were back, it felt like they were trying to get out this time. She was only a few strides from her bedroom and was pretty sure she didn't want to go any farther. Any courage she'd found had left her.

She stayed glued to her spot in the hallway, heart and butterflies pounding. As the moments ticked away and the house remained quiet, all of the pounding inside Aggie slowed. She listened for the sound to repeat and for any footsteps or signs of someone else in the bedroom. There were none.

Aggie searched down deep in her gut and tried to muster more courage, anything, a small chunk would do, "He... Hello?" It came out as a whisper. Clearing her throat, she tried again, "Hello?" It was easier, and louder, the second time.

Aggie listened for, but dreaded, a reply. She hadn't planned on what to do if someone answered her. *Run, I guess, or hide.* In the silence, a familiar line from a holiday poem ran through her mind: Not a creature stirred, not even a mouse. *Funny time for that to pop into my head.* The inner dialogue helped to divert her attention, albeit only a small fraction, from her situation. She took a deep breath and blew it out slowly. Then again.

I can't stand here all day, I've got to either go forward and face this or backward like a big, chubby chicken. She reached out and placed one hand on the wall so she could take the weight off of her bad ankle, it had begun to throb slightly. She shook her head and chuckled at her predicament and at herself.

Go on, Aggie. Just do it fast before you have time to talk yourself out of it!

Aggie let go of the wall and stood up straight; taking her own advice, she began to move toward her bedroom. She wasn't moving at light speed, but she *was* moving as fast as her throbbing ankle would allow. She supported herself as she went by holding the wall, and then the door frame, as she got closer. *There's only one way in or out of the bedroom, I would have seen anyone leave.* The thought did not comfort her, nor did her next one. *Aggie, how did you get this far without a weapon?*

Aggie stopped all forward motion and paused just outside of the bedroom doorway. She looked around for something solid she could throw or use to stab or whack an intruder. The hallway was bare except for a small table with a crystal vignette she had just put together the previous week. She scanned the small table for something useful; the pillar candle and small crystals from Payson wouldn't do any good. She eyed her amethyst geode. It was the only thing with any weight to it and beggars can't be choosers. She grabbed the geode as quickly and quietly as she was able. She tested it in her hand. It had some heft to it, was hard and had some nice rocky edges that could leave a good mark on someone if you hit them with it.

She made her way back to the doorway and braced herself against all of the unknown possibilities that might await her on the other side. Geode in hand, she took a deep breath and entered the bedroom. Sure, she only had one move if she wasn't alone, but at least she had that.

Her heart pounded as her eyes darted around the bedroom. There was no one there and not a thing out of order. Aggie exhaled. Her hands trembled so she set the geode on the bed to keep from dropping it on her good foot. Still doubting that she was alone, Aggie took more time to examine the nooks and crannies of her room more closely. She even looked under the bed, and no one wanted to do that.

She was alone and everything seemed in its place. *Huh. What the hell?*

CHAPTER TWENTY-ONE

AGGIE LOOKED AT HER NEW CELL PHONE'S MAIN SCREEN AND CHECKED the Reminders App. She was due for her weekly conference call into the office and she was dreading it. Once a week, there was a conference call between all of Judith's department managers. Aggie had always been part of the call; as Judith's right hand she took notes and helped to keep everyone on target. Now, all of the managers reported to her as Judith's successor and she had a right hand who took notes.

The calls were usually held in the late morning, about an hour before lunch. Judith had set it up that way so that everyone would be forced to get to the point and not ramble off topic. People usually wanted to get to lunch on time, so it was a pretty good system. The calls tended to be productive, on topic and short.

Now, however, Aggie was trying to fill Judith's much-too-big shoes and she felt lost. She knew the key points of each topic and could speak knowledgeably about them. Judith had taken her under her wing and had been a great mentor, but Aggie felt she had a long way to go reach Judith's level. Judith's husband had started Brewster Management shortly before they got married and she joined him after they wed. They built the business together. When he died, she continued to grow Brewster Management, it was now one of the most successful, privately owned real estate management firms in the valley.

In the last few years, Judith had been setting herself up to retire from Brewster Management. She was well past retirement age and was finally ready to let some things go and relax. Preparation for her retirement included granting many of the department managers more authority, decision making ability, along with healthy raises and yearly performance bonuses. Her managers, already loyal, became even more invested in Brewster Managements' success. Because of that, the place practically ran itself.

Judith's passing had happened quite unexpectedly and many were still grieving her loss, especially Aggie. Yet, everyone seemed to trust Judith's judgement of her taking the over the reins and appeared to take it in stride. Everyone but Aggie. Maybe Judith knew something she didn't, but she still spent a lot of time worrying that she wasn't doing enough to make Judith proud.

Aggie forced her way up and out of her thought cycle. Blinking away dry eyes, she checked the time once more. Thirty minutes to go. Aggie had a brief thought that perhaps most of the dread and stress about the conference calls was self-imposed (Rider's words rang in her ears); nevertheless, it felt real and it weighed on her heavily. She stared at the lake absentmindedly while clutching a stray couch pillow against her stomach to quiet the butterflies.

She was back in her thought cycle soon enough: staring at the lake reminded her about last night's sighting of the lights, that reminded her about the unidentified banging upstairs that followed. She came back around to the lights on the lake, then to both of the times she'd seen them in the woods. That reminded her of her dream. *Or was it a vision?* It was all a bit overwhelming, so she continued to sit on the couch, with a decorative pillow smothering butterflies (she hoped) in one hand and her phone in the other. At least she had distracted herself from the call for a few moments.

At three minutes before the hour, the ringer on Aggie's cell phone sounded and dispersed the thought cycle for good. A glance at the

Caller ID informed her that it was her right hand back at the office, Susie. *Time for the call. Great.*

"Hello, Susie. Conference Call time again so soon?" She forced out a small chuckle, hoping it sounded natural.

"Good morning, Miss Bailey. Yes, it's that time again." Formalities and no return chuckle, she was all business. Susie always called her separately and then connected her to the rest of the group. "Everyone is present on the call, shall I connect you now?"

A lightbulb went off, Susie was giving her a choice. She had a choice! Why hadn't she thought of that before? *Maybe just this once, since there's so much going on...*

"Ma'am? Miss Bailey? Shall I connect you?"

"Ah. No." Aggie paused, searching for an appropriate excuse but decided no excuse was better than a white lie, "I am not going to be able to participate today. Please make my apologies to the managers and tell them I'll be back on next week. In the meantime, please send me a copy of today's notes after the call, OK?" Aggie listened hard to the response for a tone or an objection.

"Certainly, Miss Bailey. I hope you have a great afternoon. Good bye." With that, Susie was gone. It was *that* easy. No tone, no questions asked. Easy as pie.

As the call disconnected, Aggie felt some of the weight lift off her shoulders. She took a deep breath and then blew it out hard. A coworker had labeled it her 'decompression breath'. *Looks like I've got some extra time on my hands. Now what?* Aggie's stomach rumbled, and she rested her hand on it for a moment, smiling. *The butterflies have left the building. Problem solved, time for food.*

CHAPTER TWENTY-TWO

AGGIE MOVED TO THE KITCHEN AND GAVE THE FRIDGE AND CABINETS the once over, there wasn't anything very exciting. Dieting was hard enough without it being boring, too. She saw a left over chicken breast, grapes and apples and an idea started to form: modified chicken salad in a pocket. It had been awhile since she'd had it, something Rider had come up with back in the day. It sounded just right at the moment.

She set about cutting up the ingredients and preparing the chicken salad; she cubed the chicken and halved some grapes, cut a few slices of apple and cubed them also. She added a tiny bit of mayo (*can't have chicken salad without mayo - diet or no diet*), mixed it all together and stuffed it all in a pocket. Her stomach rumbled again in anticipation and she laughed. It was a carefree sound and it filled the kitchen for a moment. She stopped and soaked in the moment, she hadn't had too many carefree moments in the last several days and it was nice.

She realized if anyone had been watching her, they'd think she was being corny or melodramatic, but that was OK. It was what it was. Aggie poured herself a diet cola with lots of ice and sat down at the table to eat. Normally, she'd sit in front of the TV while she ate and watch the murder channel. She resisted the urge now, partly because she was afraid she'd just end up staring at the lake again and that would get her nowhere fast. The other, more interesting reason, was that the little bowl of crystals from her hike had caught her eye. She recalled the non-crystal that she had apparently picked up. The one that Rider had pointed out. Perhaps she could finally give it a closer look.

As she ate, she dumped the little bowl over near her plate. She pushed the crystals around and looked them over again just for fun. Yup. There were five smallish quartz crystals and one dirty, chunky piece of something else. She guessed it was a pendant that had fallen from someone's necklace. It sure looked pendant sized and it had a loop for the necklace, but it needed to be cleaned up first. It had many layers of tarnish and muck built up on its surface. Muck being the technical term for all of the icky stuff from the woods like mud and caterpillar poop.

Aggie's lunch hit the spot. Her stomach had stopped growling, finally, so she decided to get to work on the pendant. She placed a small glass bowl two-thirds full of hot water on the table. She added a heaping spoonful of baking soda and a shot of white vinegar for good measure. A quick stir had the solution fizzing nicely. She dropped the piece into the bowl and let it sit there while she hobbled off for a few more supplies.

She returned to the table with an old toothbrush, and old worn, but clean cotton rag, and an awl. She grabbed the box of baking soda and set it on the table beside the other things. Impatience got the best of her and she plucked the item out of the fizzing bowl. She inspected it closely, some of the muck had come off in the bowl, but there was much more still left to remove. Aggie grabbed the old toothbrush, wet it in the bowl, and then tried scrubbing the pendant. Wet muck splattered the table, her hands and her face.

Ok, new plan. She grabbed her paper towels from the counter and placed a few sheets on the table and blotted the muck from her face with another. Aggie donned a pair of gloves kept at the sink, placed the bowl on the towels and pulled it close. She dipped the pendant in the water and held on to it as she scrubbed it with the toothbrush. She was less vigorous this time and most of the water and muck stayed in the bowl. She pulled it out of the bowl after several scrubs and noticed she was making progress. Any large chunks of muck were picked off with the awl and she took care not to damage the surface below. The solution began to get murky, so she dumped it out and replaced it, minus the vinegar this time.

When the water got to be murky once more, she dumped it again. This time, though, she only put in a very little amount of water and a lot more of the baking soda. She gave it a stir and was rewarded with a paste. She rinsed the muck off toothbrush, dipped the toothbrush into the paste mixture and then applied that to the pendant. This process was repeated many times and eventually she replaced the toothbrush with the worn out rag. The last step was directed at removing as much tarnish as possible and she kept on until the paste was gone. Cleaning the pendant had turned meditative, any worry and concern of the past few days melted away as she scrubbed.

Finally, Aggie felt that she had gotten off all the muck and tarnish that was going to come off. She was even wearing some of it. She rinsed off the pendant thoroughly then blotted it dry. Her hard work was rewarded and she held a beautiful piece of jewelry. It was indeed a pendant and it had a handmade, artisan quality to it. Something about the style told her it had been made many years ago. She was pretty sure it was silver because of the way the baking soda had lifted most of the tarnish. Aggie finally removed her rubber gloves and the pendant felt cool to the touch. In her hand was a honeybee perched on a chunk of honeycomb. The underside appeared to have initials, or some type of signature mark, but it wasn't quite legible. Her hand closed protectively around the pendant and she made a mental note to tell Rider about it.

Aggie's head began to ache and she put it down to eye strain from working on the pendant. *I didn't have a concussion.* She sat back in her chair and closed her eyes. With her eyes closed, she became aware of the weight of the pendant in her hand. She pictured it in her mind's eye, it really was beautiful. She imagined who its owner might have been and how upset they must've been at having lost it.

The temperature in the kitchen dropped as she sat there, prompting a few goosebumps to appear. *Must be a breeze off the lake.* Eyes still closed, she smiled and enjoyed the breeze. It was only going to get hotter as the days went by. Sitting quietly, she became aware of an ache in her neck and shoulders. Tension had built up over the past few days and made itself at home. *What I really need is a soak in a hot tub and a cold drink.* Rolling her head around on her neck released some of the tension and produced several cracking noises that were very satisfying.

Aggie groaned at the headache, it didn't seem to want to go away. *Time to take something for it.* She sat up in her chair and rolled her neck one more time. She was rewarded with two smaller cracks as she opened her eyes.

Beside her at the table stood a tall young man, long dirty-blonde hair, wearing a T-shirt and cut off fatigues; he was barefoot and held something small in his hand. He looked directly at her with peaceful eyes and a half smile. In the fraction of a heart beat that it took Aggie to react, he flickered and was gone. Aggie blew out a quick breath of relief and the scream that was building turned into a nervous laugh. Another fraction of a heart beat passed and he was back. Aggie's heart was in her throat. The man was much closer to her this time and he had metamorphosed into something dark and empty. Blood poured from a wound in his neck and soaked his T-shirt. His peaceful eyes were now lifeless.

Aggie let out a startled scream. She tried to jump from her chair but got hung up on the arms. As she stumbled and fell back, trapped by the chair's arms and his proximity, she dropped the pendant she had been holding. With both hands free, a moment of clarity prevailed; she grabbed the arms of the chair and thrust it back and out of her way as she stood. Her mind raced to make a plan. *Run? Stand my ground? Fight? With what?*

She looked up to see how close he'd gotten, raising her hands to fend him off. He was gone. *Gone?* She looked around. *Is behind me?* Her heart leapt at the thought and she spun around as the thought occurred to her. *Nope, gone.*

Aggie fell back into her chair, one hand covering her mouth. She dropped her hand after a moment and took several deep breaths to calm her nerves. *What the heck is going on?* When her heart beat returned to normal, she concluded that she was going to have to find a different way to ask that question. It wasn't very original anymore.

CHAPTER TWENTY-THREE

AGGIE NEEDED SOMETHING TO CLEAR HER HEAD, THERE WAS WAY TOO much going on lately and she needed to put it out of her mind. For a few minutes, anyway. Just long enough to decompress. Especially after what had happened in the kitchen earlier. That was a little too close for comfort. Ignoring it probably wasn't the best idea, but it was what she needed at the moment. Rider was busy prepping for his trip. He didn't have much time and she didn't want to hold him up or burden him. Reality would rear its ugly her soon enough. In the meantime, what she could do was read.

She was sitting on her bed in a tank top and underwear; some of her pillows propped up behind her, a big fluffy one in front of her. On top of the fluffy pillow was a murder mystery she had been wanting to read for a while but just hadn't been able to get to. Against her wishes and before she could even open her book, her thoughts began to drift. Thoughts of orbs, dreams, crystals that weren't crystals. A knot began to form in her gut as each thought ran through her mind. She was able to catch herself, though, and pushed them out of her mind so she could focus on her book and relaxing.

She crossed one leg in front of her and let the other one dangle off the side of the bed. If she sat with both legs crossed, the circulation would get cut off and she'd get pins and needles. She pulled the pillow in close and over her crossed leg. She closed her eyes and soaked in the moment: peace and quiet (for a change), soft pillows behind her and soft bed below, a diet cola with ice (and a snack) on the bedside table, a cool breeze blowing in off the lake through the open windows, and a new murder mystery to carry her thoughts away. She focused on those things and tried to manifest calmness throughout her body.

TAP TAP

No. No. Not again. Aggie's senses fired up, but she paused and waited. Maybe it's coming from outside? She crossed her fingers, hoping it would go away. She needed a quiet night. *Come on, just one night? Please?*

Her plea was answered soon enough, and she was quickly reminded that not all answers are the ones you want to hear.

TAP TAP

It was louder this time.

Aggie's head and shoulders drooped, she sighed, opened her eyes and looked around for the source of the tapping. A line from an old movie popped into her head: "It's coming from inside the house." She laughed to herself, but it wasn't funny. A chill crawled down her spine and stayed there.

"What now?" She attempted a sarcastic tone, but the butterflies in her gut betrayed her and it came out sounding weak. Her heart started to beat a little faster, too. It wasn't racing like before, but it was revving its engine just in case.

WHAM!

Aggie flinched and pressed herself back against her pillows as if she could escape through them. She didn't realize she was holding her breath until she needed to let it out.

She didn't want to believe her eyes, but she'd have to. She'd had the perfect view. Directly in front of her were the windows that overlooked the lake and directly in front of the windows were window seats. She happened to be looking that way and was witness to one of the window seat 'lids' raise up on its hinge and slam back down again. All by itself. In the almost light of day.

Aggie was tempted to run from the room and head downstairs. But that didn't feel safe either. Not now. Not after that man appeared and then disappeared. Safety was an illusion. As much as she had wanted to put this all out of her mind, however temporarily, something out there wasn't having it. She sat for several minutes and gathered her thoughts.

She concluded that the noise she'd heard the day before, and thought was a box of books falling over, must have been the window seat slamming down that time, too. Avoiding the thought about how it opened and slammed by itself, she further reasoned that the window seat wanted her attention. Well, it had her full attention now.

Well, I have to go look now, right? You're not going to leave me alone until I look, huh? The window seat didn't answer her, but it didn't slam again either. She pushed away the pillow and mystery book and bid them a silent farewell. She patted the book lightly, as if it were an impatient child waiting for her attention.

I'll be back to you soon. She glanced at the window seat. *Probably.*

Aggie slid over on the bed until her dangling foot hit the floor, she swiveled and the other foot followed. She stood up and faced the window seat, squaring her shoulders as one would (she imagined) against an adversary.

Courage, girl! She slowly worked her way across the room to the window seat. Suddenly the breeze blowing in off the lake was too chilly, goose bumps appeared on her arms and stayed there. She told herself it was the breeze anyway, and she *was* in her underwear, after all.

Now, she was in a stare-down with the seat. Sure, now it wasn't going to open all by itself, it wanted her to do it.

You picked a great time to be quiet. Still, she just stared at the window seat. She had to open it, she knew that. But what would she find when she did? An animal? A rat?! A tiny little boogeyman? She had no clue what she'd find but wondering about the possibilities was not helping the situation at all.

Remembering how unprepared she was the first time this had happened, she looked around for some sort of weapon or manner of defense. The only thing she could locate was a hard cover book. She grabbed it, realizing at the same time, its inadequacy. *If this is going to continue, I'm going to have to at least get a baseball bat.* It was going to have to do. She hefted it, trying to reassure herself of its potential lethality. If need be, she could at least use it as lever.

Next item: fast or slow? She weighed her options and decided on fast, thinking that would surprise whatever was in there, if it was alive, that is. She realized it sounded foolish, whatever was in there obviously wanted her to open the seat. The only one around here that was going to be surprised was her. Aggie chuckled to herself at the thought and realized if she could joke at a time like this, maybe she'd be OK after all.

Aggie held the book firmly and placed it under the lip of the window seat. She paused only for a second and then, at a regular speed, lifted the lid. She lost her nerve only at the very last moment and flung the seat back with a little bit of force. As she was lifting the lid, it occurred to her that her arm would be hanging defenseless over the open window seat for a moment and she didn't want to take any chances. Much like making sure your feet don't stick out from under the covers when you're sleeping. There are just some things that are common sense.

She quickly stepped back half a step, an imagined safe distance, and peered cautiously into the open space. A damp, musty essence rose from it and wafted up to meet her. The space was empty except for a small book about the size of a paperback, it looked like it had fallen in a big puddle or gotten rained on and then dried out. The covers and the pages were quite warped. It occurred to her that it hadn't rained in quite a while and, further, that she didn't think she had a leak in here.

Ok. That wasn't so bad. You look harmless. Aggie's courage and confidence rose. The butterflies quieted themselves, finally. She reached into the space and pulled out the book to get a closer look. It was light blue and had a hard cover with a faded rainbow in the center above the word "DIARY". It looked damp, but felt dry. She flipped through a few wrinkled pages, they were dry as well; but, every bit of it had water stains. Aggie lifted the diary to her nose and wrinkled it against the damp, musty smell, confirming that the smell in the window seat had been coming from the book.

She brought it back to her bed and sat down on edge. As she stared at it she tried to discern from it what all the fuss was all about. *Why was it in the window seat? How did it get wet? When was it placed there?* She'd already checked out the window seats when she moved in, they'd been empty then. And last, but not least, *what did it want?*

As these thoughts rolled around in her mind, she opened it to the first page. Written in a bold, neat script was the name Winifred.

Ok, Winnie's Diary, what do you want with me?

CHAPTER TWENTY-FOUR

AGGIE ADJUSTED HERSELF ON THE BED SO THAT SHE FELT comfortable. She wasn't so sure she should be looking through someone else's private diary. If they were like her, writing anything and everything that came to mind, there'd be a lot a private thoughts in there. It wouldn't feel right. If someone read through her journal without her permission, she'd be very upset at the intrusion.

Holding it gently in one hand, she brought it up to her chest and held it over her heart. She imagined the emotions, sentiments, *intent* contained in the diary seeping through the book into her. *Give me a hint*, she whispered to the diary, *what do you want me to do with you?* She half expected, half hoped for something to happen (which would be par for the course around here lately) and looked around the room expectantly; but like the window seat, it was silent now too. *Ah, if it were only that easy.*

Aggie was already feeling protective of the orphaned diary, the same way you would a lost puppy or a fallen baby bird. She wondered if she was supposed to give it to someone, to find Winifred or one of her relatives perhaps. How could she know for sure? Other ideas started coming to her: maybe it held clues to an unsolved murder, or a disappearance, or an adoption... Chuckling to herself, she realized those ideas were a bit extreme and coming from the mystery nut part of her, so she shifted her focus back to what she knew now. Rather, what she *thought* she knew.

The most obvious answer was it's just a diary that Winnie left behind, or forgot. Maybe it was there the whole time. Maybe she just missed it before. *But what about the seat banging? The diary obviously wanted her attention.* That thought stayed at the forefront of her mind and it pushed for an explanation she didn't have.

What if she just skimmed a few pages here and there? Surely that could do no harm. Maybe there was an address or phone number or some other clue. That wouldn't really be an invasion of privacy, not if she was trying to locate the owner. Right? Aggie thought maybe she was pushing the boundaries with that one, but it was all she could think to do. At least it was a plan. "Besides," she held the diary up in front of her, "you called me.*"*

Ok, here goes. Aggie opened the diary to the first page even though she'd seen it before. She shook her head, nothing new. She turned to the next page and saw that was where the diary entries began. No address, no phone numbers. *Maybe the back cover?* She flipped to the last page, nothing.

Flipping through the diary's pages quickly, she tried to scan them without reading them. Which turned out to be a lot trickier than she expected. Several words popped out at her and she couldn't help but read them: Stephen, memory, my scar. How could she not want to read more now?

The diary was only about half full, Winifred had never finished it. Aggie felt a small pang in her chest, the unfulfilled potential of the diary was kind of sad. There was so much room left for so many more thoughts and memories. What could have caused her to stop writing in it or to leave it behind?

Something caught her attention on the top of the page of the last entry, the date was from September, 1975. *That explains the rainbow on the cover.* Images of hippies, protests and peace signs floated before her mind's eye. She had been just a kid in 1975, so these memories were from a child's perspective. This intrigued Aggie completely and it made her curious about Winnie and her life and what had happened to her in 1975 that might have made its way onto her diary's pages. Every minute that went by brought more questions and piqued her curiosity.

Crap, now I want to read it.

Who am I trying to kid, anyway? I've wanted to since I picked it up.

Maybe just one page.

CHAPTER TWENTY-FIVE

MONDAY - MAY 19, '75

I should be dead. At least that's the way I see it based on what I've been told.

The doctors think that writing my thoughts down might help to jog my memory and I agreed to give it a try. One of the nurses was sweet enough to get me this diary, it's blue and has a rainbow on the cover. It's not really my taste, it looks like it was made for a teenager. But, it serves a purpose, I guess.

I've never been one to keep a diary, but I'll give it a shot. Who knows what'll happen? Woulda, coulda, shoulda. If I'd been in the habit already, I might get back some of what I've lost of the past year.

I'm not really sure if I'm doing it right. Or, even where to start. That leaves me wide open for someone to say: at the beginning. But that's a whole other ball of wax. What beginning? I'm not sure exactly where that is. My real beginning was back in New Mexico. That's what I remember, but that was over a year ago. My recent memory? It's gone. The extent of it only goes back a few days - to when I woke up here - that feels like my beginning right now. Or, would it be what I know from the police and the doctors? That goes back a little further, to that night. The night that I can't remember, no matter how hard I try. The night that changed almost everything, from what they tell me.

I woke up in the hospital about a week ago (and not to sound like an old cliché, but I'm going to say it anyway because it applies in this case) with no memory of how I'd gotten here. As I woke up, I looked around and slowly became aware of my surroundings. Light green, industrial style walls, a couple of windows overlooking a busy parking lot, important looking machines blinking and beeping occasionally. A television on the wall opposite my bed, turned off. A stand by my bed with medical stuff on it like gauze and tape. Ever present, of course, is the underlying general medical smell you only get in a hospital.

I looked myself over and saw that I had a tube sticking into my veins; feeding God-knows-what into my arm. It felt intrusive and foreign but I've come to appreciate the way it sends magical pain medication through my system. Even still, there's pain, and it flows through my body playing dodgeball with the medicine. I'm not sure how bad it is without the meds, but I don't want to find out. I've heard the phrase "dull ache all over" but that's not quite accurate. To me, it's like a sharp ache all over. There's nothing dull about it. It is constant and only lessens when I nap. The coma must have been wonderful. I guess that's how the body protects itself - it just shuts down and takes a big nap.

I'm finally able to sit up without too much pain. After a few days of trial and error, my body and I have reached an agreement. I try not to move around very much, or too suddenly, and it doesn't fill me with shooting pains. It's a precarious truce at best, but it's all I've got right now.

4 p.m.

Somehow, the news that I'm finally awake up got out and the news spread quickly amongst my friends. I know that's who they were because they told me so. They showed up in small batches throughout the day, as much as the nurses allowed. When it got to be too much for me (it's incredible how exhausting just lying here can be), the nurses noticed and would make them leave. Soon enough, though, a new batch would appear.

First, it felt like a practical joke, but then it was frightening. Which, I found out, is also exhausting. Of course, everything these days is exhausting. The scariest part was not knowing any of their names or faces. They could have been anyone. I did my best not to let on, I could tell by their expressions that they cared for me. Several of the girls were crying ("happy tears" they said) and I got a lot of hugs.

I wondered if I was going crazy. I didn't recognize any of them. Not one. They spoke to me as if we shared a history. Nothing was familiar. I tried to follow along in the conversation, but I couldn't. So, I just kept quiet and smiled. I decided not to make any excuses or apologize for being out of it, I figured they could draw their own conclusions.

They seem like really nice people. They brought cards, flowers and well wishes. Their feelings for me seemed genuine. I lay there like a fraud not being able to reciprocate; nodding and smiling, hoping they couldn't tell. I'd be lucky to have them as friends. I have no idea what to say or do if they come back. Tell them the truth, I guess.

CHAPTER TWENTY-SIX

Today I had another visitor. I don't think he was part of the crowd from yesterday. He had dark brown wavy hair and I'm guessing he was at least thirty. He'd brought a small pink and green plant and he was looking at me with worry in his eyes. I finally decided to come clean. All of the pretending yesterday, to recognize people and follow strange conversations, was just too much for me.

"I'm sorry, I just don't recognize you." I tried to look as apologetic as I could, so he wouldn't be insulted. "My memory isn't what it used to be."

He gave a small laugh and I swear I could see a glimmer of relief in his reaction. He set the plant down nearby and gave me a reassuring look, "Th-there's no need to be sorry. I didn't expect you to remember me, I just came to see how you were doing."

I'm sure I looked confused, "how do you know me?"

"I was with you that night. I sure am glad that you're going to be OK."

In an instant, fear clutched at my heart and gave it a big squeeze. I tried as hard as I could to remain calm on the outside, my instinct though, was to back as far away from him as I could on the bed. But, my body and I have this agreement, so I just lie there, unmoving.

I sat there processing what he said. I tried to remain calm, grasping for memories of that night, anything. Just one. Nothing came to mind but what I was told by the nurses, and briefly by the cops.

I took as deep of a breath as I could manage, looked him in the eye and said, "They told me you were killed. I think they said your name was Billy." I pulled the lightweight blanket closer in a feeble attempt at protection. My fingers clenched the material. I looked around casually for the call button, just in case.

My guest sat back in his chair and returned my stare. He clasped his hands together, as if in prayer, held them out to me for a moment and then let them drop to his lap. "No. Oh my God." He shook his head side to side, his right hand now covering his heart, "I'm so sorry. That wasn't me. Didn't they tell you?"

When he realized I had no answer for him, he proceeded. "The police told me that the man who died was your friend. I tried to help you both. I want to tell you how sorry I am that I wasn't in time to help him too."

I sat stunned for a few moments, taking it all in, trying to recall anything I could. I had nothing. No memory of that night, of him, of my friend. I didn't even have any tears. I should be mourning my friend, I should be saddened that he lost his life trying to save mine.

Of course, I'm grateful. Only, I have that same feeling inside me as when you hear a terrible story on the evening news: something bad happened to someone and they were hurt or killed. You are removed from it, so it doesn't really hit home. Sure, you feel bad. Think, poor bastard - why did that have to happen? But, again, you're removed from it so you go on about your day and don't give it another thought, for the most part.

Yesterday, my friends steered clear of any talk about that night. It didn't occur to me until just now, as a matter of fact; I was too busy trying to figure out what was going on with all those strangers in my room. I think they had all agreed ahead of time to just talk about the good times. Certainly, if the man who was killed was their friend also, they'd hidden it well. Or, perhaps they had already done their grieving.

All at once I was overcome with a yawn, there are some that will just not be suppressed. I apologized and gave him a few more moments before I asked if he could please excuse me so I could take a nap. I didn't have to pretend to be tired, I truly was. Suddenly and unavoidably exhausted. I hope I didn't come off as rude.

He did ask if he could drop in again to visit and I told him that would be fine. I might just as well visit with a stranger as my friends; at this point I know about the same amount about of each of them. He left the pretty little plant on one of the little bureaus and I felt him leave rather than saw him. My eyes were already shut. I don't think I remembered to thank him. For the plant or for helping me. I don't even think I got his name.

CHAPTER TWENTY-SEVEN

FRIDAY - MAY 23, '75

I'm going to have to tie a string around my finger until writing in this diary becomes a habit. I forgot yesterday, another busy day with doctors and tests and the poking and prodding.

Had a few visitors yesterday, but not as many as the day before. Just a few of the girls came back, the only one whose name I can remember is Clara. I started off our visit by admitting to my amnesia and saying that was the reason for acting so weird the day before. She patted me on the hand and said that they already knew (the nurses told them), but they were my friends and were going to be here for me. She added that she was impressed with the way I had handled myself yesterday, and if it helped, that it reminded her of the old me. Brave and strong. I suppose that's a good thing to know about yourself. Hope she's right.

Clara is the kind of girl you notice in a room full of girls. She's pretty, of course, but that's not what draws you in. It's the energy about her, a sort of subdued electricity. I get the feeling she'd be a real firecracker if she let loose. It's in her smile, her eyes, her conversation. Something just below the surface; like she knows the secret to happiness and you want in on it. She says we're best friends and showed me a few Polaroids of us together. You think I'd remember a girl like that. She left me with a kiss on my cheek and promise to be back. It will be nice to get to know her.

It was about mid-morning when I got another visitor: Stephen, the man who found me on the beach. He came in timidly and asked if it was a good time to come in. I told him it was as good as any, and offered him a chair near my bed. He introduced himself, officially, and we made small talk for a bit. I finally remembered to thank him for what he did that night. I also apologized for not saying it the other day. He played it down. You know, small talk.

After an awkward moment of silence, he smiled and said, "since you aren't able to tell me a little bit about yourself, how about if I go first?" I laughed and I told him that would be great. That broke the ice and we both felt a little bit more comfortable from then on.

I found out he travels for work, a salesman I believe. I'm not sure he said what his product is, though. He lives in southern Arizona and travels mostly through the southwest. He likes the independence and opportunity to see the scenery along the way. He asked me how my friends were handling my amnesia and if the doctors had told me when I could go home. (Pretty well and not yet).

I watched him as we talked. I noticed that he grew more relaxed as our visit went on, but I could tell it was an effort. Below the surface, he was uneasy, nervous. He kept his hands in his lap, one resting on each thigh. Occasionally, he'd slide one palm back and forth like it was sweating. I suppose he's just shy, which makes what he tried to do for me even more impressive. My heart went out to him and I made a conscious effort to make him feel more at ease around me.

Stephen left unprompted when I started yawning. I thanked him for visiting and he took my hand in his (it was soft and dry!) and said it was his pleasure. Kind of corny, kind of sweet.

CHAPTER TWENTY-EIGHT

TUESDAY - JULY 15, '75

Ugh! I am so tired of coming up against a brick wall. All I have to show for my efforts are headaches and hangovers. I still can't remember anything about California, or that night. Nothing.

I need something good, something happy. I need to know that my memory does work. I feel like a failure and it's taking a toll on me. It's not just the missing memories, it's all the wondering and worrying about them. It's also the what if's and the fact that the attack is still unsolved. I'd really like to know what I've been missing. I've never liked that, I always wanted to be included. "Be careful what you wish for." I can hear Granna's voice in my head as I write that.

I had a thought. Instead of beating myself up for having a broken brain, or moping around about what I don't remember, I'm going to give myself a break. Today I'm gonna write about the things I do remember. Maybe that will help my brain to work a different way and not struggle so much? It's worth a shot. At the very least, I will have written down something positive for a change.

Granna. My grandmother Anna. My Mom's mother. A free spirit. Husband died in the war, never remarried. Raised me after my parents died.

Granna raised me in a stable, loving home in the high desert of New Mexico. I remember happy years filled with friends and family and lots of laughter. It's only looking back now that I realize how hard it must have been for her to take me in while grieving the loss of her own daughter. Just because I don't remember seeing her break down, doesn't mean she wasn't sad at times.

She was a great example of strength. We had our share of tough times over the years, like everyone does, but she never bowed under the pressure. Granna kept a smile on her face and would say 'every cloud has a silver lining' and that you 'just had to remember to look for it'.

Granna was a nurse and that paid her bills, but her passion was clay. She 'threw pots' in all of her spare time and decided to raise honeybees after an early retirement. We learned how together, and I cherish those days with her, give or take a few bee stings.

Between the clay and honey bees, Granna and I stayed pretty busy. She kept her kiln full while I gathered honey. We'd bring both to the local co-op to sell, but mostly we went for the fellowship. Granna would meet up with her friends, neighbors from the surrounding area who'd bring in their products, as well. Produce, pies, tinctures, soaps and creams; you get the idea. They made out pretty well, too, but that's not why they kept going back. They went back for the same reasons we did: friendship, coffee and the card games.

They played a variety of card games over the years, but my favorite memories are from the times when I was old enough to join them. They taught me to play Rummy, or as Granna called it, 500. They said learning this card game was a good base for others requiring more skill. And I did learn other card games, but none of the others matched the fun I had playing Rummy.

There was always a game going at the co-op and each of the ladies had their special quirks. Granna watched the others like a hawk, certain if she'd let her guard down, one of them was sure to cheat. There were two old sisters, Mary and Louise, who would argue strategy in French and about why the other played a certain card or not. If anyone else dared to take a side, Mary and Louise would stop their infighting and redirect their snipes to whom ever had been so bold.

The funniest part was the gossip; there wasn't really a hair salon in our small town, so this is where it all happened. And boy, those ladies lived for gossip. They frequently got it wrong, but they all just hungered for the next exciting piece of news. I guess it was their form of today's soap operas. I felt snug and warm and loved during those games; they took me into their hearts and I was one of them. I miss those days. Rummy will always have a special place in my heart because it makes me feel like home.

Remembering back, I think I understand a little bit more now about Granna. She retired early, but no so that she could relax. She was always on the go, one way or the other. I don't recall that she ever let life get her down, she was too busy enjoying herself. My grandmother filled her life with the things that made her happy: her art, her honey bees, her friends and loved ones. She didn't dwell on what wasn't there.

There are lessons for me in those memories, so maybe this walk down memory lane is helpful. If Granna was here, she'd scold me for feeling sorry for myself and for trying to drink my problems away.

Maybe that's my lesson. Maybe I'm focusing on the wrong stuff. Maybe I'm trying too hard. Maybe I just need more Rummy and less Rum.

CHAPTER TWENTY-NINE

I know that it's going to make me sound crazy, but I need to get out of here. Out of this house. Out of this state. It doesn't make sense, I know. This seemed to be the perfect spot to heal and recover; up to now, it has been just that. There's no one around to bother me for miles and I have felt very safe here. Up to now.

Now I just feel trapped. From the outside looking in, I'm sure most people would think I have it made. I have this great big house to roam around in, by myself most of the time, a nice little dock on a nice little piece of the lake (which I also have to myself most of the time). Amazing sunsets, especially now since it's Monsoon Season. Somebody might ask, "what else could she want?"

Well, that's what they get for judging a book by its cover. Right now I want my freedom. I do have some freedom, to a certain extent. I am free to come and go wherever and whenever I want, so far as my feet can take me. Which is not as far as it used to be after the surgery.

I have no transportation, so I can't go into town or for a ride. I even dragged myself out to that gross old shed. I was hoping to find a bike tucked into a corner somewhere, because I'm pretty sure I could handle a gentle bike ride. At least it would be <u>something</u>. There's never been a bike here, as far as I can tell. Not even spare parts. That shed was nasty, what it does have is an abundance of cobwebs and they won't get me far.

Everyone out here besides Stephen is a stranger to me. Well, they are back home too, for that matter. By back home, I guess I mean California. Now that I think of it, it's kind of funny that I would call a place I can't remember home. At least back home, *they* know me and I'm sure I could get someone to take me for a ride or lend me a bike. Clara seems like she'd be the best bet. I could even get a bus pass. Out here in the boonies, there's nothing. No friends, strangers or buses. If I had known that Stephen being gone so much would turn into a bad thing, I might have thought twice about accepting his offer. I figured this was the best option: no "friends" around to confuse me, I'd be away from the place where it happened (and I'd feel safer), Stephen would be on the road for his job a lot (so I wouldn't have to endure his looks of pity).

All I have out here, it seems, is time, my thoughts (which I'm trying to get down and into this diary) and the whiskey. Don't get me wrong, it serves its purpose, but it's not going to get me out of the house (or out of my head). It's not like I have to go into town, I just need to know that I can. I know, self-pity is gross. One problem at a time.

The more I dwell on where I can't go, the more I feel I need to get away. I know I left California for good reason, I'm not so sure that I am emotionally ready to go back there, yet. I could go back to Granna's old house in New Mexico, but that's a little remote also. I would just be swapping out one lonely place for another. Also, I would be surrounded by her memories, which are many (and happy) but they are not the memories I need right now. I know I would just be distracting myself. Staying here, with this overwhelming feeling of being trapped, is doing the same thing.

I have saved most of the money I got from Granna after she passed away. It's not a huge amount, but I thought I might be able to use some of it to get a second-hand vehicle. Maybe I could get a station wagon or a van, that way I could just head off somewhere and sleep right in the back if I want to. That would save on motel money. I always wanted to see more of the country, now might be the best time.

When I read back over these last few paragraphs, I think maybe I don't know what I want after all. Maybe I'm just coming up with different ways to distract myself from remembering. Amnesia is a cold bitch. I didn't ask for this and I'm out of ideas. I thought I was strong enough to do this. I also thought that Arizona would be an adventure. And I think it would, if I could see more of it.

Stephen is not going to be happy about this. We both know that the condition upon my accepting his offer to stay here was no strings and when I was ready to go, I'd go. He's been great so far, but I've been getting the feeling that he's growing more attached to me the longer I stay. I hope he's not expecting more than I can give him. His classic forehead kisses are starting to last a little longer than they used to and feel a bit creepy. I should be able to just talk to him, but the thought of it makes me very anxious. I can't just stay here and play Rummy with him forever. He had to know that.

Something has to change soon, I know that much. I can't seem to drink enough to make it either all go away or make it all OK. I guess I need to come up with another strategy.

CHAPTER THIRTY

AGGIE STOPPED FLIPPING THROUGH THE DIARY AND SET IT DOWN ON the bedside table. She was just slightly ashamed of herself for reading way more than 'just one page'. However, reading those entries made her feel markedly closer to Winnie. She was almost flesh and blood now, not just a name in the front of the diary.

She got up from the bed and walked over to the selfsame window seat that birthed the diary. Without hesitation of any kind, she climbed onto the seat sideways, adopting the half-cross legged position she'd used on the bed. Sideways, she could look out over the moonlit lake while she thought things over.

Her mind was already processing the diary entries she'd just read. On the surface, there was at least one similarity: they'd both inherited property. Winnie, from her grandmother and Aggie, from her friend and boss. But reading between the lines, there were also not-so-obvious similarities between them. Neither of them, and she hated to admit this about herself, could make an important decision to save their asses. Even the decisions they needed to make were not that different.

According to her diary, Winnie couldn't decide if she wanted to stay where she was or to take off. It was turning in to a similar thought process for Aggie, although for much different reasons. She wanted desperately to stay here in her new home. She had loved it from the very first time she'd visited Judith here. It was a beautiful, old fashioned house. It was secluded and peaceful, and the fact that it was right on the lake put its charm over the top. She had always envisioned it as a B&B, a perfect getaway for those caught up in the city's hustle and bustle. She'd even told Judith so. Now, she had a chance to try to make it happen.

She had been completely unprepared for Judith's passing, and even more unprepared for Judith to have left her anything, never mind everything. She was still trying to make sense of it all. But, one thing that was clear was her feelings about this house. She absolutely loved it. If she was going to spend any of the money, it would be on that.

Now, her dream was being threatened. Things were curious at the start, but as the days went by it had gotten more and more frightening (she pushed away a flashback of the man in her kitchen). She feared that soon she would be too on edge and too scared to stay here. If things didn't let up soon, she would have to make some hard decisions. The thought of having to leave broke her heart.

Since her inheritance, she'd felt pressure to meet everyone's expectations. She felt like every financial or business decision would be met with looks of disapproval, followed by unsolicited opinions from colleagues and family alike. The stress of trying to do the right thing had overwhelmed and immobilized her.

Knowing she needed to figure it out one way or the other didn't ease the decision process any. Reading about Winnie's flip-flopping made her feel like she was at least among friends. She had even thought about making a list of pros and cons. No matter how the columns balanced out, it always came down to knowing she'd have to explain herself to them. "Them' being all the people she felt wanted to help her make the smart choices with her inheritance, thinking they knew best. Thinking they had her best interests at heart.

Attempts at establishing boundaries seemed to fall on deaf ears and so she second guessed almost every decision these days. Rider had been the only person close to her who had been silent on the matter, if you didn't count their recent conversation on Italy. And she didn't.

Of course 'they' were happy for her. Now she was, to quote her sister, 'all set'. There hadn't been any requests for loans. Yet. There had been tons of advice on how and where to invest, even though her family had been middle class their whole lives and hadn't had to deal with anything quite this large. The money had been a blessing and a surprise; she'd be forever grateful to her friend and boss for even considering her, never mind making her the sole heir. But, it was truly a double edged sword.

She wasn't lacking for ideas on how to spend the money, if she was so inclined. She and Rider had played the 'Lottery Game' many times over the years. Any time they'd bought lottery tickets that had a really large jackpot, they would take turns telling the other what they would do with the money. They'd talk about what they would buy first, where they would go, who they would (and wouldn't) share it with. They had always agreed to make sure the other one was taken care of. Of course, you never really expected it to happen, but one wanted to be ready. Just in case. Yeah, she had plenty of ideas of what to spend it on. Too bad they hadn't played the "Investment Game".

Aggie realized that the answer wasn't going to present itself tonight and it was getting late anyway. She stood up from the window seat and stretched out her cramped-up leg then bent over and touched her toes. That always loosened the stiffness in her back. Standing back up, she glanced at the alarm clock on her bedside table and wondered if Rider might still be awake. He didn't know about the guy in her kitchen, the diary, or the events that led up to its discovery in the window seat.

"WELL, YOU'VE HAD A BUSY DAY. HOW ARE YOU HOLDING UP?" RIDER paused to sip his drink (ice coffee, she guessed), "aren't you the least bit creeped out?"

Aggie had managed to recount the day's experiences calmly and matter-of-factly.

"Well, yeah. I mean, what the Hell, right?" Aggie paused to give it some more thought. "there's been some really scary stuff going on around here. I find myself waiting for the next thing to happen; but, at least this turned out to be something I could actually do."

"Don't you think it's over? Finding the diary, that's not what it was all about?"

"Well, yeah. I'm sure part of it is about finding the diary. But, it just feels like there's more. I have a permanent rock in the pit of my stomach, the small hairs on the back of my neck never really relax and I'm in a constant state of alert."

"You must be ready for a nap or two," Rider chuckled, he understood. "So, what going on with brunch this weekend?"

CHAPTER THIRTY-ONE

THE HOMEMADE CHILI WAS SIMMERING IN THE CROCKPOT AND IT WAS coming together nicely. Aggie gave it another stir and couldn't help but enjoy the spicy, robust smell wafting through the downstairs rooms. She took a small bite with the spatula to test the flavors, then put the cover back on so it could finish cooking. She gave the spatula one last lick and then put it down on the saucer to rest. She wasn't worried about spreading germs, this batch was all hers.

Mmmm, so good. Even if I do say so myself. Aggie chuckled because it sounded vain, maybe it was. She didn't care because she was pretty pleased with her recipe; it was super easy and it always came out great. She had found a few recipes on line and kept the ingredients she liked and got rid of the ones she didn't (which would be the onions and peppers). A few of her secrets were to use the premixed packet of mild chili spices from the supermarket and a can of vegetarian baked beans. That kept it from being too spicy. If she felt like going crazy, she would add mushrooms, carrots and ground turkey to thicken it and make it more hearty. This batch was going to be super hearty.

She headed to the fridge and pulled out some shredded cheddar cheese and some butter. The butter was for the cornbread which had been calling her name ever since she picked it up at the supermarket the other day. The cornbread was the whole reason she even made the chili; if you have cornbread, you might just as well have some chili to go with it. Right? It wasn't necessarily on her diet, but what are you gonna do?

Aggie noticed that she had another headache coming on and made a mental note to take something for it. She was getting tired of them.

She opened the cabinet with her bowls and pulled one down, her favorite: a pretty yellow one that looked like an upside down bee hive. Next, she grabbed a fork and butter knife from the silverware drawer and walked to the table to set everything down.

CRASH!

Aggie flinched, involuntarily dropping the items in her hands. Once again, her senses were instantly on high alert. *What now?* She stole a half second to glance at the table; luckily, her favorite bowl had landed safely. Her eyes then darted around the room looking for the source of the noise. The goose bumps were back again and her stomach was up in her chest. *Deep breath, Aggie, deep breath.* This was a new noise, it was much too loud and much too close to be the window seat again.

She had only another half second to determine that it had come from the hallway. *Near the stairs, maybe?* Now she heard a man's voice, speaking low. Was the bloody man from the other day back? She was frozen in place, but was able to reach for the butter knife. She held it out in front of her, aware of its futility as a weapon, but it was something. She really needed to get a baseball bat. Maybe one for each floor.

The sound of her pulse pounding in her ears did not diminish the sound of the low, shaky voice coming from the hallway. It was a man's voice, filled with shock and disbelief, "Freddie?"

Aggie heard a shuffling sound, and then the voice again. This time louder and angry. The disbelief was gone as was the tremble, "Freddie!"

She flinched again, in spite of herself, and backed up a step or two. With a trembling death grip on the butter knife, she thrust it out in front of her once more.

The shuffling sounds had stopped and with no time to wonder what was next, she heard footsteps: heavy, running footsteps. They were headed her way.

Her heart was beating out of her chest, she was backed up against the counter and trapped behind the kitchen table. She looked for an escape route; to her left was the pantry, the back door was ahead of her to the right. It was directly opposite of where the sounds were coming from. By the time she decided to make a break for the back door, it was already too late. The trip from the stairs to the kitchen was short, especially if someone was running.

"Fred…!" The shouting man appeared in the doorway of the kitchen and came to an abrupt stop at seeing Aggie. He was out of breath, his clothes were disheveled and an ugly depression in his right temple was gushing blood; it streamed down the side of his face and over a banged up eye. Or rather, what was left of an eye. She grimaced at the sight, but couldn't look away. Something was faintly familiar about him. She tried backing up further but the counter stopped her.

He ignored the butter knife being waved at him and demanded, "who are you?" He turned to look around, "where the Hell is Freddie?" Aggie chose her moment and made a break for it. She ran out the screen door as quickly as she could, on her almost healed ankle, butter knife in hand. She was halfway to the dock before she took a chance to look behind her. The shouting man hadn't followed her.

She stopped running and faced the house. She shifted her weight to her good leg, knife at the ready. Slowly, her breath and heartbeat returned to normal. Well, almost normal; could she ever go back to normal after all this?

Why are there so many bloody people in my kitchen? What now? That seemed to be another favorite question lately.

Aggie assessed her situation. She was pretty much screwed. Everything she needed was in the house: car keys, cell phone, change of underwear. *OK, so maybe it's not that bad if I can make a joke.* She had to go back to the house no matter what, it was just too far to walk to a neighbor. Even if she did, what was she going to say? Some scary guy with a bashed in head ran through my house looking for another guy and yelled at me?

The walk back to the house took considerably longer than the trip out of the house. Aggie would take a few steps then stop and listen for the shouting man. The adrenalin was ramping down and she could feel her ankle starting to throb, so she took her weight off it at each stop. She repeated the cycle until she was just outside of the kitchen door. When she got to the screen door, she stepped as far to one side as she could and still be able to look into the kitchen. She took a deep breath and peered through the doorway in what she hoped was a stealthy manner.

Aggie was able to see all of the kitchen, as well as into the hallway, and it looked like the angry man was gone. She stepped back from the screen door and exhaled, her free hand went over her heart. *What the hell is going on here?*

Several minutes passed as she tried to convince herself to go back into the house. She considered how she had dealt with the banging of the window seat. She thought she'd handled it pretty well; sure, she had been afraid. Who wouldn't have been? But, she approached it logically as she could and, in the end, found the diary. Since that night, banging had stopped. Of course, it had only been a couple days. But still, it was a plus. And she hadn't been so upset that she stayed away from her bedroom. *Yeah, but there wasn't someone with a bashed in head yelling at me, either.*

A chime sounded somewhere in the kitchen and it pulled her back from her thoughts. She had just received a text message. Like one of Pavlov's dogs, she always responded to the bell on her cell phone; it was time to go in. She looked once more and, seeing no sign of the shouting man, entered the kitchen.

She crossed the kitchen and smiled as checked her cell phone. It was Rider, "just wanted to find out how it's going over there."

CHAPTER THIRTY-TWO

SEEING RIDER'S TEXT GAVE AGGIE A BIG SENSE OF RELIEF, JUST thinking about him lifted a weight off of her shoulders. She thought she had gotten it under control and was fully prepared to get through the rest of the evening on her own, but deep down, she was kidding herself. Talking it out with Rider would help settle her nerves. Of course, she also wanted to hear more about his trip and how his preparations were coming along. *It can't always be about you, Aggie.*

Aggie called Rider and before they could get into a long conversation, as was their habit, she asked him if he would meet her out some place. She had to talk to him and she really needed to get out of the house. She heard a heartfelt "uh-oh" from the other end of the connection and they made plans to meet at a diner they both liked, which was at a halfway point between both of their homes.

She turned off the crockpot, grabbed her purse and keys and headed out to meet Rider. She was so deep in thought on the way to the diner that she never even turned on the radio. She kept seeing the shouting man running into the kitchen. It played back in her mind in slow motion, the hostility was palpable. A shudder ran down her spine. She could still feel the anger seething from him, see the red and grey bits dripping down the side of his face from the dent in his head. The one horrible, ruined eye. The worst part, the part that really brought on the goosebumps and turned her stomach, was when he looked right at her, right in the eye. There was a moment of connection between them when she felt pure darkness. That had scared her the most, and she gripped the steering wheel a little bit tighter just remembering it. Aggie had been sure he was going to charge her.

Rider's car was already in the parking lot when she arrived. He'd gone inside and gotten them a table already. It was a little system they had, whoever arrived first (if they were traveling separately), got the table. Or the tickets, if it was a movie, and so on. It evened out, for the most part.

Aggie entered the diner and looked around for her friend. He'd found a good table in the back and it looked like he'd ordered her a soda.

"Hey, Bud, thanks for coming out." She smiled and sat down across from him, waiting for the calm his presence would bring to her.

"Hi Ag, you look a little shook up." He smiled back at her, cocking one eyebrow.

"I'm OK, I think." She wasn't very convincing and they both heard the tremble in her voice. She cleared her throat and they looked at each other for a moment.

She tried a reassuring smile on for size and he handed her a menu. Neither of them really needed it, they had eaten here plenty and knew what they each liked from the menu. But, it gave Aggie time to calm herself so she could tell her story with a steady voice.

The waitress took their orders, patty melt for Rider and a turkey burger with mushrooms for Aggie, and they sat in silence for a moment. There was no hurry to fill the void with meaningless small talk, they were comfortable enough with each other to continue the conversation when they were ready.

Rider's text was the main reason they were sitting her tonight, so she wanted him to go first. If it hadn't been for his text, she'd be at home with a big case of the creeps. *And an even bigger case of boogeyman, one with a bashed in head.* A shiver ran down Aggie's spine as she thought about her own wounded forehead. She stifled an urge to touch it, to reassure herself it was different, hers would heal. It would be nice to have something else to focus on for a little while. "So, tell me about your trip. How are your plans going?"

"Are you sure? On the phone, you sounded pretty rattled. Why don't you go first?" He looked her in the eye and she could tell he was being sincere.

"No, it's OK. I need to let it settle first. You go. Really." She flashed her best reassuring smile, accompanied by raised eyebrows for good measure, which made him chuckle (which was what she was going for). She could never get just one eyebrow to go up, like he could. No matter how hard she tried, they both always went up at the same time. Aggie took a sip of her soda and waited for him to begin.

Rider took a quick breath and his eyes lit up as he spoke, "Well. Of course I already have my passport," he met her eyes again, "and I still have to book the airline tickets, but I'm still waiting for an actual start date."

Aggie encouraged him to go on with a nod while she steeled herself to hear the details. She had said no to joining him and she had no right to be upset. She promised herself to be happy for him instead of sad for herself.

"Work has been really understanding and they say they won't make me work out a full notice if I can't work it out. But I am trying to get it as close to two weeks as I can." Rider paused and watched her expressions, he could almost see the conversation she was having with herself play out across her face. He fiddled with the silverware as he continued, "Aggie, really, there's not much to say. There's just packing, which I can't do yet. I have to get someone to check on my place every once in a while. I was hoping, maybe, you could get someone at Brewster Management to help me out." He smiled and tried to sound offhanded about it, ramp down the excitement he could feel in his voice. He didn't want to upset her with talk of Italy; even though she'd declined his offer, he almost felt like it would be rubbing it in to talk about it.

"Really, it's Ok Rider, I can take it. You can be excited, I'm excited for you. I'm the one who said no." There. It was out in the open, she had named the awkwardness both of them felt. It helped and she unconsciously sat a little taller in the booth now. She still had a little rock in the pit of her stomach, but she told herself it was from the shouting man and not Rider's leaving.

Rider smiled at her, but didn't respond. He was still playing with the silverware. She gave him a half-smile, but it was genuine. "So, we've got just under two weeks before you're off. I can come over and help you pack, whatever you need. And, of course I can get someone assigned to check on your place regularly. Consider it done." She reached across the table and put her hand on his, which stopped his fiddling with the silverware. She nodded and raised one eyebrow at him. "Crap," they both went up again. She could tell because he chuckled. Just once, couldn't she get it just once? "I'm never going to get it." She chuckled back at him and she knew they were good again.

They were interrupted with the delivery of their meals. While the waitress served them, Aggie watched her friend and began to feel lonely and sorry for herself all over again. This time, she caught herself before it had a chance to show on her face and she managed to push those thoughts as far away as she could. For now. *You can always fix the situation if you want to, Aggie, right? So, stop it. You made your choice.* She took a deep breath, as nonchalantly as she could, and smiled. This was going to be tough.

Rider was the first to speak again, after they'd both had a few bites of their food, "Ok, let's talk about Italy later. What happened tonight? What was it this time?"

Rider listened as she told him about the loud crash in the hall followed by the shouting man, her death grip on the butter knife, the sense of familiarity, and running out of the house when she thought he was going to charge her. She sat on her hands to hide the trembling that had returned and she tried to fight off the shakiness in her voice, but he noticed all of it.

"I heard your text just as I was working up my nerve to go back into the house."

"Well, at least you still had your butter knife with you for protection." They both laughed, he was trying to lighten the mood.

"Rider, this was the scariest one yet." Aggie pushed her still full plate away. "At least the other guy didn't charge at me. I've never been through anything like this before. It's getting worse each time, I don't know what to do. And another thing, why are they all bleeding?"

"I don't know." He paused and then gave her a big smile, "You know, you can get away from it all if you come with me to Italy." It was a half-hearted attempt, but he thought it might distract her for a moment or lighten the mood.

Aggie did smile, but it faded as she placed a hand on her stomach. "Seriously, I think I might throw up a little." A tear spilled out and she laughed at herself as she wiped it away.

Rider reached across the table and gave her hand a reassuring squeeze. "I'll come back to your house with you after and we'll go from there."

CHAPTER THIRTY-THREE

"I FEEL LIKE A PUPPY," AGGIE WHISPERED. RIDER WAS WALKING through her house looking for anything out of place (as much as he could tell) and she was following him. She had gone over the window seat episodes again, retraced the steps of the shouting man, showed him where the flickering guy stood, and just for the heck of it, she pointed out the spot on the lake where she'd last seen the lights.

"It doesn't look like there's anything going on now, Ag. I think the coast is clear for the moment."

How would you know, really? You didn't see the lights, either. The snappy, ungrateful thought ran through her mind before she realized she was thinking it. Fear and stress was her only excuse. She regretted it immediately and reminded herself that he was here now. Helping her.

Instead, guilty conscience and all, she nodded in agreement, "I think you're right. Besides, if the shouting man was here, we'd know. Trust me."

They were headed back to the kitchen when Aggie stopped and closed her eyes. "Hold on for a second." Rider stood by quietly as she shook her hands out at her side and then became still, listening and waiting. Ten seconds passed and then twenty, she took a deep breath and exhaled slowly. Ten and then twenty more seconds passed again, then she opened her eyes and looked at Rider.

"What was that all about?" He tried to conceal a smirk.

Aggie sighed and shrugged her shoulders, "It was worth a shot. I got nothing."

"What do you mean, nothing? Nothing what?"

"Nothing. No goosebumps, no headache, no chills running down my spine, no weird noises. Nothing." She shrugged and headed towards the kitchen, "What I do have is the creeps. It's all been so random. I don't get it."

"I really wish I knew what to tell you. This is out of my league."

"Yeah, my league too." Aggie walked to the fridge, "do you want something to drink?"

~

AGGIE AND RIDER SAT ON THE BACK PORCH WITH THEIR DRINKS. Casual conversation dropped off as they watched the sun go down behind the hills and the lake change from blue to golden and then to black.

"Aggie. I don't want this to come out wrong and I don't want to upset you at all. But, I'd like to say something."

"Go ahead, it'll be fine." She sipped her drink and waited. This was going to be about Italy again, she was sure. Well, good. She could use the practice.

"Ok," Rider stalled and ran one hand through his hair. "I know you've made your decision, and I wish you'd change your mind, but I accept that you said no."

Aggie looked at him and waited, he wasn't finished making his point. But, so far so good.

"I've been thinking about what you said about 'one of these days'. You've said that a lot lately and I wonder if you're setting yourself up."

"Setting myself up? For what? I don't understand."

"I think you say that when you don't really know the outcome to something. No. That's not really it. Let me try to find the right words."

Aggie stayed silent and but acknowledged to herself that she thought she knew what he was getting at. She set her drink down and started picking at an imaginary hangnail. "It's like you want something but, for one reason or the other - fear, doubt, guilt - you put it off by saying 'one day' or 'someday'. I'm worried that you're setting yourself up for a quiet, safe life where you live up to everyone else's wants and expectations but yours."

Aggie felt her face turn red and she wanted to deny everything he said but she couldn't find the words. She kept from facing her friend as he spoke so he couldn't see the truth.

"Ag, I'm not saying this because I want to you to come to Italy with me. Obviously, I do. But, I don't want you to think that I am one of those in your life who is forcing expectations on you. Part of me wants you to come for my own selfish reasons. But, another part of me - a bigger part, I think - wants you to come for you."

Rider paused and waited for acknowledgement.

Aggie looked up finally, red faced and tears welling up in her eyes. "It's just…" she searched for the words, "it's all too much right now." One tear broke free and ran down her cheek. Aggie dabbed at both eyes with fingertips and took a deep breath in an effort not to give in to any more tears.

"I'm just saying this because you're my friend. It's OK to do the thing you want to do. It's Ok to say no to others. Even me. I'm always going to be your friend." He smiled at her, "It's Ok not to try to please everyone else."

"I don't," Aggie interjected.

Rider chuckled at his friend, "Denial much? I know you. You're overwhelmed right now, I would be too. Just, please give yourself the chance to do some of the things you've always wanted to do. There must be a way." He made sure to catch her eye. "You can't be everything to everybody, *you* get to be in charge of *you*. No one else."

Aggie finally gave in and let the tears flow, hoping they would wash away the pressure, guilt and fear she'd been living with. Hopefully, she could take his advice, he'd hit the nail right on the head. But, old habits die hard. She put her hand on her stomach as a half-hearted chuckle came out, "I still feel like I could throw up a little bit."

She stood up and pulled him into a hug. He hugged her back as her tears soaked into his T-shirt. As she got a hold of herself she spoke softly into his ear, "I know, you're right. I just don't know how."

"Just think about it, OK? Life is too short and 'someday' might never come." She nodded her head yes and then kissed him on the cheek before letting him go. Rider made a face, like he always did, and Aggie laughed, like she always did.

CHAPTER THIRTY-FOUR

TUESDAY - MAY 20, '75

There are always nurses at me for one thing or another. Checking my temperature, changing the IV and bandages. I'm not sure how they expect you to get any rest around here with all of that going on. I haven't mentioned my other injury yet, have I? I've been trying to ignore it. It's not easy to do.

When the police told me about the attack on the beach, they were very careful with me about the details. They mainly wanted to know if I could identify anyone. As soon as they heard about my amnesia, they left with disappointed looks on their faces. Yeah. I know how you feel, fellas.

When the doctors told me about my condition, I was listening but I didn't hear them. My head was a mess, full of all this new information and no real way to process it all. I guess I'll be sorting through it all for a while.

Today the nurse came to change the dressing and, as usual, I turned away. I usually try to pick something outdoors to look at and focus on. I don't usually turn my attention back until they're done. They have a soft touch, for the most part, and it's not as uncomfortable as it could be, I suppose. I just haven't wanted to know the details, to know how bad it is (was), or what it looks like. Playing ostrich never helped anyone, and Granna didn't raise me to run away from my problems, but I'm going to have to sneak up on this one. I hope she'd understand.

If I just get it down on paper, name it, so to speak, maybe that will be a good first step. Baby steps. If I can acknowledge it, that's half the battle, right? I'll look at it later. Maybe.

Combining what I remember from the police and the doctors, I can put together a Reader's Digest version of what I think happened to me. That's all I have to go on, my memory will not help me in this case.

I was on the beach with a friend. He was killed in the attack, his jugular vein had been cut and he bled out very quickly. He still had money on him, so it didn't seem like robbery to the police. They think I heard it happen and ran to him, which is when they think I was injured. I was stabbed in my lower abdomen and lost consciousness. Eventually, we were found by a passerby and they went for help.

At the hospital, the emergency room doctors discovered a deep cut to my uterus. The bleeding couldn't be stopped and I was sent to surgery. They performed an emergency hysterectomy and I came out of surgery in a coma that lasted several days. I also ended up with a pretty good sized scar, and zero chance for children. I don't know that I necessarily wanted children, but I hate like Hell that the choice has been taken away from me. I don't blame the doctors, I am grateful that they saved my life. But, it's worse than bittersweet. I'm not sure I'll be able to find words to explain how I feel about it.

This is my limit right now. I can't bring myself to look at or even touch the scar. I'm just not ready. Why? I ask myself that and I don't have any answers.

On paper, I seem vain. Who would want some ugly, jagged, purple (I'm guessing) scar running across the bottom of your abdomen? Obviously, no, I wouldn't want that. But I'm not being vain. It's not so much how that scar is going to look on me, it's about how it is going to be a lifelong reminder of that night. The night that I can't remember, no matter how hard I try. The night that changed two lives forever. Details of that night hide along with all of the other missing memories in a quiet, dark place in my mind.

The wound or scar, whatever you wish to call it, will always be a symbol of loss, grief and pain. Frankly, I'd prefer to do without it. I've been imagining myself reliving that night's horror every time I see or touch the scar for years to come. I wonder how a person could endure that over and over again. Then, I tell myself that I can't really remember the actual event; I think, maybe it'll be OK. But, the mind is complex, and instead, I'd replay what I think happened in my Reader's Digest version of that night. That seems to be just as bad.

My memory is just as bad of a loss, in my opinion. I didn't even realize I was in California when I woke up. Last thing I knew I was packing up Granna's house in New Mexico. It's a bit of a shock to the system when you're told that you've had a whole life experience over the last year or so and you have no memory of it. I almost don't believe it, except here I am in a hospital in California (which is definitely not New Mexico). I don't remember coming here or meeting anyone. I have no memory of where I live or if I have a job. It's disorienting and overwhelming. They want me to see someone so I can talk about it. "Talk about what?" was my initial response, "I've got nothing here." Maybe they're right, though; maybe I'll talk to someone. Baby steps, right?

They say you're not given any more than you can handle. It's supposed to be a comforting phrase, meant to fill you with strength and courage; a promise that you can get through this. To me it has a darker connotation. If that's true, then why have my memories been taken from me? Am I being protected from them? Was that night, all this time in California, so terrible that I am not supposed to remember? If that's the case, should I keep trying to remember? What will happen if I do?

CHAPTER THIRTY-FIVE

Monday - May 26, '75

I hope they don't think that I am going to be writing every day. I'll do what I can, but I'm exhausted. They told me that writing might help jog my memory, so more is better. According to them. Well, I haven't jogged any memories free yet. I'm sure I'll know if and when it happens.

Right now, I feel like my brain is protecting me. I'd kind of like to keep it that way for a while. So, why am I doing all this writing? It's because I'm torn. I would like to have some of my memory back, the good part. I have no memories of anything California. The last memory I have is of leaving New Mexico to come here; almost a year of my life is missing. But, life is not fair and the universe is all about balance. There can't be light without the dark and I guess I can't have the good without the bad. I get that. It'll be interesting to see how it works out in the end.

It does scare me a little, not knowing who it was. I heard my story (our story? Poor Billy) made the papers. I haven't seen any articles myself, and I have been hesitant to ask for copies; but I do wonder if they printed anything about my amnesia. Part of me hopes not, because

I like my privacy. Another part of me thinks it wouldn't be so bad. If the attacker is still around, they would know I can't identify them at all. So then, maybe, I'm not in any danger. That's my one big fear right now, even though I should be safe here in the hospital.

6 p.m.

I had a nap, a visitor and supper. I'm almost ready for another nap. I wonder if I'll be able to get away will all these naps once I go home.

Clara came to see me again today. I can see why we became friends. She's thoughtful, caring and so full of life. She told me that the others will be in to visit soon, but they are taking turns so I don't get too wiped out. She said they are all pulling for me to heal quickly so that I can get out of here and that they are all sending their love. I wish I could remember all their faces and names, they're a bit of a blur. Clara's is the only one that stands out from the crowd. I'll have to work on remembering the others. Maybe Clara can bring me photos to study. I'd hate to lose touch with anyone, they all seem so sincere.

We had a great chat. She tells me we work together at The Diner waiting tables. I said what diner? She said The Diner, that's its name. We laughed about how dumb the name was and she said we have that same conversation and laugh with all the tourist who come in. At least people are talking about it, maybe it's not so dumb after all. It was good to laugh.

She pulled a little rectangular package out of her purse and handed it to me with a big smile. She had wrapped it in tissue paper, but I actually had an inkling as to what it could be. My heart soared - something I remember! I tore away the tissue paper the second it was in my hands. It's a memory from New Mexico, but somehow made its way here. Could it be? How did she know?

Clara giggled and clapped her hands as I held the small package. In a second flat I was holding my favorite old deck of Beekeeper Playing Cards. It was worn around the edges from years of use, but it was as familiar as the back of my hand. I held it to my chest with one hand and motioned for a hug with the other (still not making sudden movements). I cried happy tears and I laughed at how foolish it was to be crying over a deck of cards. Clara, bless her, understood and told me that's why she brought them. She had hoped it was something connected to California that would be a memory.

I asked her to tell me about it. Clara held my hand while she spoke, I told her once it was my Granna's deck from back home and I specifically brought the Beekeeper Deck to honor our hives. I always had it with me at the diner, during the slow times I'd pull the deck out. Sometimes, I'd play solitaire; but more often than not we'd play a quick hand or two of Rummy. Not for points, but just for fun and to pass the time.

Then she said, "Ronny misses you." She didn't wait for my inevitable question, but continued on with her explanation. Ronny is our friend. He is in the third grade and has been coming in a couple days a week for a few months. He would sit in his booth sipping soda, eating french fries, and working his way through all the southern rock on the juke. He only mumbled or shook his head in answer to any attempt at conversation. Sensing a challenge, I had made it my business to befriend him and try to pull him out of his shell.

She said I started by singing along to the music he played and complimenting him on his good taste. Eventually, I got a smile out of him and he started to be less withdrawn. After several attempts at conversation, it was clear he had a stutter, which she said I ignored. After earning his trust, he confided in me that he came into The Diner to avoid bullies. Poor kid. My heart went out to him.

Clara continued with her story. She told me that in almost no time at all, I had won Ronny's trust and we'd gotten him to play Rummy with us. Finally, I had gotten him to sing along with us to his favorites and, as if by magic, he didn't stutter when he sang. She said that when his proud smile filled the diner, a few of us teared up and the regulars cheered him on. To cap it off, she said, the diners join in when he sings now. It's not to be missed, she said. Apparently, he still had a small stutter when he speaks, but he's more patient with himself these days and is making progress.

By the time she had finished her story, I was shaking my head no and crying again. We laughed together for a few moments when I told her that her story couldn't be true. She squeezed my hand and promised me that it was. She finished by saying that Ronny and his mom send their love and wish me a fast recovery. The woman in the story sounds like someone else.

CHAPTER THIRTY-SIX

SATURDAY - MAY 31, '75

The days do tend to run together here. If it wasn't for the occasional visitor to break up the monotony of IV's, dressing changes, blood pressure checks, it would be extra boring. I've been thinking about what's next for me and I'm a bit overwhelmed. All that I remember is back in New Mexico and that's what I want right now. I want Granna and comfort and familiarity. But that's not what I'll get if I go there, there's no one left. I closed her house up over a year ago and she's been gone longer than that, although it doesn't seem as long to me. I'm grateful to at least have my memory from that time; I don't think I could handle learning she's passed on top of all I'm going through now. The grief is fresh but I've already mourned her. Well, I guess I still am, at least I don't have to start over.

So. Where does that leave me? Here. Alone in Southern California, surrounded by strangers. Strange friends? Friend who are strangers? What do I call them? Friends? I don't know them. Not really. They say they know me, but it's not the same. Do I stay here and accept the help everyone's been offering? Do I go it alone? I can't stay in the hospital forever.

The people from back home that I could depend on aren't around anymore. There are still people around, but they were casual friends. Not the type you could go to with something like this.

Then there's work. What do I do about that? I have no idea how long it'll be until the doctors will let me go back to work. If I even want to. I'm not even sure I'll remember what to do or where stuff is located. I don't even know where The Diner is.

I thought that maybe the doctor was right and writing it down like this would help me sort things out, but all it's doing is making me more upset. I have flirted with the idea of using some of the money Granna left me and going somewhere altogether brand new. Somewhere that I don't know them and they don't know me. A do-over with no expectations from anyone. A clean slate has a certain appeal.

4 p.m.

I guess I had myself a little bit of a pity party there, didn't I? I re-read what I wrote down earlier and, honestly, it's embarrassing. Who is that girl? I was strong enough to come here from New Mexico on my own. I didn't whine and cry about it. I made friends (apparently), got a job and started another phase of my life. I'm still that person. I can do it again. Right? Granna would be shaking her head at me if she were here. Hopefully, I got it out of my system.

I discovered that I can move around on the hospital bed a little bit more now without too much pain. So I've taken to lying on my side and curling my legs up a bit, instead of just lying there on my back. Variety is the spice of life, as they say. I was mid-pout, curled up on my side and wiping away a few tears when my new friend Stephen showed up. The door was open, so he tapped on the door as he entered and caught me like that. It was pretty embarrassing.

He apologized for intruding and started to back out, I stopped him and called him back into my room. I tried to laugh it off and say it was nothing. He was a gentleman but I could tell he didn't buy it. I didn't buy it, either. I gestured for him to sit and thanked him for coming by. He clasped my outstretched hand for a moment (dry palms again) and gave me a warm smile before he sat down. Sweet.

"Are you sure this is a good time? I can go." he looked me right in the eyes and waited for my answer. I appreciated that because I know he meant it. If I said so, I know that he would have split. I gave him the most genuine smile I could muster, nodded yes, and motioned to the chair again. He finally sat down and I worked myself into a sitting position.

There was a brief moment of awkward silence then we looked at each other and chuckled at the same time. It was a perfect ice breaker. I asked how work was going (slow, but that left more time to visit) and he told me I looked like I was doing better (thank you, I think I'm making progress). He said he'd tried to come up with something more original, that everyone must ask me how I'm doing; but, that was the best he could come up with. He said he'd work on it. That made me laugh again and it put me at ease.

We talked for a while; him about what he liked about being on the road, and me about life in New Mexico with Granna (which is all I have to offer conversationally). He makes me feel comfortable when we talk. I don't have to apologize for not remembering him, or the last year. I guess you could call him a sort of clean slate.

After a bit, he noticed the Beekeeper deck on my side table and pointed to it. He got a faraway look in his eyes and said that he hadn't played cards since he was young. He smiled and told me about how his older sister taught him some of her favorite games and how much fun they'd had. She'd even let him join in games with her and her friends sometimes. He loved her for that, it had made him feel so grown up. We compared notes and both landed on our favorite being Rummy. How's that for a small world? He said the runner up was Poker, but he could have just been shining me on to be sweet. I have a feeling Poker is number one for most guys.

Stephen got up to leave when I started to get tired. He said goodbye with another small squeeze of my hand and I thanked him for visiting and promised him a game of cards the next time.

CHAPTER THIRTY-SEVEN

AGGIE WAS BACK IN THE WINDOW SEAT, JOURNAL AND FAVORITE PEN IN hand, diet cola with ice on the seat beside her. Rider had gone back home and she appeared to finally be alone. She hoped. Such an ironic thing to hope for with Rider's trip looming large. It felt like the dust had started to settle some; and for the moment, there weren't any strange sounds, or stray people, in her house.

She thought back over the past few days and all that had happened in that short period of time. As was her habit, she had written it all down in her journal each night before bed. It had helped her to deal with it. By putting it all down on paper matter-of-factly, it didn't seem as overwhelming as it could have. A lot of thoughts about the past week still chased her and weighed on her mind. It was time to try and sort them out some more. Aggie took a deep, decompressing breath but it caught in her throat, making her cough. She paused to wipe away a stray tear and chided herself for getting overly emotional. Even if it seemed appropriate, in her opinion. She took another cleansing breath and started a new entry.

Judith, what have you done by leaving this house to me? Did you know about Winnie? Or the lights? Or the men in the kitchen? Did you experience any of this? You never said anything to me. Journaling about it all hasn't helped all that much, yet, either. I'd be lying if I didn't admit to a certain amount of curiosity about the whole thing.

I have great trust in you, so I have to think that you knew what you were doing by leaving me so much (and leaving so much up to me). I'm trying very hard to not let you down. There are so many things going on right now and they're coming at me from all sides. I'm afraid something will get by me one of these day. Rider has been great, but he'll be gone soon. The friends I made at work have been great, but as you know, I have this new position (*clears throat) and that makes it awkward now. Once Rider leaves, I will feel truly alone here. Not counting my new friends in the kitchen.

I wish you were here. We could sit and chat and I could tell you what's been going on and we could bounce ideas off of each other, like before. Like when we'd watch the murder channel. It was so much fun watching those shows with you, someone like me who never met a mystery she didn't like or a puzzle she didn't want to solve. I love that you got it, that you didn't think it was morbid. It's always an intriguing mix of human nature and motivation for someone with a curious nature.

The last show we watched together sticks out in my mind, it was an episode about a serial killer cold case from the '70s. Mostly I remember it because you weren't acting like yourself that night. You seemed to withdraw into yourself as the episode wore on and I've wondered if it was because you had started not to feel well. You were gone so suddenly after that. I regret not talking with you about it now.

I miss you terribly.

Aggie stopped journaling for a few minutes to regroup and take a few sips of her drink. She thought some more about how Judith acted that night. At first, her gut told her that Judith hadn't been getting sick that night, but it wasn't too long afterward that she passed. Had it happened differently, she would have sworn that something else was going on with Judith. She seemed focused on the show and, normally, they would fill the commercial breaks with observations and guesses and counterpoints. This time, the normal back and forth conversation with Aggie dwindled as the program went on. It was odd enough behavior that it stood out in her mind.

Aggie had decided to wait for the right moment to ask her friend about it; in the end, she waited too long and never got the chance. Of course, afterwards and because of the suddenness of it all, Aggie second guessed her ideas about that night. Perhaps Judith wasn't feeling well after all?

Now that some time had gone by, she wasn't so sure, again. As usual, her curiosity tended to get the best of her. She flipped back to the front of her journal and made a note on her 'To Do' list to look for that program on line so she could rewatch it. Maybe it would turn out to be nothing, but Aggie's curiosity was still piqued. It just didn't feel right to let it go.

Leg cramps were beginning to settle in from sitting cross-legged on the window seat, so Aggie gathered up her things to move over to the bed. She paused long enough to let the pins and needles have their way with her legs until the sensation dissolved. Aggie set everything down on the nightstand, settled herself comfortably on the bed and took another sip of her drink. Turning her attention back to her journal, she reread the last bit and then drew a short line under the last paragraph signaling a change of subject.

CHAPTER THIRTY-EIGHT

THE FLOOR IN THE DEN WAS CLUTTERED WITH OPEN STORAGE BOXES, Aggie sat on the floor surrounded by them. The boxes were full of stuff she had taken from Judith's main house. This house, the one Aggie lived in now, had also been hers. It reverted back to Judith after the death of her brother many years ago. She used it only occasionally, and mostly in the spring and fall. It had been left to Aggie with all of the furniture; there hadn't been many personal items because Judith had used it only sporadically. All of the boxes held stuff from her main home. They were filled with memories, paperwork and all the little things one gathers over the years. They still had to be sorted and decisions had to be made about what to do with each of them. Judith had no family to leave them to and her will hadn't specified, so it was up to Aggie.

This was not the task Aggie was taking on today, though. Aggie was searching for two specific items: a shoebox and a photo. Since reading more of the diary, something had been nagging at Aggie and she thought they'd help clear her thoughts a bit. The photo was of Judith's late brother and the shoebox held some old letters and a few postcards.

Judith hadn't spoken much about her brother, so finding these items while packing up her house stood out. Aggie had seen the photo many times before, it always sat prominently on the mantle in Judith's living room. When asked about him, Judith would only answer vaguely: years ago, he'd had an accident at home, he never regained consciousness and died a few days later. That was all she would ever say.

Judith always had a fond, yet sad, smile and a faraway look in her eyes when she spoke about him. That in itself was curious. Aggie wondered what else there was to her brother. Surely, they'd played together as children; surely, there was a life time of memories in the period before his accident? It struck her odd that his life had been boiled down to these few sentences. But, that's all Judith would ever say about him. The strange thing is, when Aggie was clearing out Judith's home, she found the cherished photo face down on a shelf in a storage closet.

The shoebox she was looking for had been found in the same closet, Brother's photo resting on top. Aggie gave the box a quick look when packing up and when she saw that it contained old letters and postcards, she just couldn't toss it. If she remembered correctly, most of the letters appeared to have the same block-style handwriting and she had a gut feeling they were from Judith's brother. She had packed them up together, planning on deciding their fate 'one of these days'. Today was that day. She'd have to tell Rider, he kept telling her that 'one of these days' might never come. What did he know?

Aggie paused in her search and looked around the room at the mess. She had been through almost all of the boxes and soon became worried that she wouldn't find what she was seeking. There were still a few boxes left to go through and she was holding out hope that one of them held the needles in the haystack.

She read more of Winnie's diary last night and then slept on it. This morning, over breakfast, her thoughts returned to the visits by her kitchen men. That train of thought led her to all the other activity, in and outside of the house. Those thoughts intertwined with the diary entries. She had to try to make sense of everything. It had to be connected. If she could find the link, maybe she could find some answers to her questions. Maybe she could stay in her home after all.

After breakfast, on a hunch, Aggie went back to her journal entry about the last night she'd been over Judith's to watch TV. After journaling about it last night, it still weighed heavy on her mind. She wanted to see if she remembered the evening correctly, to see what her initial impressions were of her friend that night. She had written that Judith seemed quite distracted by the time the program ended, even though she brushed it off when asked. Aggie had also written that Judith said something offhanded that night, almost to herself and not necessarily intended for Aggie. At the time, Aggie thought it was in reference to the dark nature of program they'd been watching. Now she wasn't so sure.

Judith had said, "I guess the universe does have a way of evening things out in the end." Aggie had asked her how so, as the show indicated there had never been a resolution to that case. Again, Judith brushed it off as 'nothing' and added, "just random thoughts."

Aggie shifted position on the floor and pulled one of the last unopened boxes to her. She crossed her fingers as she untucked the flaps of the boxes. She whispered a quiet plea, "please be here, please be here," and reached up to tip the tall box towards her so she could see the contents.

Jackpot! Sitting at the very top was a bubble wrapped frame and it was still lying on top of the shoebox full of letters. Aggie smiled as she pulled both items out of the box and set them beside her on the floor. Her mood lifted instantly and she felt a tingle race down her spine. Soon, she would have answers!

She pushed the box forward, out of her way, and sat down on the floor cross-legged. She placed both items safely in her lap, then took a deep breath and closed her eyes for a moment to banish a headache that was making itself known.

No, no, no. Not now. Please, not now. Aggie hesitated and held her breath, the tingle and the headache meant something was coming. Probably. *I must be getting the hang of this.* The headache grew stronger and she slowly let her breath out. *What now?* She steeled herself, waiting, watching and listening to her house. To her left was the opening to the living room, ahead of her and beyond all the boxes was the brightly lit hallway and the stairs to the second floor. A chill crept over her as her attention was drawn to the stairway. Sunlight shone in through the colored glass in the front door and was playing tricks on her. That must be it? How else to explain all those colors moving about on the landing?

Without looking away from the hall, Aggie gripped the frame and shoebox to her chest as one item. With her free hand, she pulled the large storage box close and she crouched down behind it. The colors moving about on the stairway started to solidify, a blue shadow turned into jeans and a shirt, a bright area turned into a white dress. Next, people formed inside of the clothes and Aggie felt a jolt as the volume turn on. The angry, shouting man from the kitchen was struggling with a petite woman in the white dress. He had ahold of her arm and she was trying to pull away; despite the difference in their sizes, she was holding her own.

"Fr-Freddie, p-please! You can't go!"

"Let go, Stephen, you're hurting me." Her voice cracked as she looked around for something to grab, anything, to help her. The railing was just out of reach. She stopped struggling when a young man with long, dirty blonde hair appeared behind Stephen. Freddie and Aggie both noticed him at the same time, Stephen did not. Aggie held her breath, she could feel her pulse pounding in throat. It was the other man from the kitchen. The quiet one.

It took a moment for Stephen to realize Freddie had stopped struggling, it took another to realize she was no longer focused on him. He turned to see what held her attention and his grasp on her arm loosened.

Freddie was not so distracted by the quiet man that she wasn't able to seize the moment. She felt Stephen's grip loosen and pulled herself free. The quiet man acted quickly, pulling Stephen into a choke hold. This kept him from turning around all the way. Freddie turned to flee down the remaining stairs while the quiet man held fast to Stephen. His eyes never left Freddie as she made a break for it.

Freddie held on to the banister as she descended. She pulled herself to a stop when she hit the first floor. Her free hand flew to her neck and she clenched a familiar looking pendant on the necklace she wore, her eyes opened wide. Freddie turned and looked above her at the landing, "Billy!"

"Run, Baby, run!" Aggie and Freddie both startled at the unexpected outburst, the quiet man had finally spoken.

Freddie didn't need to be told twice, the urgency in his voice was clear. Still, she hesitated just a moment longer, taking time for a last look.

"Let me go," Stephen growled as he struggled to free himself from the mysterious man's grip.

"You can't have her either," the quiet man growled back. His sudden appearance behind Stephen had given him the upper hand and he was able to maintain his choke hold with little effort.

Freddie gasped at the quiet man's words, dropping the pendant and turning to head out the back door. Aggie caught a glimpse of the swinging pendant as she turned the corner, the sight of it hit her like a jolt of electricity. It was a silver bumblebee.

The jolt was followed by a rush of emotions from the fleeing girl. They washed over Aggie like a rip tide. At once, she felt a sense of recognition and confusion. Then, sadness and finally, grief. Heart crushing grief. The tears streaming down Aggie's face mirrored Freddie's but went unattended as the scene on the landing played out.

Stephen struggled against the quiet man's hold, they appeared to be matched in strength and he could not break free. The very moment Freddie had moved safely away from the bottom of the stairs, the quiet man spun Stephen around a quarter turn and, in one swift motion, brought Stephen's head down sharply on the corner of the landing's balustrade. The unexpected blow stunned Stephen and ruined his eye, blood began to pour from the wound. The quiet man used this moment to finish his mission.

He pushed his knee into the back of Stephen's to throw him off balance and then gave him a hard yank downward before Stephen could regain his footing. It worked. In the time it took Stephen to fall to one knee on the landing, Aggie saw the quiet man change. His quiet, calm demeanor was gone. He tightened his grip on Stephen until he was white-knuckled. Now his face was red, his nostrils flared and he was gritting his teeth. The most notable change, however, was physical. As in the kitchen, blood now poured from a wound in his neck covering his T-shirt, and it was dripping onto Stephen.

The not-so-quiet man leaned down to Stephen's ear, spittle lubricating his words and the side of Stephen's face, his words came out in a loud growl, "you can't have her!"

In one smooth motion, he hooked one of his legs behind Stephen's and pushed him head first down the stairs. Aggie and the not-so-quiet man both watched as Stephen fell in a slow, awkward somersault. The fall took longer than one would expect and Aggie fully expected the large man to rise once he came to a stop on the first floor.

Aggie crouched lower in her spot and braced herself for that inevitability. At any moment, he was going to jump up and either charge the quiet man or run after Freddie. She wasn't ready to place bets on which option it would be.

As it happened, she would have lost money on either bet. Stephen landed in a heap, his head impacting a decorative iron door stop at the base of the stairs. His face was turned towards Aggie at an awkward angle. She watched as bright red blood and small grey bits poured from his newest injury. It mingled with the blood from his eye and spread out into a puddle on the hallway floor.

Aggie forced herself to look away from the gore for a moment. When she got up the nerve to look back at Stephen, he was gone. So was the quiet man, the iron doorstop, and the puddle of brain matter and blood. So was her headache.

Aggie looked around her urgently, desperately. She found what she needed close by, almost at her elbow, where she'd placed it earlier. Relieved, she leaned over the plastic waste basket and threw up.

CHAPTER THIRTY-NINE

TUESDAY - JUNE 10, '75

I've been home for just a day now. I should be saying "home sweet home" but even this is unfamiliar. I don't recognize my place. I know it has to be mine because it's filled with objects from New Mexico, things I brought with me: Granna's pottery, some of our honey is here, photos, furniture, knick-knacks, some of my clothes. You get the idea. It's like a strange adventure. What will I discover around the next corner?

The funny thing is, though, that if I'm wondering where something might be I can usually find it. Then, just when I'm starting to feel comfortable and get all cocky about it, "look, Ma, no hands," I'll stumble across something I don't recognize (something I must have picked up since moving here), just to have it knock me down a peg. I never really liked see-saws.

If I do say so myself, I picked out a cute place. It's a two bedroom cottage with a small porch. It's older, but has been kept up pretty well. The rooms are painted in soft, soothing colors. If I had a bike, it would be biking distance from the beach (why don't I have a bike?). It has big windows with white gauze curtains, which let in all the sun and makes it very bright. The big windows are just the right size to let all the bad guys in, too. Right? I don't think I was worried about that before. I think about it a lot now. I shut all the windows yesterday and locked them, but it has gotten kind of warm in here. The little fan I found helped move the air a little bit, but it wasn't ideal.

I know I shouldn't let fear rule my life, I get it. But, logic doesn't help, or make sense, when you're afraid. I was awake most of the night listening to every little sound, trying to figure out if it was someone trying to get in. I didn't get much sleep so I am making up for it with extra naps today. I have to figure out a way to deal with this. I can't spend the summer roasting in the cottage instead of enjoying the breeze from the open windows. I'm not able to relax about it yet.

I felt safer in the hospital than I do here in my own home. It's funny. I am worried about people getting in, when I was surrounded by bunches of people at the hospital, most of them strangers. I should have been afraid there, too. My head and my emotions are scrambled up and I don't like it. I feel like I can't trust my gut, nothing is familiar. I'm so disoriented.

WEDNESDAY - JUNE 11, '75

I am forcing myself to deal with being alone. For a little while, anyway. I need to prove to myself that I can do this. Be on my own. My first inclination is to surround myself with people. But then, what people. Clara? Stephen? My other friends? Who?

Clara has made great strides to bond with me, she's a wonderful girl. But, I still haven't been able to remember her yet. I don't know that I can trust myself to let her in. I only have her say so that we were friends. She does make me want to believe her, though. I'd be lucky to have a friend like her.

Stephen has only been in my life since that night. If actions speak louder than words, then I should be able to trust who he is. He has been so sweet and thoughtful and attentive. I had many visits from him while I was in the hospital, and that's while he's supposed to be busy working. He's become a nice, new friend in a short time and I don't have to try to remember him from before. It's refreshing.

Having amnesia messes with a person. Do I take everyone at face value, or just some? How do you choose who to trust and who not to trust. When I woke up, everyone here was a stranger to me. I know shutting myself off from everyone isn't the answer, either. I thought some time by myself might help me sort these thoughts out.

I know I should feel grateful. Both Clara and Stephen wanted to see me home from the hospital and help me get settled. I was shouting, "Yes, please!" from deep inside. Either would have been great, and they would have stayed with me, either one guarding me from the living room couch, too, if I asked. I probably could have gotten a team of people to take turns.

I turned them both down, even though the thought of coming home alone was scary. I'm still scared, to be honest. Deep down, I knew I had to face at least a few days head on, by myself. I just thought, the old me had the strength for this. She needs to show the new me the way. It's only been a day and boy, she's got her work cut out for her.

The hospital set up a cab to bring me home when I asked. I got a few odd looks when I told the nurses I was going home by myself, but I held my ground (shaky as it was) and I have a few proud moments to show for it and to hold on to when I get wobbly-kneed. It's proof that I can do this. I splurged and had some groceries delivered so that I wouldn't have to stop on the way home or ask for any favors. I'm set for several more days. I will have to use that time figure out what I'm going to do next. Do I ask a friend for help or brave the streets (and the bus system?) by myself. It's very tempting to organize another delivery, but that road leads to hermit-ville. Right? Baby steps.

So far, Clara and Stephen have respected my request to give me a few days and some space. But, it's only been one day. Guess we'll see how I manage. I have to admit, I have their phone numbers taped to the wall by the phone like a security blanket.

Maybe I can start by opening one window. It's getting hot.

CHAPTER FORTY

THURSDAY - JUNE 19, '75

The walls haven't started to close in yet, I kind of expected them to. The days pass pretty quickly with mindless daytime TV. That and naps. It's more like my little home is my very own protective cocoon. I have kept to the house, but it's only been a few days. Matter of fact, I've mostly kept to the living room and kitchen. I make a snack or meal, get a drink and then head back to the couch.

I haven't slept in my bedroom yet. I've only been in there long enough to get fresh clothes and my favorite pillow. I'm still not completely comfortable here. The bedroom are in the back which is darker and further from the street. Anyone could be hiding back there. That sounds irrational when I write it down, but I feel like if I had to call out for help, nobody would hear me from back there.

The other reason is, this doesn't feel like my house. It's like I'm a guest and the host is away. It feels like I'm just here temporarily and that I'll never feel settled.

I found a compromise for the windows. I have opened a few of them a little way to let the breeze in, but not far enough for a person to get through. So that I'd feel safe, I put a dowel (found some in a closet, don't know why they were there) across the top of the window diagonally to prevent the window from being raised any further. I thought that was pretty clever. I think it should hold OK.

I know that I should be working towards something. Avoiding the issues by watching TV is not going to make them go away. Which I get. When I stop and focus, I can feel them lurking. I haven't done much besides writing in this dairy, even that seems so futile. How is my little diary going to fix this? I can't remember, there's nothing there. End of story. I've been keeping this diary, like they said I should, but it doesn't seem to be working any magic. How am I supposed to write about the dark empty parts of my memory? How do you make peace with a giant ball of nothing? I will keep at it for a while longer, they assured me I would get some benefit from it. Not sure what that will be. We'll see, I guess.

3 p.m.

I have a little pile of objects next to me on the couch. I gathered them from the kitchen and the bathroom. A few of these are definitely not mine. The smallest item in the pile is a Polaroid photograph, I had it stuck to the fridge with a few magnets. It's a picture of a young man with blonde hair, he's wearing camouflage pants and a white T-shirt. His hair is cropped close and he's smiling at the photographer and giving them a peace sign with his fingers. I don't recognize him, but I think this must be Billy. Clara told me he had been in Vietnam and this guy has a military look about him. He has a quiet confidence about him. Nothing specific in the photo, just a feeling I get.

The next thing in the pile is a man's razor. It was on the stand next to some shaving cream. The cream could be mine, but I wouldn't be shaving my legs with this huge contraption. It's moosey, the kind that ratchets open so you can switch out your blades. It looks like the kind my grandfather would have used.

I also found a pair of boxers and a wife beater folded up on a shelf in the bathroom. These are definitely not mine. It seems like the evidence is pointing to Billy being very comfortable here, even staying over, maybe. Hmmm. I've been looking at, and touching them, to see if it would bring up any memories. Nothing so far.

Midway through the day, I felt a pang of sadness. Not for my lack of memory, but because of it. We were obviously very close, I should be mourning him. I can't muster up the emotions I must have felt for him, they just aren't there. I do feel terrible about it, but I won't pretend for the sake of mourning. That would be dishonest.

I do feel something. There's a certain sense of loss. And of gratitude. Which is weird and I don't quite understand it. I can't put my finger on it exactly, but maybe I will understand better one of these days. I want to be able to mourn him properly, the way he deserves. I may not want to get my memories of that night back, but if I could choose, I'd want my memories of him. If only for that reason. It feels wrong not to say goodbye properly, honestly.

It finally occurred to me that he had to have had a funeral or memorial service by now. It's been a few weeks. Clara hasn't said anything, it's an awkward subject to say the least. Frankly, I don't know if I'll bring up the subject right now, but I am curious and when I figure how to do so, I'll ask.

He must have family, a mother and father, *someone* that would have made the arrangements. It's maddening not to know any of these things. Did I know them? Did they know me? Do they know what happened? Do they know the reason I haven't sent my condolences? I probably should figure out a way to do that. I can see it now: I'm so sorry for your loss, we used to be close but I can't remember him at the moment. That'd go over nicely.

CHAPTER FORTY-ONE

THINGS HAD NOT GONE AS HE'D HOPED ON THE BEACH. EVERYTHING started out fine, but it went bad quickly and he'd been beating himself up about it for weeks now. She'd gotten hurt and it was his fault. He never would have forgiven himself if she hadn't made it. She was supposed to be his, he knew this just as he knew the stars came out every night. It was just so, he felt it in his bones. The fact that he had had to take some action, clear a path, was just a small factor that he easily accepted. Nothing came to anyone without a few challenges or a little bit of work. You had to meet life halfway, make your own luck.

He was doing just that very thing again. If he didn't act again, soon, he'd lose her for sure. She had locked herself away from everyone. It was a ridiculous attempt on her part to be independent. To prove that she was strong. She needed someone to look after her right now, take care of her, protect her. He was meant to be that person. But, she had shut down any chance of him getting to prove that to her.

She was holed up in her cottage; she wasn't going out and she wasn't accepting any visitors. He needed to nudge her his way. Gently but firmly. Being direct wasn't going to work, she'd need a push in his direction. His thumb stroked the side of his knife nervously as he reviewed his simple plan. It was all he could come up with. If it didn't work, he'd have to ramp up his efforts. First things first, though.

This plan depended on stealth. Again. He was anxious about it and upset with himself. He couldn't stop reminding himself how that had worked out last time. He did not want to take any chances of hurting her again. He ran the scenario though his mind again. It was a quick and simple plan and he was confident that it wouldn't do anything more than it was supposed to: nudge her his way.

The man was standing in the shadows on a darkened street across from her cottage, observing it. Dusk had turned to evening while he'd been standing there. Although he hadn't seen any signs of her, exactly, he was sure she was inside. The lights were on in the front of the cottage and the blinds were pulled down tight. She was still recuperating and wouldn't have left on her own. There was nowhere else for her to be right now and she shouldn't have any visitors, she'd made it clear that she wanted to be on her own for a bit. He double checked that factor by looking for cars parked in front of her cottage. There were none at the moment.

He took a deep breath and dropped the knife into his pocket. No time like the present. He adjusted the dark cap on his head and zipped his black sweatshirt all the way up as he crossed the street to her back yard. He pressed himself up against the back wall of the house and paused, looking and listening for any other movement or signs anyone else was about. The back yard was dark, still and quiet. *Perfect, that should help the noise to travel.* The man nodded to himself and turned his attention to the back of her cottage.

CHAPTER FORTY-TWO

AGGIE WIPED AWAY THE TRACES OF TEARS FROM HER CHEEKS WITH THE back of her hand and then she wiped her mouth. Only then was she able to take a deep breath. She grimaced and rolled her eyes at her surprising reaction and pushed the waste basket away from her until it was out of harm's way (and out of sight). She'd take care of that later. And then, she just sat there. She wasn't ready, yet, to process what she had seen. She needed a moment.

She ignored her stomach, which hadn't quite returned to normal. She ignored the sound of blood pounding in her ears and rushing through her veins. She told herself that she really couldn't smell the blood in the hallway. Not really. Still, she wrinkled her nose at its lingering, slightly metallic scent.

Finally, she looked down at the objects she'd been clutching so tightly. Aggie held up the photo and removed the bubble wrap. She could at least handle that. She concentrated on the man in the photo when something in the hallway caught her attention, a flash, or flicker of light, out of the corner of her eye. Her grasp on the photo tightened as she looked for the source of the flash. She gasped and tossed the photo away as if it had burned her fingers.

Aggie immediately regretted it. The frame skittered across the top of the box, heading off the other side. A perfect time to be without bubble wrap. "Crap," she lunged forward to prevent it from falling, but by then, it snagged on something and stopped by itself. She sat back and breathed a sigh of relief.

Aggie became aware of that a crop of goosebumps had popped up across both arms, so she rubbed them away. She stretched out of the crouch she'd been in and, as her ever present headache faded, glanced at the almost nearby photo. The photo stared back.

It was just as she remembered from Judith's mantle. The photo was cropped to a headshot, but in the background was evidence of a party; confetti and balloons peeked out from the corners. Judith had told her once that her brother didn't like to have his picture taken, so there weren't many of him as an adult. It showed a man with short, dark, wavy hair, high cheek bones, strong jaw, brown eyes, and a strangely appealing (but unsmiling) cupids mouth. The soft curves of his mouth were distinctive and unusual and was always the thing that pulled her in when she looked at the photo. That was what she had noticed about the shouting guy in the kitchen, but couldn't put her finger on. Of course, the bloody dent in his head and the messed up eye could have thrown anyone off.

As Aggie sat there, her mind began to put the pieces together. A few pieces, anyway. Realization hit her like a ton of bricks. Judith's brother, the bloody, shouting guy from the kitchen, and the Stephen from Winnie's diary were all the same person. Winnie! Another light-bulb went on. Winifred. Winnie was Freddie, wasn't she? It never occurred to her that Winnie was the Freddie Stephen was calling for in the kitchen. That's what she got for assuming.

Her mind was spinning. She needed to go back to her journal. What else had she missed or gotten wrong?

Aggie stood up from her spot on the floor and gently touched the photo. She shook her head when nothing else happened. Finally, she picked it up and pushed a few boxes out of the way, clearing a path to the couch.

She set the photo down on one of the cushions, pausing for a moment to focus on the whereabouts of the other items she wanted to gather together. A theory about this whole business was starting to come together and a plan was forming; but, she needed a few items before she could say for sure. Aggie wiped her palms on her shorts and then shook them out at her sides. She took a cleansing breath and told herself to get going. No time like the present.

Two of the items she wanted were in her bedroom, so she headed that way but stopped at the last moment at the base of the stairway. Her intention was to have a respectful moment of silence for what she just witnessed. It was the right thing to do, considering. As she stood there with her head bowed, she began instead to search the floor, stairs and wall for evidence. She was looking for an old speck of blood, a dent in the floor from the iron doorstop, a mark, anything that would prove that what she'd seen had really happened.

The fact that she found nothing, she realized, didn't seem to bother her. How many years had passed? She wasn't sure, but time has a funny way of erasing certain things from the reality of the present. But erasing it, by definition, means that something had to have been there to begin with, right?

Aggie felt as if a mark had been made, on that very spot. She felt it deep in her gut. If not on the floor or the stairs, then in space and time. What other explanation could there be? Trauma on that level had to leave some kind of trace. The kind of trace that could be felt by the small hairs on the back of your neck, or played back like a memory. That's what she had just witnessed.

Out of respect, after chastising herself for getting distracted, she resumed her moment of silence for a respectable amount of time and then proceeded upstairs. There was no more time to waste, she had a plan. Maybe she could get her house back, after all.

CHAPTER FORTY-THREE

I'm still on the couch, just barely. It's taken me quite a while to calm down even this much. There's a giant lump in my chest and the hairs on the back of my neck are standing on end. I heard something outback earlier and it sounded like someone was trying to get in. I'm sure of it. I heard a few thumps, like something (someone) was up against the side of the house, then there was a scraping noise and some rattling. I know I've been hyper alert, and someone could say my imagination is working overtime. But, I know what I heard.

I wanted to go back there and scare off whatever it was. I really did. The old me would have. The new me wasn't having any part of it. I tried to gear myself up for it, but I just stood there in the middle of the living room, immobilized. My heart was beating like crazy and I strained to hear more sounds, I looked around for a weapon of defense - a bat, a hammer, anything. Nothing. I couldn't make myself move. I was empty handed and positive that someone would come bursting in at me from one of the bedrooms at any second.

I forced myself to count to ten, took a deep breath and then ran to the bathroom. It has a very small window and a lock on the door. It wasn't a great plan, but it was a plan. It took me 'til a count of 13 to get moving, but I did it. I sat in there for quite a while trying not to cry, trying to calm down, all the while straining for signs someone broke in. Finally, I was able to convince myself that no one was there and cautiously made my way back to the living room. I have to say, my house doesn't feel like a nice safe cocoon any longer.

I don't know what to do. I want to check the bedrooms, but I don't know if I have the courage. Surely, if someone had broken in I would have seen them by now. I can't call the police, they would just laugh. So much time has gone by that it doesn't make sense any more, but I can't quite convince myself that there's no one lurking in the shadows for me.

Meanwhile, I've pulled the phone off the wall and have it propped up on the back of the end table. It's within reach if I have to use it. I also have a giant carving knife at my side on the couch. The knife is not my favorite choice, having had the experience I did, but I couldn't find a bat (everybody should have a bat). I'm going to have to think of something, though.

Bedtime

I'm still a little shaken, but I also feel a bit like a fool. No one is here. No one is hiding in either of the bedrooms or trying to get in through the windows. I let my imagination get the best of me. In the heat of moment, though, I sure was convinced of it.

How do I know all this? Did I summon my courage and check the bedrooms, knife at the ready? No, hardly. I was still sitting on the couch, trapped by fear, when there was a knock at the door. I was about to jump out of my skin, and I even grabbed for the knife, when I saw that it was Stephen. Thank God there's a window in the door. When I saw him standing there, I could finally take a deep breath again.

I ran to the door with tears in my eyes, too relieved to care if he saw them. I let him in and gave him a big hug. I felt better instantly, safe. I just realized I was so grateful to see him I never did think to ask why he stopped by.

I invited him to come in and sit down. He looked at the giant knife, then back at me. So, I told him what was going on.

Stephen listened carefully, held my hand when I got teary, and best of all, didn't tease me. He told me that he understood how frightened I must have been and told me he was sorry that I had gone through that. He said all the right things and I started to feel better. He offered to check out my bedrooms and then take a walk around the house (he smiled at me when I raised my eyebrows and said "no, you don't have to come with me").

He reported back after he made the rounds and declared both bedrooms, and their closets, empty, all the windows secured. He made his way around the outside of the house and came back in with the offenders in hand. He stood in the doorway and held up a shovel and garden rake. He guessed they had been propped against the house and fell over, making the scraping noise I'd heard. That doesn't really explain the thump, but it made me feel better that I wasn't hearing things, (but not so much better that I don't feel a fool for jumping to conclusions so easily).

Stephen set them somewhere in the back yard (I didn't follow him) and when he came back in I hugged him again. I told him I hate being afraid and feeling unsafe. I told him that this is all new to me and I'm still trying to figure out how to get along. I told him that I felt like I should apologize for not being stronger or more independent. I mean, that's who I used to be.

He told me it was perfectly understandable after everything I've been through. We talked for a bit more, and even though he was still there, I found myself a bit on edge. As I am now.

He did give me something to think about. Now, he's asked me before, but I dismissed it. This time, though, after today's events, I'm giving it serious thought: he's offered to have me visit him in Arizona. I can heal and recuperate there and be away from what is strange and foreign to me here. I will have a chance to relax and get better. I can work through these issues without being afraid at every turn. I'll be safe.

He also told me that the offer is coming from a friend and that there is no pressure and no strings, that I can trust him.

I guess the ball is in my court. I have to admit that I am tempted. Arizona sounds less scary than California at the moment. Initially, my reaction is "but what about my life here?" Then, I realize how funny that sounds. Why not take some time and see how it goes? On one of her visits to the hospital, Clara told me our boss sent his best wishes for a speedy recovery and that I should take the time I need to heal and come back when I'm ready. So I've got that going for me.

I'm going to sleep on it. On the couch. With my knife beside me.

CHAPTER FORTY-FOUR

SHE GRABBED WINNIE'S, NO - FREDDIE'S - DIARY. AGGIE MADE A mental note: it's Freddie. She repeated it a few times to herself. She'd thought of her as Winnie for so long, considered her almost a friend, switching to Freddie was going to take some concentration. She also grabbed her own journal and headed back downstairs.

In the kitchen, Aggie grabbed a bottle of water from the fridge and took a few sips, swishing the liquid around in her mouth a few times. Then, she plucked the Bumblebee pendant from a small bowl in the center of the table and headed back to the living room. There, she grabbed the shoebox and then set everything down on couch next to the photo.

Aggie was trying to convince herself the reason her heart was beating faster was because she'd just run around the house, but the fact was she was anxious about her idea. And a little excited.

Aggie sat on the couch next to the gathered items. She took a deep breath and closed her eyes for a few moments, she had a plan but was unsure how to begin. She had never done this before and wasn't sure what the standard procedure was, or even if there was one. Her mind started to drift and she went with it.

Why had she started seeing all these strange - she searched for the right word - visions? She thought back to the first time, the night in the woods with the red lights. She'd had a dream (vision?) then, too: the crying lady wearing a white dress in the rain. After that she had been drawn to the diary. Drawn being a slightly less scary word for how she was actually led to find the diary. Were they connected? If so, how? Not to mention the two, quite different men who appeared to her. She'd seen the lights three times, and now today, the terrible scene on the stairs.

It was a lot to absorb in a short period of time. What was the catalyst? She had been in the house before with Judith and had lived here for several uneventful months. Why, all of a sudden, was this going on? What had changed?

Aggie's theory was that, yes, they were all connected. She wasn't sure how, yet. Part of her theory was that someone really wanted her attention, they had something to share. She thought it all began for her with the fall in the woods. She'd smacked her head pretty hard, had been unconscious for a while. Maybe she had shaken something loose up there that allowed her to see what she'd been seeing. Maybe. It was her best guess.

She'd heard of this sort of thing happening to people who'd had a near death experience, or similar. Her experience was far from near death, she was confident of that. Who knows what's possible though?

Aggie still wasn't sure if she was happy about it, seeing things that is. But, it was what it was and she was too curious now not to get to the bottom of it all. If she could.

She compared it to a time her and Rider had gone on vacation together. They'd been at the ocean and when they got in the water, they were told to keep their feet moving a little. There were fish and small 'rays down there and you wanted to make sure they knew you were there. Ok. "No problem," she thought, "it's their ocean."

On the second to the last day, Rider had rented some snorkeling equipment and he floated around for quite a while finally checking with her to see if she wanted a turn. She thought about it and decided to turn him down, floating on water and being prone to seasickness helped her make the decision. Standing, and even swimming, were fine; the problems began when she started to float.

Well, Rider has a way of convincing Aggie of things, and in the end he talked her into it. She agreed with the stipulation that she was going to stop the minute she got queasy. He laughed at her and handed over the snorkel mask, she would do without the flippers.

Up to this moment, Aggie knew there were fish this close to the shore. She had seen their shadows, moved among them. She was ready. She reminded herself to breathe through the snorkel, and only the snorkel, and then stuck her head in the water, her arms out beside her and her legs behind her. But, there weren't just fish in the water, there was A LOT of fish. A lot. And several 'rays. Right there below her.

She found herself in a small state of panic. She wanted to stand up right away, to get out of the water fast, but she also didn't want to put her feet back down. That's where the fish were. So, she continued to float there, fighting panic, trying decide her next move, and trying not to drown through the snorkel. She finally got a hold of herself and stood up. Still, she'd almost been afraid to put her feet back down. It was an awkward dance.

She looked around for Rider, wanting to admonish him for not telling her how it really looked under water and simultaneously preparing herself to be laughed at or teased. But, he had swum off to another section. She felt relieved and foolish. Obviously, they'd been there the whole time. Deep down she'd know that. She never expected there to be that many, though, and right there in her little part of the ocean, practically touching her.

It had taken her quite by surprise, she had a lump in her throat and her heart was pounding to beat the band. It took a bit of convincing herself to try again. There was no danger, she had been fine the whole time. What would she say to Rider? That she had been afraid to even look at the fish? That'd go over big. She'd been in the water all week long anyway. Don't miss out, she told herself, because you were caught off guard. Besides, you've never seen a 'ray this close up (that one turned out not to be the best argument for going back in).

In the end, perceived peer pressure from her friend, and a little curiosity on her part, won out. Aggie floated on her belly and stuck her head back in the water, actually remembering to breathe through the snorkel and trying not to wimp out. She held out as long as she could until she began to feel the onset of seasickness. She tried to appreciate the experience, but it had startled her deeply. She had to admit, she appreciated being able to use the excuse of being seasick if Rider were to comment on the short amount of time she'd been snorkeling. He'd understand that.

What had been going on at the house and in the woods and the lake was like that time at the ocean. She'd hit her head on that rock in the woods, and when she came to, it was as if someone had put a snorkel mask on her. She'd always thought that there was something else out there. She'd had no proof of it, just a feeling, faith (maybe even hope) that it didn't all just end when you passed. The difference was that now she could see it and hear it.

CHAPTER FORTY-FIVE

AGGIE FIGURED SHE KNEW HOW SHE HAD COME TO BE ABLE TO SEE what she'd been witnessing. What she didn't know was why. Why these visions (guess she was going to use that word after all)? And why at all different times? That was the next part of her theory.

When she thought back over all of her experiences until now, she saw a possible pattern. Now, she was going to try to test it. With only a few exceptions, such as finding the diary, she'd been touching or holding something. Something that connected her to them and, possibly, them to each other.

Aggie opened her eyes and glanced at the objects beside her on the couch. Which one? She scanned all the items once and then her eyes landed on the Bumblebee pendant. That had been in her pocket the night she had to stay in the woods. She just hadn't realized it then. She picked it up and held it reverently in her right hand. She closed her eyes again and focused her mind on the pendant, envisioning its shape and design. Aggie focused on the way it felt in her hand and strained to feel any energy coming from it, a small vibration, anything. Her mind went in a small loop, focusing on each in turn. Nothing happened.

She opened her eyes and her clenched fist, which had slowly tightened while she'd been concentrating. She examined the pendant, it was

OK. It looked the same. But she was getting squat, nada, nothing. Not even a headache. She switched the pendant to her left hand while she shook the pins and needles out of her right. She wasn't giving up that easy. What next?

Aggie went through the same steps again, this time holding the pendant in her left hand. Nothing. She tried again with it cupped between both hands. Nothing.

You know what they said about trying the same thing over and over again and expecting different results. She chuckled at herself and realized that's exactly what she'd been doing. Time to try something else.

Aggie shook her head. She had really focused on it, though. Hard.

She tried to regroup, which is tricky when you don't really know what you're doing in the first place.

Maybe she should try something else. Her eyes landed on the framed photo of Stephen. A butterfly zoomed around in her stomach at the thought of it. *What if it works?*

"That's the point, Aggie. Isn't that what you want?" The sentence hung in the quiet room for a moment while she considered it.

"Come on girl, this is not the time to wimp out, either." She nodded, agreeing with herself and took a deep, cleansing breath. "OK. Ready." Aggie set the pendant down carefully and picked up the photo.

The butterfly had traveled from her stomach to her heart and lodged there. *Great.*

She concentrated on Stephen. She thought about what she knew of him from Judith, the episode in the kitchen, the most recent episode on the stairs, his injury, how he'd never come to after his 'accident'. She put one palm on the glass, directly over his head in the photo, and said his name out loud.

She tried to have empathy for him, for the way it had ended for him. She tried. She just kept seeing him charge into the kitchen, bloody, screaming and angry. More butterflies joined the first one, she took a few deep breaths and tried to ignore them. "Come on, Stephen. Where are you when I need you?"

Aggie listened to the house, looked around for any shimmering lights, or changes in the room. She held the frame tight, one hand still on the glass. She focused on him, whispering his name like a mantra. Nothing happened. Part of her, she hated to admit it, was relieved. The other part of her scolded the first part.

It wasn't working. Why not?

"Crap." Aggie set the frame down beside her.

AGGIE GLANCED AT THE CLOCK, SHE'D BEEN AT IT FOR OVER AN HOUR between both efforts. It was very frustrating. And exhausting. She felt tired. Bone tired, as her mother used to say.

Her mind drifted as she tried to figure out what to try next. She moved her head in a small circle until she heard and felt her neck crack, releasing the tension it held. She sat back into the cushions of the couch while her mind wandered. Her eyes looked out into the room, but focused on nothing in particular. *What now?*

Minutes passed and as her thoughts went to the earlier visions, they replayed in her mind on a loop. Maybe it had to do with location, a few things had happened in the kitchen. What if she tried again from there?

With a small second wind, she gathered everything up again and relocated to the kitchen table. For good luck, she set everything down on the table in front of the same chair she'd been sitting in when she'd first seen Billy, 'the quiet man'. It was nice to know his name, finally.

Aggie stretched her arms and then arched her back before sitting down. She cracked her neck again. Two cracks this time, it felt good. She realized she was procrastinating, but she couldn't help it. She was still nervous about the whole thing. Mostly, though, she was afraid she wasn't going to be able to do it.

She took the Bumblebee pendant in hand and examined it for the umpteenth time. It was so beautiful, amazing craftsmanship. Obviously, a labor of love from a talented artist. Her thoughts drifted back to finding it on Western Hill, at the time she had been convinced it was a crystal. She had seen a dirt encrusted crystal on the ground, just like the others in her pocket that day. It was the only reason she grabbed it. It was her sixth for the day and she had been pretty happy with her haul because she hadn't really even been hunting crystals. She just always happened to be watching for stuff on the ground because, well, you just never knew what you'd find.

Aggie paused and rubbed her eyes, she was beginning to get tired and this whole thing was giving her a headache.

She was getting a headache! Butterflies appeared in her stomach and her pulse began to race. Was it happening? She forced herself not to move a muscle, she continued to just sit there and tried not to tense up. She kept her eyes open this time, in anticipation, and she let herself focus on the room around her. As much as she could, without moving her head. She didn't want to jinx it, in case whatever she was doing, or not doing, was working.

Aggie held her breath and waited, hoping she was right. Her headache had gotten stronger and she closed her hand protectively around the pendant. Her eyes darted around the room, not wanting to miss it if it happened. *When it happened*, she silently corrected herself.

In a moment, she saw him, the quiet man from the kitchen and the stairway. Billy. He was close, a little over an arm's length away. He looked as he did the first time she'd seen him. Long dirty blonde hair, T-shirt and cutoff fatigues. There was no blood, so far. The same peaceful eyes looked her way, but unfocused, he was looking through her.

Stunned, she let go of the breath she'd been holding. Aggie smiled to herself and waited. Would he do anything more or would he morph again like he did both times before? At least, if he changed this time, she wouldn't be caught off guard. She was tempted to call out his name, but she didn't want to spoil the connection.

"Billy." She couldn't help but whisper his name to herself and regretted it the moment it escaped from her lips. She winced and waited for him to vanish. Aggie watched him like a hawk, now he was looking right at her, *seeing* her. He had heard his name.

He held out his closed hand to her and slowly unwrapped his fingers from what he had secreted inside. The object he was holding was small and shiny and it gleamed in the light coming through the window. She leaned forward so she could make it out. It couldn't be.

Her grip tightened around the pendant in her hand; yes, it was still there. But, it was also just a foot from her, in the palm of Billy's hand. A brand new Bumblebee pendant on a silver chain.

She gasped and looked up to try and catch his attention once more. He was still looking at her and this time he was smiling. Aggie, feeling bolder now, said his name out loud. She couldn't think of anything more intelligent at the moment, her mind was spinning a hundred miles an hour. He nodded and held the necklace out to her once more, then he closed his fist around the shiny, new necklace and held it over his heart. He looked her in the eye and raised his eyebrows. She stole a glance at the fist over his heart, just to be sure, and then up at him again. He was still waiting. She nodded 'yes' and Billy smiled as he vanished. Just like that, and as quietly as he had appeared. Right before her very eyes, as they say.

CHAPTER FORTY-SIX

TUESDAY - JULY 1, '75

We're on the road! After the incident with the garden tools (and even knowing that it was just garden tools falling over), I should be fine staying in my house. Logically, writing it down here, I get that. But, still, every strange noise has me imagining a stranger trying to get in. Trying to get to me. As long as I can't remember or help the police to identify the attacker, I won't feel comfortable there.

So! I've decided to go on an adventure and I'm taking Stephen up on his gracious offer to stay with him for a while, while I recuperate, at his place in Arizona. I suppose it will be similar to New Mexico, but I guess I won't know for sure until I get there. He lives on a lake and I'm looking forward to being near the water. It'll be neat to see if it's much different. I've been wondering what types of cactus are nearby and if there'll be any palm trees. Stuff like that.

I'm also going to miss Clara. She doesn't think I should be going, but it's not forever. I get the feeling she doesn't like Stephen. I chalk it up to her memories of Billy and the way things were before that night. I know she hopes it could be like it used to be. I don't have those same feelings right now (I don't know if I ever will) and I have no reason not to trust Stephen. He's been a gentleman the whole time that I've known him and we've grown to be good friends in a short time. He has been watching out for me and I'm a bit more at ease with him around than I am alone. Maybe I've grown too dependent. To be honest, I think I'll be a bit more at ease away from Southern California in general. Right now, I just want to not be afraid or feel like I have to look over my shoulders. I want to not have to worry about things going bump in the night and if it's someone trying to get in.

I know I have a life to rebuild here. From what I've gathered, it sounds like I was doing well and having a good time. But, I can't start over until I get through this; heal up, get my memories back, and leave fear behind me. Who knows, maybe by then they will have caught the guy and I won't have to worry about some random killer lurking around trying to finish off what he started that night on the beach.

I told Stephen I would accept his invitation but he'd have to agree to my conditions first: no hanky-panky or strings of any kind, I can get a bus ticket back any time I want, and he's to be my friend not my nurse. He agreed to them all and said that he was just happy that he could help provide a safe, quiet place for me to get better.

He said that his job takes him on the road a lot (which I knew) and asked if I would prefer him to take time off to stay there with me. I told him not to change his schedule for me (hence the no nursing clause in my set of conditions). I don't want to be a burden or put him out at all. Plus, I told him, I think the time alone will be good for me in the long run. It'll give me time to sort through all these things that have happened and find a way to deal with them. I think I was trying to convince myself, as well. I'm moving forward on blind faith that if I keep trying, I will heal up and my memories will sort themselves out. That's what they say, right? Time heals all wounds? We'll see, I guess.

I'm writing this from the passenger seat in Stephen's car, he's driving and narrating. We are headed East on Interstate 8. He said it used to be called Interstate 80, but they've been working on it over the years and was renamed not too long ago. I have to admit, it's a nicer road than I thought. We've been driving through a lot of unpopulated desert areas with a lot of nothing scattered in between remote small towns. I'd be nervous if it wasn't for the fact that Stephen knows this route by heart due to his job. He's very comfortable with the drive and so I'm at ease. We talked for a bit when we left California, but there's only so much conversation you can have before you start repeating yourselves. We've got the radio on and occasionally we pick up a local station. Mostly we get static, though. Stephen doesn't seem to mind the quiet times in between and doesn't force conversation just for the sake of it. I think it's because he's used to being alone in the car so much.

I picked up my diary to pass the time when conversation died, but I'm going to try not to just write babble. He says we've got a six-hour-ish ride today, not including pit stops. We'll stop in a bit to gas up and get a bite to eat at our halfway point, Yuma, Arizona. It's interesting how close this highway gets to the border. I've never been this far south before, I feel like I could reach out and touch Mexico.

∾

2 P.M. (7-1-75)

We just had a pit stop in Yuma. Stephen stopped at a combination roadside diner/gas station that he knew about. It was about a 45 minute break. Longer would have been nice, but then we'll never get there. We stretched, ate, and went to the restroom (they weren't as bad as they could have been, but they weren't as clean, either).

We ate our take out on a picnic table in the shade near the diner. It was nice to be out of the car after three hours and the breeze was nice. Stephen also picked out a postcard and bought a stamp for it. He noticed me watching him and smiled, saying it was for his sister. He must have mailed it at some point when I wasn't looking, because I didn't see it again after that. He probably wanted it to have a Yuma postmark.

Stephen was chatty over lunch and told me again how happy he was that I took him up on his offer. He said he didn't get much company out there and was looking forward to me being his guest. I just smiled and thanked him again. It just felt awkward. I should be thanking him, not the other way around.

I know I'm not explaining myself clearly. He just keeps thanking me and telling me how happy he is. I'll have to work on him a bit, let him know I appreciate him and this offer more often. I'll try to beat him to the punch next time, maybe he'll relax a bit.

An odd thing happened at lunch when I got up to use the restroom. There was a small line, so I had to wait my turn. I turned around while I waited, and saw Stephen. His side was towards me and he was picking at something on the table. I couldn't quite make out what he was doing, but he was very focused on it.

Soon, my turn came and I forgot about him and the table. When I returned, he was eating his sandwich again and was no longer concerned with the table. It was nothing and I would have forgotten about it. Except, when we got up to leave and he cleared the table, the spot he'd been fiddling with was uncovered. Something had been carved into the surface of the picnic table. It looked like an apostrophe.

I caught his eye when he returned from the rubbish and pointed at the apostrophe. "Hey, what does that mean?" I asked and he looked where I pointed. For a split second, his face flushed and he looked like a deer in the headlights, like he'd been caught red-handed at something. It was pretty funny. I mean, it's just a picnic table. When he turned back to me, the look was gone. He shrugged and said, "yeah, that's weird" and continued on to the car without looking back. He definitely didn't want to talk about it. No big deal, Stephen. I guess we all have our little quirks.

I'm going to stop for now because this is starting to make me a little car sick. Besides, we're almost there and I want to watch the scenery.

CHAPTER FORTY-SEVEN

AGGIE'S HEARTBEAT BEGAN TO SLOW, ALTHOUGH THE BUTTERFLIES remained. Billy had vanished, but his image was fresh in her mind. She very clearly saw the brand new necklace in his hand. The same necklace she'd seen on Freddie during the stairway vision. It swung from her neck as she was running away and it caught her attention.

She uncurled her fingers from the pendant in her hand. It had been Freddie's. She pondered the mysterious circumstances that brought her to be holding it in her hand now.

She thought about Billy again. He wanted her to know the necklace was Freddie's, even though it was also connected to him. Freddie. He wanted her to focus on Freddie, she guessed. But, hadn't she been doing that? She'd been reading the diary, getting to know her. She had spent a good part of the afternoon holding the pendant and trying to "see" something, only to have him appear again. What was she doing wrong?

Aggie put the pendant down on the table and spread everything out. She was stumped for the moment, maybe something else would come to her if she just waited. She gave herself heck for that thought. *That's not very proactive, is it, Agatha? Come on girl, think.* But she had nothing else up her sleeve.

She reached out and touched the other items one by one, beginning with Freddie's diary. Her touch lingered. Had she missed something in there? She didn't think so. Soon, she was holding it.

She had held it so many times, now. Each time she'd read an entry. Apart from how she was brought to the diary, nothing had ever happened. She'd never had an appearance or vision when she was reading it. Why would now be any different?

Aggie was exhausted, but she was willing to try anything. She wanted and needed her house back and this seemed to be the only way to get there. *I've got nothing to lose, right?*

She pulled the diary to her chest and held it loosely. She closed her eyes and tried to let her mind wander. She waited, expectations high, stomach full of butterflies.

She breathed in and out slowly but only picked up the faint, musty smell that still lingered within the diary. She looked out at the room with one eye and then closed it again. No hint of another headache, the previous one faded along with Billy. Nothing.

Trying not to focus on something wasn't as easy as she thought. Maybe she was still 'doing it wrong'. She huffed and tried not to try. It was confusing. And frustrating. When Billy showed up, she figured she'd done it, and could do it again.

Aggie opened her eyes and set the diary down on the table. "Crap," she wiped away a stray tear, "crap." She thought about her home. If she couldn't figure this out, what was she going to do?

Freddie. It was all about Freddie, according to Billy. Why shouldn't she believe him?

She thought back to earlier, to the scene on the stairs. It seemed like something important had happened with Freddie. Aggie had seen it on her face, had felt it rush over and through her as Freddie ran out the back door. For a few moments, she had shared Freddie's emotions. It was a whirlwind of emotions, and they had been quite powerful. She had been caught off guard but those feelings were still with her. They were rolling around in her gut like a bad meal.

At first, there had been a feeling of recognition. Someone lost had been found. Then she felt confusion. She knew in her heart that they'd been lost to her forever; how could they be back? Next was sadness as she understood what that meant. It was bittersweet to have this moment, one last moment, with the lost one at last remembered. One sweet, yet terrible memory, at last. The final, but lasting emotion, agonizing grief. It roiled in her gut, it was familiar and foreign at the same time. And heart breaking.

This is what Freddie had felt at the bottom of the stairs, there was no question in her mind. She had seen Billy and had finally remembered him. Remembered their love. And then, finally, she grieved for him.

The feeling of grief had been sudden, overwhelming and agonizing. Aggie hadn't felt anything as powerful since her friend and mentor, and almost second mother, Judith, had passed. She had pushed it aside, best as she could in the midst of the stairway scene playing out; but, it hadn't left her. It had been sitting there this whole time, waiting to be acknowledged. Waiting to be attended to. Doing so meant facing her loss again, as well as Freddie's. Time passing had helped her deal with her loss, but now it was back and fresh. A scab pulled off an old wound, painful and bloody once more.

Aggie was sobbing again. She shed quiet tears for herself and Judith, for Freddie and for Billy. She felt closer than ever to Freddie, they had both suffered a terrible loss and her heart went out to her again. She had already promised herself, but now she promised Freddie: she would figure this all out one way or another. Yes, she wanted her house back, but now she wanted to help Freddie just as much. She just had to figure out what it was she wanted.

"Crap." Aggie dried her tears as she voiced her frustration to the empty kitchen. "Maybe I just need a break, I can't think anymore."

She began to gather up the items, she'd come back to them later. She placed Stephen's photo on top of the box of his letters because they belonged together. She put her journal to the side for her to work in later. Aggie smiled and placed the pendant on top of the diary because she knew they went together. They both belonged to Freddie.

"Oh my gosh," Aggie smiled and grabbed them both in a rush, "that's it."

CHAPTER FORTY-EIGHT

AGGIE SAT BACK IN THE CHAIR AND SMILED AT HERSELF. SHE HAD BOTH the diary and pendant in hand and a fresh wind of inspiration blowing at her sails. Maybe she was getting the hang of this after all.

"Ok, how did I do that?" As Aggie retraced her steps just prior to Billy's arrival, she realized she hadn't done anything. That was the secret. Her mind had been wandering at the time, she hadn't been focused at all. She'd been overdoing it before and that was mucking it up. The diary wouldn't work without the pendant, and vice-versa, because they belonged together. That's what she hoped anyway, strength in numbers. It felt right. She was ready to give it another go.

Aggie repeated her preparations: she stretched and cracked her neck, took a deep cleansing breath and let it out, she sat back in her chair and tried to quiet her mind. Eyes shut gently, she told herself to let her mind wander. *Wander off the path, if you want, just let go.*

She held the diary and pendant to her chest, sure to keep them in contact with each other, her arms crossed around them. With each breath she left her tears and grief from a few minutes ago behind. She imagined a white space in her mind's eye, a clean slate, and let her mind take it from there. She relaxed, breathing steady, passing time but not being aware of how much. She stole a quick peek around the kitchen, seeing nothing interesting, she closed her eyes again.

A touch of a headache began and she knew she was on the right path. Butterflies appeared in her stomach again, but they hadn't been too much trouble last time. As her headache grew stronger and then steadied, the white space in her head grew dark. The butterflies worked their way up into her chest and took the place of her heart, but still she followed her mind's lead. Slow, even breaths helped.

Aggie saw a woman in a white sundress sitting in a jeep, she was crying and holding the lower part of her belly. Aggie recognized Freddie. She was repeating one phrase over and over between sobs, "oh my God," and shaking her head side to side. "Stephen." She took a breath, "no, I won't believe it."

The road was wet from a recent storm and rain drops dotted the wind shield. She watched Freddie drive down her very own street and was surprised when she turned off the road after only a short distance.

For Aggie, this would have been a grown over trail in the woods, but for Freddie, this was a well-travelled dirt road and the jeep was handling it fine, for the most part. Freddie cursed the balding tires as she continued up the muddy road. She took it slow and was able to make it, albeit with a little slipping and sliding.

Aggie was familiar with this route and anticipated Freddie's destination, although having only travelled in on foot herself. Sure enough, Freddie eventually pulled out into the clearing at the top of Western Hill and parked. She left the jeep running, set the emergency brake and left the headlights burning.

It was early evening, but the monsoon rain clouds had further darkened the sky, blocking any moonshine there might have been. As if on cue, it began to rain again. Freddie paid no attention, there was no top on the jeep but she seemed not to notice her hair or her dress, or the interior of the jeep, getting soaked. She reached into a pocket of an overnight bag on the passenger seat and pulled out a small, blue book. It was her diary, the very same one, though much newer, that Aggie was holding in her hands.

Freddie flipped the book open to the first page and something small slid into her lap. She tossed the diary back on to the passenger seat without looking and picked up the item, it was a Polaroid. Aggie recognized Billy. She held it to her lips and kissed it, her lips lingering on the surface. She continued to cry and through heaping sobs, cried out, "Billy. Oh my God, I really have lost you."

Freddie tucked the photo into the top of her sundress and reached up to her necklace, one hand closing over it tightly. She called out his name one more time and it came out as a sad, choked cry. She pushed wet hair away from her face with her free hand and tried to catch her breath.

Aggie could feel goosebumps rising on her arms but she ignored them, as she did the butterflies. She didn't want to disrupt this vision at any cost. Freddie was guiding her now, she just had to hold on for the ride.

Through the dark and rain, an object began to appear in Freddie's headlights. As on the stairs, a light swirling area appeared. Freddie watched as it became a T-shirt and cutoffs and then in a heartbeat, Billy materialized inside them.

"Billy!" Freddie's sobs were cut off and she reached for the door handle. She jumped out of the Jeep to greet him, oblivious to his method of arrival. The memory of his fate forgotten. All she knew was that he was there, in front of her, within arm's reach. In her haste to reach him, Freddie's still clutched hand pulled the chain from around her neck.

Aggie watched as they approached each other. Freddie went to Billy, calling his name with her arms outstretched. As the lovers closed the distance to each other, Aggie saw the necklace slip out of Freddie's hand and fall into muddy oblivion. At that moment, Billy disappeared and Aggie experienced instant deja vu.

This was almost the exact vision Aggie had the night she'd stayed in the woods, even though she'd thought it was a dream at the time. A woman in the rain, in a white dress, calling out for someone. And now she knew what the words were: "Billy."

Freddie looked to the spot where Billy had been standing in disbelief. Where had he gone? She cried out for him again and again, spinning around in the mud and rain. She clutched at her neck for his necklace, it was gone. Freddie fell to her knees and dissolved into a heap with renewed, anguished sobs.

Aggie watched as the rain let up and waited anxiously for what happened next.

Tap, tap, tap.

"Hello? Aggie?" Someone far off was calling her name.

Crap. The connection to Freddie was broken, she'd felt it slip away.

"Aggie? Are you OK?"

Reluctantly, she opened her eyes and tried to find the source of the interruption. Slowly, she came out of the fog she'd been in and focused on the room around her. She set the diary and the pendant on the table and greeted her best friend, Rider.

CHAPTER FORTY-NINE

I've made it to Arizona with Stephen. The drive wasn't too bad, we made it without any issues and beat the holiday traffic. He asked if I wanted to go into town to celebrate the 4th, but I'm not ready for a crowd of people.

It's a whole different world here, but at least there's water. The lake is beautiful, his house is pretty remote. It's a bit of a culture shock compared to southern California but it's going to be an adventure. I keep telling myself that. I can always go back, we agreed to no strings; just that I'd give it a try. There's a small dock at the edge of the lake and I can picture myself spending a bunch of time there.

Out of the blue, and out of character for me, something surprising happened last night. I'm blushing and shaking my head at the memory of it. It's ironic how much of the detail I can remember from last night versus the whole of the time I was in California. It goes like this.

I've been imagining the start of this new part of my life here in Arizona. Stephen has yet to do more than kiss me on my forehead, but I find myself longing for him with each gentle touch. I picture his soft, cupid shaped lips on mine.

Last night, I found myself outside his bedroom door, a dim light glowed from the space between the door and the floor. He was still awake. My heart leapt. I stood there in a long, lightweight tank top and cotton undies taking stock; definitely not sexy, everything covered up. What was I doing? I counted to ten anyway and tapped on his door. I told him I couldn't sleep and offered him a smile. He had pulled a robe on over his boxers as he opened his door and he was tying the sash as I sat down on the edge of his bed. He smiled and sat next to me.

"Are you OK? What can I do?" His dark eyes, filled with concern, held my stare and I was lost in them.

"I can't sleep." I broke away from his stare, he'll notice that I'm a fraud. "Maybe it's just being in a strange place?"

He laughed and I realized how that sounded. "Not that your house is strange, I…"

"I know what you meant." Stephen took my hand in his and gave it a small, comforting squeeze, like he's done before. He kissed it gently, like he does my forehead. "Can I get you something?"

My stomach knotted up. I took a breath and worked up my courage to ask the question. "This old house makes a lot of noises, it's unsettling." I paused and took another breath, staring at the floor, "Can I just stay with you until I get sleepy?"

I clasped my shaking hands in my lap, and finally got the nerve to look him in the eye again.

"Of course, whatever you need." He smiled a gentleman's smile, a girl can tell the difference you know. He gestured towards the left hand side of the bed and I moved to lie down on the pillow there. He walked around the the far side of the bed and sat down. After a few moments, he asked if I wanted any water, a magazine or an extra blanket. I said no and that I was fine now that he was there.

The silence was awkward. Neither of us knew what I really wanted. He was trying to accommodate me and be a gentleman at the same time. My heart! I reached over for his hand and he held it in his. I gave it a small tug to indicate it was OK for him to lie down, too. We had some silly small talk about the day and after some time had passed, we both grew quiet. The light in his room was already dim, which was conducive to sleepiness. Part of me intended to go back to my room at this point, but I was so comfortable that the thought had completely left me.

I rolled over on my right side, away from Stephen, but only out of habit. I favor my right side. Soon I heard him breathing rhythmically and realized he was sleeping. I took that moment to shimmy closer to him, not realizing the he was on his side, too. I felt safe next to him. We were practically little spoon and big spoon, separated only by a thin wall of gentlemanly space. I felt so comfortable that I backed up as close as I could to him. He woke slightly and placed an arm around me for the first time. My heart leapt again.

The next move was mine to make. I almost chickened out. Almost. When it felt right, I moved my left arm back, under his, and rested it on his thigh. After a few moments, I got braver and spread my hand out and traced the muscle beneath it. I let my hand stray even further back and caressed the cheek of his buttock. Stephen let out a small moan and shifted himself even closer to me. He leaned forward and kissed the back of my neck gently, the scruff of his whiskers caused a chill that ran down my back. My turn to moan. Such a small thing can feel so good! He paused at that, allowing me control what would happen next, if anything. I sank back into him, wanting him, needing him. I grew bolder and moved my hand between us, grasping him.

"Kiss me again, just like before," I implored. He complied and I felt a second chill.

My heart sped up, my breath caught in my chest. Yes. This. More of this!

I felt him grow hard in my hand, but the rest of him remained stock still. My heart was beating faster and my anxiety level was rising, but I pushed my way through it. I reminded myself how much I trust Stephen and I relaxed a little. He whispered "are you sure?" I gave him a "mmm hmm" and brought my left hand forward on top of his, which was still around my waist. I told myself that I was ready, I was excited, this is a good thing. I stayed still, on my side, being the best little spoon I could - anticipating his next move, my pulse reacting with my nerves.

I didn't flinch as his arms loosened their hug and his hand moved under my tank top and over my breasts; his movements were soft and gentle. Slow. Patient. I leaned back into him and waited for what came next. Another kiss, this time to the tip of my shoulder. Yes, this is nice. I moaned to let him know all was well.

His hand moved down to my stomach, lingering for a moment at my bellybutton then gliding lower across my skin and down. At that moment, his touch set off a live wire inside me and my heart clutched in upon itself as his hand brushed over my scar. I gasped and pulled away from him, rolling over onto my stomach. I buried my face in the pillow, sobbing from embarrassment and shame, whispering I'm sorry, I'm sorry.

I woke up with a start, tears in my eyes. I stole a quick peek behind me and was disoriented to find myself in my own bed, alone. No Stephen, no kisses, no touching. It was a dream. A reprieve!

I rolled over onto my back feeling mortified, slightly frustrated, and relieved at once. There was a soft green glow coming from the alarm clock and it washed over my body as the dream replayed in my mind. I covered my face with my hands and groaned with embarrassment. If only to myself. Why have a dream like that? The brain is a funny thing.

I have to admit that he's foxy, anyone would say so. He's tall and has dark eyes and hair, even darker lashes, kissable lips meeting in the middle below impossibly high cheekbones. Yes, I've noticed. I'm human. But, but I have no plans to do anything about it. We are just friends and I am not ready for anything more. Really. I'm still healing.

I can barely handle the occasional holding of hands. Which, I think, can sometimes be very intimate. Part of me, in time I'm sure, will begin to crave a bit more and long for the closeness and comfort that it brings. Right now, though, it doesn't. The scarred and wounded part of me needs the safety and comfort of aloneness, protection from a curious stare, or an intimate, careless touch.

I climbed out of bed as quietly as I could and stood there for a few moments, naked (because, unlike my dream, I sleep that way). I looked down at the offending scar, source of my embarrassment and shame, aglow from the light of the clock. Its jagged, barbed wire-like lines run from my lower left abdomen across to my lower right abdomen. An ironic and constant reminder of a memory I don't have. The green glow gave it an alien-like life of its own. How can that be part of me? My hands, which had been at my side, moved to my hips, hesitating. I wanted to, but didn't, couldn't, make myself touch it.

The day may come when I can look at my scar, perhaps even touch it, and not have panic, grief and anger wash over me; right now though, I can't imagine when that will be. Up 'til now, I've done my best to ignore it. I certainly don't understand why I would dream about something so intimate. I clearly would never put myself in the position of letting anyone else near my scar when I can't even deal with it myself.

I paused, listening to the sounds of this new, strange house. All was quiet. Only the alarm clock was there to witness my struggle. I slipped into the robe I'd left on the chair beside my bed, tightening the sash protectively around me as I headed downstairs. Now it's after 4:00 a.m. and I'm in the living room waiting for daylight to arrive; I've got a few candles burning and a whiskey rocks on the coffee table. It's not easy to write by candle light, by the way, so I'm stopping for now. Too many thoughts are keeping sleep at bay. Hopefully, the whiskey will take care of one or the other (or both!).

CHAPTER FIFTY

SATURDAY - JULY 12, '75

Stephen has finally left on his first road trip since I've been here. I could tell that he didn't want to leave. I think he was waiting for me to ask him to stay, to tell him that I was nervous to be alone here. But I have to admit, I feel pretty good about it. The house is remote, sure, but that's a good thing. No one's going to find it by accident. And, we're so far from California that I'm not on edge about my attacker still being 'out there somewhere'. Stephen took me grocery shopping, I stocked up and sent him on his way.

I'm relieved, actually. I've had the dream again twice. That dream. The one with all of the touching and sexy stuff. Both times, they ended the same way the first one did. And then I ended up analyzing them for the rest of the night. I'm hoping, with him gone, I won't have that dream again. I have enough on my plate, without my own dreams adding to my problems.

On the other hand, however, it's forced me to come to terms with my scar. I've been touching it and looking at it, trying to accept that it's now a part of me. It's not easy and I find myself softening the edges with a whiskey rocks. But, I am making progress and that's no small potatoes. I'm hoping that, eventually, the scar will no longer have any power over me. I'm crossing my fingers.

I've gotten to the point where I can touch the length of the scar without my heart beating through my chest or having ever changing images flash through my mind about the night it got there. I have yet to be able to do it without thoughts of the babies I will never have running through my head. My heart breaks for a family that I will never have.

It makes me so mad. What gave them the right? What inspires a person to do that? Was it random? Worse, what if it wasn't random? Are the police still looking for him? Is he still looking for me?

Then, my thoughts turn to Billy, who's lost everything, and I'm sorry. Sorry that he's gone, sorry for his family, sorry that I still can't remember him, sorry for myself and my missing memories. It's a giant pity party of one.

Well, I am making progress but it's going to take a while. In the meantime, I'm crossing my fingers that it's enough to stop the dream. That, and Stephen being on the road. We'll see how that goes.

CHAPTER FIFTY-ONE

"YEAH, I'M GOOD." AGGIE SMILED AT HER FRIEND AND THEN RUBBED her face with both hands, partly to get the blood flowing again and partly to momentarily regroup. "What are you doing here? Shouldn't you be home packing?"

"Yes," Rider made a face and shrugged, "and no."

Aggie stood and went to meet Rider who was about halfway into the kitchen from the back door. She greeted him with a hug, "no? What does that mean?"

"It's a long story," the sparkle that had been in Rider's eye since getting the new job was gone.

Aggie sensed he had some bad news to share and a knot formed in her stomach. Instead of waiting for the story, she began running possible scenarios through her head. The knot grew bigger.

"Uh oh." Aggie gestured to the living room, "Let's go in here where it's more comfortable. I need a change of scenery."

He shrugged again and headed towards the couch. Aggie's curiosity piqued, he was definitely moping and that was not like him. She followed him in to the living room and waited while he chose his usual spot on the couch. She sat in an easy chair across from him so they could see each other comfortably while they talked. She waited for him to begin his story, he never needed prompting. He'd speak when he was ready, that's why he was here.

After a few moments of silence, Rider began to speak, "the job in Italy is gone."

"What do you mean gone? Just like that?"

"I was getting to that, Nellie," his nickname for her when she jumped the gun. Aggie bit her lip and stifled a chuckle, she nodded to him to continue.

"The assignment is gone, I should've said. The client took a sudden turn for the worse and passed away a few days ago. So, I'm not going to Italy." Rider looked down at his hands, which were folded in his lap.

Aggie took that as her cue to respond, "Oh no. I'm so sorry. I know how much you were looking forward to the job." She paused and waited to catch his eye, "did they say if they had any other possible assignments for you?"

"I asked and they are looking in to it. But," he shook his head in disbelief, "they said that because they had been so understaffed, they'd put a lot of effort into recruiting, and now they have more nurses than they do assignments."

"You've got to be kidding."

"I know." Rider threw his hand up in the air, "so now that I've taken a leave from my first job and this assignment has been cancelled, I'm out of work."

"You're old job won't take you back?"

"They've already filled my shifts with someone else. They hadn't planned on me being available until next year, so they moved as quickly as they could, too."

"What about the new place, do they think they'll have any new assignments coming up for you?" Aggie was trying to come up with suggestions for him, but she was pretty sure he'd already considered all of these options.

"They might, but no guarantee. They apologized profusely, of course. For all the good that does me. I know it's not their fault…" He ran one hand through his hair and let his bad news hang in the air.

"That sucks. I'm so sorry." Aggie felt helpless. She hated to see him so depressed. She was already trying to come up with something to make him feel better, but she'd have to wait. She could tell he wasn't ready to switch moods yet.

"I can't believe they cut it so close, another couple of days and you'd have been on the plane." She wanted to get up and sit next to him on the couch, put her arm around his shoulders or hold his hand and tell him 'it'll be alright' or 'things will work out'. That's not what Rider wanted, though, in these situations. He knew, as well as she did, that things work out the way they were supposed to in the end, it's just hard to remember that while you were going through the crappy times. If he was meant to have a traveling nurse assignment, he would get one. Perhaps, it would be an even better opportunity. You just had to wait, and have faith. That's the tough part.

"I'm not sure what they expect me to do now. For a few minutes, I had two great jobs. Now, I have none." He shook his head, "I know I can get another job nursing. Somewhere," Rider waved his hand randomly, "I was just really looking forward to this. I've wanted it for so long."

Aggie nodded sympathetically, "when did you find out?"

"This morning."

They looked at each other in silence. Aggie was out of questions and he knew she understood his disappointment. This was one of the benefits of a longtime friendship: familiarity. The silence between them was comfortable, just not upbeat at the moment. Aggie's mind continued to swirl with thoughts about what she could do to cheer him up. She couldn't help it, she was a problem solver.

"Do you want a coffee? I can put some on for you," Aggie offered as a distraction.

"No," Rider rubbed his stomach, "I'm going to drown in it as it is. I've already had several today." He realized she was attempting a subtle change of subject, he silently agreed that it was a good idea. He'd wallowed enough for the day. "By the way, what were you up to when I got here?" he chuckled, "I thought maybe you'd been overcome by a nap at the kitchen table."

Aggie laughed, "I could really use one." She looked at a clock on the bookshelf and noted the time, "it's been a really long day. You won't believe what's been going on."

THE TWO FRIENDS HAD MADE THEIR WAY THROUGH THE MAZE OF OPEN and unopened storage boxes in the next room over and were now both sitting on the couch in the den. Aggie brought him up to date on the scene on the stairs and how she'd been holding onto the photo and the shoebox the whole time. She told him how that had given her a theory on what had all been happening. Rider listened and nodded in all the right places, commented and questioned in others.

She even told him about the snorkel mask comparison, which he understood. He had laughed at her retelling of the part about the scary amount of fish in the sea, but not for too long.

"So, I had an idea to try to make a vision happen on purpose," she explained, "it didn't go so well, though."

"Why?" Rider asked, "what happened?"

Aggie laughed, "that's easy, nothing. A whole lot of nothing."

Rider laughed with her then raised his eyebrows at her. He was waiting for the rest of the story, the one that ended with her at the kitchen table with her eyes closed.

So she told him. Everything. Like she always did and vice-versa. She started in the den with the pendant and trying too hard and ended with the vision of Freddie alone on top of Western Hill in the dark and the rain. "That's when you walked in. It seems like it could be the end of the story, but it's not. I have a feeling that there's much more to it."

"Wow," Rider was running his hand through his hair again, taking it all in, " I had no idea that's what was going on. I'm impressed. No wonder you look like that, you've had a big day."

Aggie laughed, "Yeah, I guess I did."

"Do you want me to go?" Rider offered.

"No," Aggie reached out for his hand and gave it a small squeeze, "I'm done with that for the day, I think. And I'm too tired, really, to sleep. Plus I miss you."

CHAPTER FIFTY-TWO

SATURDAY - AUGUST 2, '75

I've come out to the dock to soak up some sun. I've been cooped up in the house for a few days because it's been rainy and cold. Well, cold for Arizona. Stephen says it the onset of Monsoon Season. Today the skies have cleared and it's warmed up quite a bit, so here I am. I brought a snack (cheese and grapes, with a few cubes of bread in case the ducks swim by), a drink (cold bottle of beer, don't judge - at least it's past lunch time), today's mail (I got a letter!), and a little radio I found inside (It has fresh batteries and is playing some good ole southern rock. It reminds me of Clara's story about Ronny. Keep on rockin' kid!).

Stephen is traveling again for work, this time to New Mexico. He left this morning and told me he expects to be back before next week-end. I've gotten to the point where I don't really mind him being gone. It's not like he gives me time to miss him, what with his nightly tele-phone calls (he tells me about his day, asks about mine, how do I feel, etc.). I sometimes just feel like shouting: "I'm fine!"

Really, the only tough thing about him being gone is the lack of transportation. Since he takes the car with him when he goes, I'm kind of trapped here and it's too far to walk into town. So I make sure I'm stocked up on groceries and such before he takes off. I've got it down to a system now and I'm used to staying at the house by myself.

Now that I've adjusted to it all, I think I actually prefer it. The house is so out of the way that no one ever comes by or bothers us and I can appreciate the solitude. I've actually come to prefer it; sometimes, even having Stephen here is annoying. I like having no one else to worry about or check on or to have to keep to a schedule for anything. I can do what I please, when I please. I can sleep in if I want or stay up late and not worry about bothering him.

I guess it kinds of sounds like I'm complaining about Stephen. I'm not, really. He's been good to me, he's considerate and protective. Maybe that's not the right word; he's not so much protective as - well - he treats me with kid gloves. A little too much. I'm far from being my old self (I'll give him that he didn't know the old me), but he makes me feel like I'm fragile, like crystal or china. It's annoying!

I'm beginning to feel like he's holding something back. I've tried talking to him about it but he just denies it. He'll only say that he wants me to be happy here and feel safe and provided for. I know he's not being completely honest with me; I get the feeling he wants to say something about my drinking. For example, I picked up a few bottles of Jack and some beer along with the groceries before he left for the week. He helped put away the groceries and when he got to the bag with the booze in it, he made a face. It was only for a second and I don't think he noticed that I saw him. When I looked again, his expression changed back to "normal" but his mood was off for the rest of the afternoon.

I can feel his eyes on me whenever I pour a drink. I'm annoyed because it makes me feel self-conscious. I don't think there's an issue, I really don't drink that much and I'm not taking my pain killers any more. I'm not a drunk, I know what a drunk is. You can't tell me he doesn't have a drink or two with his clients when he's on the road, so I don't appreciate the looks he's been giving me. At least I can have a drink in peace this week. Hey, there's another reason I'm not upset that he's traveling.

Later... (8-2-75)

I took a break from writing to have my snack and open the mail. This is the first piece of mail I've gotten since I've been here, not that I was expecting any. It's postmarked from California and I guessed that it's from Clara. Out of courtesy, I exchanged address with a few of the old crowd and promised to stay in touch, but, I have already broken that promise.

I do get the sense that we were good friends. I still don't have any recollection of Clara from before, but the nature of her visits in the hospital and the tone of this letter are the same: she's my friend. Clara hasn't let my memory loss bother her, and she has kept in touch, like she said she would. I'm going to have to hold up my end a little better.

The letter began with a curious apology: "I know you wanted to take time away from here to heal and work on regaining your memory, forgive me for breaking my word to Stephen, but I miss you and wanted to reach out. I didn't want you to feel lonely and I thought that a letter would be less intrusive than a phone call." I'm curious what she meant about breaking her word. I didn't think her and Stephen even knew each other.

Most of the letter was a bunch of 'small talk': tips at the coffee shop are good and she's saving as much as she can for school, so-and-so has gotten a good job with a construction company and is very excited, this other one keeps asking if she's heard from me. On and on like that for a few paragraphs. Not to be ungrateful, but I don't remember any of the people she mentioned which makes it a little boring. That makes me sound like a jerk and I'm ashamed of myself. They meant well, obviously, and it means a lot that they still care enough to ask after me. I am grateful for the effort and the sentiments from home - I will focus on that and cherish this letter. I feel terrible for not staying in touch from my end. I'll try to do better.

Having said that, though, the last part of the letter did have meaning for me. Surprisingly. Towards the end of the letter, she mentions that the old gang is still reeling from the events that night. She says that they all miss us both terribly and how could anyone have guessed that such a happy night would have turned into such a terrible tragedy? She was glad that at least I still had the Bumblebee Promise

Necklace that Billy had given me that night and hopes that it gives me some measure of comfort. She ended the letter by saying that they all hope I'm doing well and healing quickly, followed by a plea to give her a call or to write back soon.

After I put the letter down, I remembered one of the nurses at the hospital giving me back the few possessions I had with me at the time of the attack. It was a pretty small bag and when I looked inside, among my ID, a set of keys and a few bucks, was a silver necklace with a Bumblebee on it. I reached in and pulled it out to look at it more closely.

"There must have been a mix-up, this isn't mine," I said, handing it back to the nurse.

"No, hon, there's no mix-up. You were wearing that when they brought you in." The nurse put it back in my hand, "it's yours."

I put it back in the bag with the other things and it sat in my bedside stand until I left the hospital. From time to time I would pull it out and examine it. I looked it over as closely as I could, willing a memory to present itself. Like my friends, and Billy, and the events of that night, I remembered nothing. I could tell, though, it was beautifully and expertly crafted. I decided that it would be a shame not to hold on to it just because I couldn't remember wearing it; plus, they said it was mine.

I've been keeping it in a little box in my room along with a few mementos I brought with me from home. I haven't worn it, and to tell the truth, I'd forgotten about it. I've decided that I'm going to pull it out and start wearing it. I figure it's the least I could do. After reading Clara's letter, it seems to have been given to me with so much meaning and emotion. Perhaps, wherever he is, Billy will see that I'm honoring him and what he tried to do for me that night. Maybe wearing it will help to jog some memories, any memory, just give me one!

Maybe I'll call Clara, after all. I'm curious why she called it a Promise Necklace. I wonder if that means what I think it does. I figured, after finding his stuff in the cottage, that we'd been dating, but I didn't realize we had gotten to that point. Maybe she can fill in a few blanks.

CHAPTER FIFTY-THREE

I found out more about the Bumblebee Necklace. Last night, after thinking about it all afternoon, I decided to call Clara. I told myself there was nothing to be nervous about (she's a friend, right?), but it still took a shot of courage to get me dialing the numbers she had written down at the end of her letter.

I almost hung up when the phone started to ring, but I took a deep breath and waited for her to answer. Nothing ventured, nothing gained, as they say. She answered quickly, before I could lose any more of my nerve, and when I said hello she gave out a small, surprised, gasp and said hello back. A small part of me tucked away in the shadows, the part of me lonely for a friend, swelled with happiness at her greeting. I could tell that she happy to hear from me and that she was trying to hold herself back from asking me every question in the book. After a small pause she asked how I was. I told her that I'm good, mostly healed. I thanked her for her letter, explained that I still have memory loss, but I appreciated her stories from home. She said she was glad that her letter had meant something to me.

After some small talk, which she cleverly directed without going into the past, I explained the reason for my call. I told her I have the

Bumblebee necklace she mentioned in her letter, but it appeared that she knew more about it, and that night, than I did. Obviously. I asked her if she could please tell me more.

Clara said "of course" in such a way that I could picture her sweet smile. She added she wished she could do more. Butterflies stirred inside me as she told me what she knew. Most of the gang was celebrating on the beach that night with me and Billy. Our relationship had gotten serious and Billy had confided in her that he was going to try to convince me to marry him. Yes, me, she said. The person who had vowed to stay single for life, a rolling stone. The person who had claimed, over and over, that marriage was a trap, and she was going to be free.

One day, Billy told her he realized he hadn't been getting any real arguments about marriage from me, he'd decided to try his hardest to convince me to get engaged. It was a start, anyway, he told her. To seal his promise, that night, he'd gotten down on one knee (very dramatically and in front of the whole gang) and presented me with a beautiful necklace (hand-crafted, by him, out of silver - a skill he'd learned from his dad). He said the bumblebee represented a part of our future together and fastened it around my neck. It was all very romantic, she said, and unexpected. At the same time, so like Billy.

Clara said we spent the night glued to each other's side and that after a few hours with our friends, we went for a walk on the beach. That was the last they'd seen or heard from us until they found out about the attack the next day. She said, at some point late into the night, they had heard the emergency sirens further down the beach, but no one had any reason to believe it had anything to do with us. Clara thought (they all had), that we had left to celebrate the night by ourselves, privately, and we had long since gone home.

I'm pretty sure I thanked Clara. I promised to stay in touch as we said our goodbyes. My mind was, and still is, swimming. It's a lot to take in, I learned so much more than I had expected to, but I also have more questions now. I gathered that Billy and I had been dating from the items I'd found in my little cottage. I didn't realize there was so much more to it, we were practically engaged. I feel numb, which, in turn, makes me feel guilty. I wish I could feel more than that. A normal person would feel more than that. A normal person would feel something.

I console myself (or am I just trying to relieve my guilt?) by imagining anyone in my place would feel the same way. Yet, I'm alive because someone sacrificed themselves for me. I grieve the hero that he was and I hope to honor his sacrifice by getting through all of this and being able to move on with my life. I hope to earn what he did for me. I'm holding back tears as I write this and I'm ashamed of myself because I wonder if they are for me or for him.

After speaking with Clara, I can't help but wonder, would it have been better to still be in the dark about him? Now I'm thinking, if I did have memories of that night and Billy, I'd be a much bigger basket case than I already am. I'm sure of it. I can't imagine how much harder it would be to try to get through this. All of a sudden, I'm glad for missing memories. That's a switch.

I feel as though, even if I'm not having memories, I am getting back a few parts of my life that have been missing. As usual, though, the universe prefers balance. One step forward, one step back. This one beer isn't going to be enough to wash away the lump in the pit of my stomach.

CHAPTER FIFTY-FOUR

THE MONSOON RAINS HAD SLOWED TO A DRIZZLE, MATCHING FREDDIE'S sobs. Her tears and cries of grief had just about run themselves dry. The rest of her, however, was drenched to the bone. Enough time had passed that the most of the storm had moved east. A few clouds parted enough to let a bit of light from the moon and stars shine through and finally the drizzle stopped, too.

Freddie began to shiver from the chill in her bones and from her wet hair and dress as they clung to her body. She took stock of her situation from her spot in the mud beside the jeep. She pushed her hair back from her face and tried to wipe the rain and tears away with still damp hands. Chuckling at herself and at the obvious futility of her efforts, she finally stood up and looked around. The hilltop was barren, save for her and the jeep. Below her, where the house and Stephen should have been, was pitch black. He had never switched on any lights, inside or out, and the darkness glared up at her like an omen.

Her heart caught in her chest at what that could mean. She placed her hands protectively over her scar. Had he chased her after all? She looked towards the dirt road at the mouth of the woods searching for another set of headlights. Was he on his way up here, too? *No. How would he know that I've come up here before? That I would have come here tonight?* Another voice crept into her subconscious: *He might have followed me here, if he'd been quick enough.* She looked to the still dark woods once more. The fact that she did not see him coming did nothing to calm her nerves.

Reason and common sense are no match for fear. It grips your soul and smothers you with illogical ideas, with thoughts that you will grasp at because that all you have at the moment. You are in fight or flight mode. Your body and mind are moving at unsafe speeds, ironically, trying to keep you safe.

Aggie watched Freddie and felt these emotions and thought these thoughts along with her. Freddie's thoughts moved at dizzying speeds as she tried to take in everything that had happened that day while trying to figure out her next move at the same time.

Clear thought finally came to her, kicking and screaming, through sheer force of will. Memories had returned to her on the stairs today. The hardest one, the one she'd feared most, among them. The memory of what had happened on the beach that night. Hearing Billy yell "you can't have her" to Stephen triggered it. That memory had opened the floodgates to the rest of them.

The memory had tried to push its way through in the jeep earlier, but she hadn't been ready to accept it then. Well, she had to deal with it now if she wanted to move one with her life. That night on the beach, the night when everything changed, it was all clear to her now.

They had just promised to be engaged, with the Bumblebee necklace sealing the promise. They'd made love and afterwards, Billy fell asleep. So, she decided to dip her toes in in the ocean for a few minutes. She soon returned from the water's edge and as she approached a sleeping Billy, she noticed a dark shadow standing over him. Then, she heard those words for the first time, "you can't have her." They came from the hunched shadow and were directed at Billy. There was a flash of light glinting off something metal and she saw Billy react. He was being mugged and was struggling with the dark shape. She broke into a run and headed towards them. She closed the distance quickly, her heart in her throat.

She heard screaming and realized it was her own voice. She was alternately calling out to Billy and pleading to the mugger, "no, stop!" She was within a few strides when she saw the mugger pull back his arm for another blow. This was her chance to save Billy, if she could. She leapt at the mugger, her only thought to keep him off her fiancé-to-be.

Freddie was already airborne when she saw the knife in his hand. She fell on the mugger as the knife plunged deep in her flesh. The mugger was Stephen. It had always been Stephen.

As she collapsed on the beach, everything in her began to dim. The mugger's faraway voice called out to her, it was filled with pain and disbelief. "F-freddie, no! Wh-what have you done?"

She needed to get off this mountain, away from that monster, Stephen. Away from the isolation. She needed to feel free again, and she needed other people. She hadn't felt that way in a long time. Memories or not, healed or not, her time in Arizona had definitely come to an end. An image of her cottage, and then of Clara, flashed through her mind. At once, it felt comfortable and familiar.

That's what she would do then. She'd head to California, to her cottage and to her friend Clara, and sort things out from there. Clara would listen, and Clara would be there for her. She would help her decide what to do next. She was sure of it. Freddie knew in her gut that she had made the right decision. Finally. It felt good.

She looked down at herself and at the mud that covered her legs and her dress, most of her really. She continued to shiver and became aware of how wet the jeep had become. She had a few belongings tucked into the bag on the passenger seat, but it made no sense to change now. She'd have to make the best of it until she could get to a bus station. Hopefully, that would be in the opposite direction of the monsoons.

She brushed what she could off her legs and climbed back into the jeep. She took off her ruined shoes and put them in the foot well of the passenger seat, she'd drive barefoot for now. Her plan was simple. There was no going back to the house. No confronting Stephen. Not until she was safely in California, not until she spoke with the authorities. She'd take what she had packed, minimal as it was, and move on.

Buy a bus ticket to California at the closest bus station, drop the jeep there and maybe, just maybe, leave a message for Stephen where he could pick it up. Maybe she'd call Clara from the road and give her the news.

Freddie reached into the top of her sundress, something was scratching her. She remembered what it was the moment her fingers closed on it. The photo of Billy. She pulled it out and looked at it, it was mottled around the edges from getting wet. But, somehow, his image was clear as day and he smiled up at her from the Polaroid.

Her emotions were immediate and raw and threatened to overcome her once again. She closed her eyes and took a deep breath in and out, then one more. She would let herself fall apart when she reached California, but not before.

She quickly placed the photo inside the overnight bag where it would be safe. She spotted her diary and put that back in the bag too. See, she was in control. Everything would be fine.

She clapped her hands together and said "Ok. Ready!" to the empty hill. She tried to sound determined, but to her ears, it had fallen flat. She threw the jeep in gear, released the hand brake, and stepped on the gas enthusiastically. The balding tires spun in the mud but made no forward movement. Not to be thwarted so early in her trip, she calmly shifted into reverse and stepped on the gas, gently this time.

The tires got purchase somehow and she moved back a foot or so, ever so slowly. She quickly shifted out of reverse into first and pressed on the gas pedal. *Easy, easy.* The jeep rocked forward and took back the foot of ground it had given up. Then the tires spun in place again.

Freddie would not be beaten by a few patches of mud and four balding tires. She calmly put it in reverse again and then stepped on the gas. Gently at first, moving backwards over that same foot of ground. She turned the wheels and felt it gain purchase once more on a less muddy patch of ground. She got excited and gunned it. Her muddy, bare foot slipped off the damp gas pedal.

"Shoot!"

The jeep jerked back in a half circle as she desperately searched for the brake pedal. She straightened out the wheel but over corrected and the jeep slipped sideways in the mud. Aggie's heart raced along with Freddie's as she tried to gain control of the jeep.

Aggie's heart sank into her stomach as she watched the scene play out from above. The rains had muddied and loosened the ground near the edge of the hill and Freddie had backed up dangerously close to it. Freddie struggled for control, unaware she had given in to panic. She was shifting into first and then back into reverse, trying to rock the jeep forward, searching for solid ground that was not to be had. She was focused on the way ahead and was either unaware of, or didn't see, that she was precariously close to the hilltop's edge.

Time slowed down for Aggie and she watched helplessly. A panicked Freddie confused reverse with first. She gunned it and the jeep shot backwards over the edge. At once, Freddie realize her mistake and cried out, "no!" Fighting against gravity, she shifted into first and hit the gas again. It was futile. The jeep's wheels responded but the jeep continued backwards. It also was going down now. This side of the hill was as bare of trees as the pine filled forest she'd driven through was full.

There were no downed branches or trunks to stop her descent. Small shrubs easily gave way beneath the jeep. Out of desperation, she tried turning the wheels to slow the slide backwards. She stepped on the brake, pulled the hand brake. Nothing was working.

Aggie wanted to scream, she wanted to reach out and stop the jeep herself, superhero style. She wished for a large boulder where there were none. She was grasping at straws. Anything to stop the jeep. She was just an observer, this was just a memory. The outcome could not be changed. She knew what was coming and it broke her heart.

The jeep's two red tail lights were the only things visible against the dark backdrop of the hillside. The round, red tail lights appeared to be gently floating down the hillside in slow motion. When they reached the bottom, they paused for a few moments, bobbing above the lake's surface. The red lights dimmed as they disappeared into the lake.

AGGIE RUBBED HER EYES AS SHE AWOKE IN THE DARK. SHE STAYED still for a moment to orient herself. A faint glow shone through the curtains throwing shadows onto her bedroom wall. She was in bed and had been sleeping half on her side, half on her stomach. Something in the covers was irritating her. She rolled all the way over on her side and saw the culprit in the moonlight. That explained the dream. She had fallen asleep on the diary and the bumblebee pendant.

She'd gone up to her bedroom after having supper with Rider. They'd gone to the diner in town so that she could get out of the house and they could visit some more. After supper, she went right home. On her way up to bed, she grabbed a few things off the table (her journal, the diary and the pendant) and went straight to her bedroom. She had planned to do some journaling, but apparently her body had other ideas. The last thing she remembered, prior to the dream, was a quick stretch on the bed.

A lump had formed in Aggie's chest and the more awake she became, the fresher the dream felt. She sat up in bed, against her pillows, and let it all sink in. So much loss and pain for one day. She knew she should write this all down in her journal, but she had a feeling that it would remain with her for good, even without being committed to paper. The weight of it held her down as if she was pinned by a large boulder. Just like the boulder that could have stopped Freddie's jeep that night, had there been one in her path.

A familiar, musty scent wafted over the bed and tickled Aggie's nose. She grabbed one of her pillows and rolled back to her side. Her eyes misted over as she spotted Freddie's diary in the soft moonlight. She drifted off to sleep once more. A dreamless sleep this time.

CHAPTER FIFTY-FIVE

I woke up before the birds did this morning. Third or fourth time this week, I've lost track. Maybe it's because Stephen has been back for a few days and the house just seems crowded with him in it. I realize that sounds rude and ungrateful, after all, it's his house. He's either around every corner I turn, or just a few steps behind me. I can't seem to get any space that's just mine; quiet, peaceful, unadulterated.

He means well, I know. He thinks that when he's gone he's neglecting me and when he returns he tries that much harder to give me attention. I wish he would stop, I am not in the mood for his, or anyone's, company lately. I am in a much better mood alone.

This week I've had to do a lot of pretending where he is concerned. Pretend that I care he's back, that I'm happy to go for that ride or this walk, that I would love to go out for dinner or play another hand of Rummy. I don't know how actors do it, pretending is a lot of work. I'm exhausted.

Every day since he's been back, he's planned something for us to do together. Frankly, it's almost all I can do this week to get up and put clothes on. I'd much rather sit by myself on the dock with the radio and a beer. Part of me knows he's trying to be sweet and I should appre-

229

ciate it. I don't want to hurt his feelings, so I've pushed those feeling away (the ones that make me want to scream 'leave me alone!', or the ones that make me want to pack up my things, run to the woods and become a hermit). But, I don't. I haven't. Yet. I stuff them way down deep inside, take a deep breath and force a smile. I've tried not to let on to Stephen, but I don't think I've succeeded completely. He's pretty sensitive to my moods and he realizes something is off. Perhaps he thinks maybe he hasn't done enough to make it up to me, so he tries that much harder. I'm the victim of a vicious cycle of my own doing.

The silver lining, if there is one, is that I haven't gotten any grief about having a drink or two. I guess that's something. Usually, I catch him giving me a sideways look with a disapproving dip of his eyebrows when he doesn't think I'm looking. I think he sensed that he better not even try this week. I'll give him a look of my own and it won't be with just a disapproving dip of my eyebrows.

Once I finally gave up on trying to fall back asleep this morning, I decided to embrace it. I put my robe on, gathered up my diary and curled up on the couch. The sun hasn't put in an appearance yet, the lake is still dark and quiet. Everything is still. I'm glad that I got up; right here and now, it feels like I'm alone in the world. It occurs to me that other people might find that lonely and depressing. To me it's peaceful and calming, I feel like I could close my eyes and be anywhere in the world and still feel safe. It's an illusion, but I'm holding on to it. At least until the sun, and Stephen, shows up.

LATER...

I dozed off at some point earlier this morning. Stephen woke me up when he came downstairs this morning. He said he thought maybe I was ill. Before I could think, I told him I'd just woken up early and couldn't get back to sleep. If I had thought fast enough, I could have ridden the lie about being sick for a day or two and might have had some more alone time. Maybe not though, it could have back fired and

I would have had to deal with Stephen the nurse. I guess it's just as well.

I let Stephen fend for himself in the kitchen and went to get dressed. While I was dressing, I remembered about the Bumblebee necklace. I located the box it was in after only a few minutes of searching and was relieved to find it safe and sound. I may have even been holding my breath. I had an irrational fear that, because I had forgotten about it, somehow I'd discover it missing and wouldn't that serve me right.

I can't explain the unreasonable attachment I have for this necklace. I'm not normally this sentimental, but the moment I fastened it around my neck, I felt like it had always been there. It reminds me of Granna's bees, but I don't think that's it. Of course, now that I know some of its history, you could say that I have reason to be nostalgic. But, I don't think that's it, either. Call me corny if you must, but since I've put it on, I feel a little bit more complete.

CHAPTER FIFTY-SIX

SATURDAY - SEPTEMBER 6, '75

Stephen is back from the road. He's been home for a day and a half and I haven't been able to get my courage up enough to tell him that I want to leave. I don't think he'll understand and I know his feelings will be hurt.

But, something is going on with him, too. When he got home he was in a very good mood. He said his trip had gone very well and had gotten a new account. He said he'd take me into town for dinner to celebrate, which was just what I needed - to get out of the house. By dinner time, I was also in a good mood. I put on my favorite white cotton prairie dress (the flattering one with the eyelet lace) and put my hair up in one of my very own hair ties. The prospect of just going into town and getting out of the house made me so happy, dinner out was a bonus.

Stephen was a different person by the time we sat down to at the restaurant. He was quiet and subdued, lost in thought. I tried talking to him about his trip to bring him out of himself. It only worked for a few minutes at a time and then he'd drift away again. We made small talk about the food we ordered and how good it tasted. We celebrated his new account with a few drinks, and then we left.

I was surprised and curious, something was wrong. We've never had that much trouble holding a conversation, Stephen was always right there to fill in any uncomfortable silences and keep me engaged. No evening stroll past the shop windows downtown, which I always enjoyed. No ice cream cone dessert. No fun. It felt like he was pouting and I couldn't get him to snap out of it. We ate and went right back to the house. Right back to feeling trapped. I couldn't even tempt him with a game or two of Rummy. He was home, the only difference now is that I feel even more alone than before.

SUNDAY - SEPTEMBER 7, '75

That was last night. This morning we had breakfast together and he was a bit more chatty than the night before. It felt better, but it still didn't feel quite right. Conversation stumbled some, but I could tell he was trying. Now he's shut up in his office making phone calls. I decided I wasn't going to hang around the house like a little puppy waiting for his attention. It's not really what I want anyway. So, I grabbed my radio, some whiskey and this diary and went to the dock to sit, sip and write.

I know I have to talk to him. Between my lack of courage and his weird mood, I don't see it happening this weekend. Maybe it's just as well, does it matter where I am? I'm kidding myself that a change of scenery will make any difference. My life feels like a Tarzan movie where I'm stuck in quicksand, grasping at vines that break off in my hand. The vines snap because they are made of missing memories, whiskey and expectations. Unfortunately for me, Stephen is no Tarzan.

CHAPTER FIFTY-SEVEN

TUESDAY - SEPTEMBER 9, '75

I can't believe how the weekend turned around! I really misread Stephen.

I had fallen asleep after lying back on the dock to watch the clouds. Stephen woke me up by calling to me while he knelt over me, shaking me gently by my shoulder, smiling. I could tell right away he was his old self and I returned his smile. He helped me to my feet and declared that he had a surprise for me.

"Dinner again?" I asked. My spirits lifted a little, it had to go better than the other night; that would be fun. I couldn't imagine what else it would be. Maybe he'd seen the disappointment on my face when we got home. I hadn't thought so, though.

He shook his head from side to side and put one finger to his lips as if to quiet my questions. He took my hand, still smiling, for a moment. I was lost in his gaze in spite of myself. His charm was infectious, all I could do was smile back. His dark eyes sparkled as he led me across the lawn to the side of the house. I couldn't imagine what had gotten in to him. A complete reversal from the previous night. I was happy to go along because it seemed to please him.

As we got closer, he asked me to close my eyes and keep them closed until he gave the word. I told him I would and held his hand a little tighter so that I wouldn't trip. Soon I could tell by the pebbles under foot that we'd made it to the driveway. I sensed him change position so that he was in front of me. He let go of my hand and held my shoulders softly, I felt him place a quick kiss on my forehead.

"It occurred to me, on this last road trip, that I have been gone longer and more frequently than I ever intended. I should have been here, helping you heal."

I kept my eyes closed but started to shake my head no, my hands reached out to him and my eyes started to water. It was almost as if he'd read my thoughts. I thought that maybe I could talk to him after all. He took both of my hands in his and continued.

"I've lived alone for a long time and I am not used to..." he paused, searching for the right words, "considering anyone else. I should have done a better job of it."

He moved back to my side, "you must have thought I stranded you out here. I hope you can forgive me."

I opened my eyes and looked at him, astounded that he could have read my feelings so well after being back for such a short time. "Stephen, of course I can. I do. That's not your job."

He nodded his head, "yes it is, as your friend." He pointed toward the driveway and its new occupant. "This is for you."

I was stunned and overwhelmed. There was a new car in the drive. Well, a jeep, not a car, and used, not new. But, apparently it was all mine!

"Are you teasing me?" I looked him in the eye. Nope, he was serious. He surprised me with a new car! I don't even know how to describe my feelings, but I haven't stopped smiling.

Hugs and Thank You's came out in a rush and then I ran to the car to look it over. It's an army green CJ5 with a soft top (that Stephen says he removed for now 'because it's much cooler that way') and gears and knobs and gauges and I love it! It's just what I need!

Stephen approached me after I'd circled the Jeep a few times. "Now, it's an older vehicle and it's going to need tires soon; but, it's sound enough to get you into town when I'm gone."

I hugged him tight, "can we go for a ride? Right now?" He grinned and tossed me the keys to my new set of wheels. I took my first, glorious drive, into town, in my own vehicle, and took him to dinner for a change. We ate and talked and laughed and it wasn't at all like the other night. We didn't walk through downtown, or get an ice cream; we did something better. I took him for another ride, it was all pretty groovy, as the kids say.

My cheeks hurt from smiling and the whole thing has given me a much needed break from the funk I was in. I can't believe I can go for a ride whenever I want! I guess I wrong about him; maybe Stephen is Tarzan after all.

CHAPTER FIFTY-EIGHT

Friday - September 12, '75

I decided to go on an adventure today and it has made all the difference in my mood and my outlook. I packed a bag just big enough to carry a picnic for one, a ham sandwich, chips, and a beverage (wait for it: a can of soda, not beer), my diary, and a pen. At the last minute, I saw the Bumblebee Necklace and threw that in there, too. I was much too excited to begin my adventure to stop and put it on.

Transportation at last! I took the Jeep and headed out, crossing my fingers that I could find the right path. Down the road, not too far from the house, I found a dirt road off to the right that leads into the woods. I put all my faith in the Jeep and its four-wheel drive and took a chance that it would take me where I hoped it would. Freedom!

I am so happy right now. The Jeep served me well, the tires held out over the bumpy road, and the trail took me all the way; I made it on the first try! There's no way Columbus felt this good when he found the new world.

I feel as if I'm sitting on top of the world. At least the top of this little part of the world. I am on summit of the hill that I've been staring at from the dock all these weeks. The change in perspective from here is amazing. I can see forever.

Over and beyond the hill, and what you can't see from the dock, is the rest of the lake. The much bigger, busier, more festive part of the lake. There are quite a few people down there, in their boats, on the shore. From up here, it looks like they're all having a great time. I can feel their excitement all the way up here.

Beyond the lake, is the rest of Arizona. Beyond that, the rest of the world. I've been operating on the idea that seclusion and quiet was the solution to all my problems. The woods, these hills, have kept the world away. All this time, I thought I wanted - no, needed - to be blocked off from the world, from people. Stephen's home was perfect for that.

Now, seeing how many people are down there enjoying themselves tugs at my soul. Watching them makes me feel as if I am missing out on something, makes me want to be part of it, part of life again. And it's tapping me on the shoulder, whispering in my ear, "that could be you, too." I don't think I knew I wanted that until just now.

I don't think secluding myself here at Stephen's is the solution to my problems any more. There was a time and a place for that, and I'm truly grateful to Stephen, but I think I have to go. He should be back tomorrow and I can talk to him then. I need to go get my life back. I'm not going to find it in his house or on his dock or even up here. Memories or not.

But, all this excitement has caused me to get ahead of myself a bit. Yes, all these thoughts are zipping around in my head and I am finally looking forward for a change. But, something happened earlier and it shouldn't be overlooked. I don't know what to think of it, so I'm writing it down. Maybe I can make sense of it that way. Maybe I'm overreacting. We'll see.

When I first arrived at the top of the hill, I was stunned. The view is amazing and peaceful and exhilarating at once. This is what I've needed. It was here all the time. Clarity. I grabbed the little bag I'd packed and found a good spot to sit and enjoy the view. My tummy was growling, so after several minutes of soaking it all in, I decided I could eat and look at the lake at the same time.

After that, I decided to get a few words down in the diary so I could come back to it whenever I needed to. When I pulled out the diary and the pen, the necklace's chain had snagged on the pen clip and came out with it. My heart sank a little bit. I worried that the chain might be broken and scolded myself. I was relieved to see that it was still in one piece. I put it on and it fell right into place. All was well with the world.

The sun was out, my tummy was full, and there was a comfortable breeze crossing over the top of the hill. I found myself holding the pendent as my thoughts drifted. In my mind's eye, I saw a pregnant woman caressing her belly, then an elderly couple holding hands, a father walking arm in arm with his daughter down the aisle. It made me realize how we hold on to what's precious with our hearts as well as our hands. We instinctively protect and take comfort from it. I held the pendant, missing a Billy I didn't yet remember, lying on the grass and relaxing. Well, you know what happened next. Yup, nap time.

I haven't mentioned this before, because I wanted to prove I could do it. It's been about a week since I went cold turkey on the beer and whiskey. It needed to be done. I have been tempted a few times to pour a small glass or open a can, but I focused instead on how much clearer my thoughts and feeling have been and was able to push the urges aside. I'm proud to say: so far so good.

I mention it now, because I had a dream during my nap. Normally, that wouldn't be a big deal, but I haven't had any dreams since the ones with Stephen and my scar (still blushing). I didn't want any more dreams after that, whiskey to the rescue.

Dreams are usually fleeting, the memory of them tends to slip away the longer you're awake. That doesn't seem to be that case this time. The pieces of this dream seem as clear to me now as they did the moment I awoke on this hilltop. The blonde man from the Polaroid I found on my fridge appears, he smiles and reaches out to me. It's Billy. I reach up and touch my necklace, his necklace. Then the scene changes, it's night and I'm on the beach running to him, I'm frightened and calling his name. I see him, he's on the ground, but there's something blocking my view. Someone is crouching over him, shouting. The only words I can make out are 'have her'. Billy's in danger and I will my feet to go faster, but they don't. I'm afraid I won't reach him in time. That's where the dream ends.

I don't know what to think. As I've said before, the mind works in strange ways. I have no way of knowing if this is just what I think it is: meaningless dream fragments. Common sense dictates that maybe because I've been trying so hard to remember that night, my mind pieced this together from what I've heard and what I've imagined.

But. Maybe now that the beer and whiskey has been out of my system for a few days, my brain is able to fire on all cylinders? What if it's a memory and not just a dream? What if I've been blocking my memories with alcohol? The old question comes mind: do you want the good news or the bad news?

I am too skeptical to believe that this is an actual memory. I'm hopeful, but skeptical. Could I actually be remembering something? Will more memories follow? I'm a bit nervous to think that this might be an actual memory. If it is, that means I most likely watched the attack. I'm torn. I want memories, but why this one? This is the one I could have done without. Be careful what you wish for, right?

It's ironic, if it's true, that my first probable memory happened up here looking out over what has inspired me to move on with my life, in spite of my amnesia.

CHAPTER FIFTY-NINE

THE SOFT SOUND OF BIRDS CHIRPING IN THE MORNING SUN WOKE AGGIE from a sound, dreamless sleep. She was still on her side, arms wrapped around her pillow. She stayed there, eyes closed, just listening to the birdsong. She absorbed the cheerful sound and let it soak into her bones. It was exactly what she needed after yesterday.

She hadn't had anymore dreams last night, but that didn't mean the events of the day weren't still fresh and present and at the forefront of her thoughts. A lot had been learned and revealed yesterday. She wanted to confront it all and figure out where that would take her next. But, she needed a few more minutes of peace and cheer. She forced the thoughts and images from yesterday back and focused instead on the birds outside her window. *Take as long as you want, you've earned it.*

Aggie was never going to be a morning person. She was a night owl and preferred it that way. But, her body had begun to betray her as she got older. Try as she might, she couldn't sleep past 7:00 am on most days. Years of being a slave to the alarm clock had conditioned her sleep habits and now her body woke up whether she wanted to or not.

She finally opened her eyes and glanced at the clock on her bedside table. It was 6:55 am. She groaned and rolled on to her back, releasing the pillow. After a few more minutes, when her back started to ache, she pushed herself into a sitting position and fluffed her pillows into a backrest. She smiled. It was her opinion that you couldn't have enough pillows on your bed.

Ok, time to face the day, Ags. She took a quick bathroom break, grabbed sip of water at the bathroom sink and returned to her nest of pillows on the bed. She rolled her neck until it cracked, releasing the cramp that had developed overnight. She was awake. Fine. But she wasn't getting up yet. That was for other people. *Morning people.*

Aggie grabbed her journal and one of her favorite pens and began writing. She put down everything she could remember and hadn't had a chance to document. It took a while. By the time she had finished, the morning sun had time to travel from behind the house to practically overhead. She had written in a furious stream, eager to get it all on paper, anxious to not miss anything. It had to be clear, she wanted to be sure of her thoughts and the plans that were coming together.

She put her pen down and stretched and wiggled the fingers of her right hand. A nasty cramp had developed from gripping the pen so tightly for so long. She cracked a few knuckles, which felt great, but always made her feel guilty. She could still hear her grandfather's voice scolding her for doing that and claiming it would give her arthritis in her old age. He was probably going to end up having been right, but that didn't stop her.

She turned the pages of her journal back to where she had started and read back over her entries. She wiped her eyes a few times, nodded a few more. She grabbed her pen and changed a few words here and there, added a few more in other places, making sure it was all neat and legible.

When she was happy with it, she turned to a fresh page and made a list. This was no ordinary To Do List, by any means. It was going to take her a day or two, but when she was done, if everything went according to plan, all would be right with the world. More right than it had been for a while.

Aggie smiled to herself and ran one finger down the page, nodding. *I can do this.* This was more of a pep talk than a declaration. *I can do this.* She touched each item on the list in turn and said a silent prayer asking for the fortitude to complete all of them.

CHAPTER SIXTY

"HELLO?"

"Hey, Bud, good morning." Aggie did a small dance in place to adjust the seat of her shorts which had ridden up uncomfortably, "what 'cha doing?"

"Not much," Rider answered her dryly, he was still upset about losing his nursing assignment in Italy. "Just sitting here thinking about my options. You?"

"Well, you are the first thing on my To Do List today. I have something to talk to you about, but I'm going to be busy today with some of the other things on my list. Can we make a date for lunch tomorrow? My treat."

"I guess so. Can't you just tell me now?"

"No. You'll have to wait." Aggie smiled at her plans, "plus, it'll take to long." She could imagine him rolling his eyes at her.

"Fine," he chuckled at her, confirming her suspicions. "The diner? What time?"

"Yeah, I'm not sure - can I text you when I'm ready?"

With that, Aggie put a checkmark next to the first item on her list. She left the journal open in front of her on the kitchen table and reviewed it. On to the next one. She stood back and checked to make sure she had everything she thought she'd need for item number two.

She was dressed for a hike: hiking boots, shorts, T-shirt and a hat. There was a backpack on the chair with a few bottles of water, a couple snacks (just in case) and a few much more precious items: Freddie's diary and the Bumblebee Pendent. There was a small tug at her heart as she remembered last night's dream, she acknowledged it with a brief moment of silence, then continued with her task.

It occurred to Aggie that she hadn't been on a hike since she'd hurt her ankle. She stuck it out to one side and rolled it one way and then the other, then back and forth. It seemed OK to her. It should be fine today. She'd actually forgotten about it.

"Crap." Aggie shook her head and grabbed her new cell phone off the table. "You never learn, do you Aggie?" Remembering her injury brought everything back to her anew from that day, especially the fact that she hadn't told anyone where she was going today. She sent a quick text off to Rider, promising to let him know when she got back safely.

Aggie was as ready as she could be. She put her cell phone in a pocket of the backpack, not in her bra like before. *Live and learn, girl.* Then she slung the backpack over her shoulders and headed out.

BECAUSE SHE WAS RUSTY, AND IT WAS WARM OUT, IT TOOK AGGIE A bit longer to reach her destination than it normally would have. She was out of breath and had to make a few more stops than she was used to, but that was OK. She wasn't in a particular rush. Sure, she was focused on the task at hand, but slow and steady would suffice.

When she came to the corner with the lightening scarred tree, she patted it for good luck. She rested and caught her breath on some of the same boulders and downed trees that she and Rider had made use of the last time they'd been in the woods.

When she passed the spot where she'd seen the lights that day, she realized that she had unconsciously begun walking along the side of the trail instead of in the middle. She acknowledged it, realizing she might be acting foolish, but she stayed on the edge anyway.

The top of the hill came soon enough and Aggie slowed her climb as she approached it. She stepped into the clearing tentatively and stopped a few paces from the edge of the wood line. She gazed out over the open area, her mind overlapping the dark, muddy layout from last night's dream on top of the bright grassy hilltop. It held so much more meaning today than it ever had before, she felt small and insignificant with that knowledge inside of her now. But, she would do what she could.

She moved to the spot where she had found the crystal, now the Bumblebee Pendant, doing her best to find the exact right place. Then, she closed her eyes to visualize last night's dream more easily. She let the dream replay in her mind until she could see where Freddie had been standing when she dropped the necklace, then opened her eyes and looked around confident she'd found the correct spot. Aggie was unsure if it really mattered, but if it did, she didn't want to blow it.

A deep breath and she was ready. She pulled the blue diary and pendant out of the bag and mentally crossed her fingers. *Please. Please. Let this work.*

Aggie held the diary in one hand and brought it to her chest. She held the Bumblebee pendant in the other hand and closed her fingers around it protectively. She closed her eyes and brought the second hand to rest over the diary and her heart. Another deep breath in and out, and a clean, white space began to appear in her mind's eye. She focused on the white space until her mind was clear of extraneous thoughts. She took slow, smooth breaths and felt the items she held so reverently. *Please, let this work.*

She let herself picture Billy and whispered his name quietly. Then she imagined Freddie, and whispered her name, too. And then she waited. She stood calmly and peacefully, picturing the white board in her mind. She pushed doubt away when it came knocking. *You can do this.*

A tingle of a headache began to appear behind her eyes and she welcomed it, knowing now what it meant. Growing more confident, she opened her eyes and waited a bit more. The headache grew and her hands began to tingle. She loosened her grip, but still felt pins and needles. Her heart joined in and began to race a little, she tried to slow it with deep breaths. It was working!

A familiar white mist circled in front of her and as she watched, a second one appeared to its side. Aggie watched, unblinking. She hadn't been sure. She concentrated on trying not to overreact and screw this up. As she focused on the connection, it felt like an invisible rope that went from her core out to the two misty clouds, her headache vanished.

She focused on the connection and Billy appeared to her once again. Within a heartbeat Freddie appeared, for the first time, outside of Aggie's dreams. They stood before her for a moment with unseeing eyes and her faith wavered. Maybe it wouldn't work after all? Maybe it was too much of a romantic fantasy? This was certainly out of her realm.

On a whim, Aggie spoke their names once more and held the diary and the pendant out in front of her. These two precious items that connected them, through time, to each other. And, somehow, in the end, to her.

Freddie was first to turn and look at Aggie, she wore a big smile and look of gratitude on her face. Billy followed suit and nodded with approval. Aggie looked from Freddie to Billy and then back to Freddie. She wasn't sure what to do next. Maybe it was up to them?

The thought hadn't so much as crossed her mind when the long separated lovers turned to each other. Their eyes locked and they reached out to each other. The moment their hands met, they began to fade from view. Aggie's heart swelled at their reunion and she watched the happy couple through damp eyes until they had vanished completely.

The tingling in Aggie's hands had reached an intolerable level, it was the worst case of pins and needles she could recall. Without stopping to wipe her eyes, she shook her hands out at her side and then open and closed her fingers until the tingling stopped. It was only then that she brushed away the few tears that remained. They were happy tears for a change.

It wasn't until that moment that she realized her hands were empty. She was no longer holding the diary or the pendant. *Crap.* She looked below her on the ground. She must have dropped them? No. She spun around and looked behind her. Nope. They were nowhere to be seen.

The only remnant was a whiff of damp mustiness that floated past her on the breeze.

CHAPTER SIXTY-ONE

IT WAS SUPPER TIME AND AGGIE, ALTHOUGH FAMISHED, WAS PUSHING her food around on the plate. Procrastinating. She looked up from her food to see her journal, still open to the To Do List, staring back at her. It was taunting her.

Item number three was next, a tough one. She'd gotten all cocky this morning making the list. All list makers know this: often, making a list is much easier than completing it. She had a lump in the pit of her stomach and it wasn't going anywhere fast. It probably wouldn't either, until she could check number three off list. She had already checked off two items today. How come that wasn't enough?

That was a rhetorical question. She knew how come it wasn't enough. There were things that had been left unresolved, unfinished business that needed to be taken care of. And she was the only one who could do it.

She had finally understood that some of the goings on lately had to do with Freddie - because of the diary, obviously. Freddie's unfinished business was Billy (and partly Stephen). And in turn, Billy's was Freddie. It explained a lot, but it didn't completely explain Stephen rushing her in the kitchen or the jolt she'd gotten holding his photo yesterday. Aggie wasn't sure if they were two separate issues, or just one. But, there was still something unfinished there and it needed to be dealt with. She was hopeful that if she faced her fears and got through this next item on her list, it would be clearer. To her anyway. Otherwise, she could never be sure that her home would ever truly be hers. She had to be sure.

Aggie had grown more confident after the success on Western Hill, but she was still pretty apprehensive about number three. One part of her problem was that she wasn't completely sure about its nature. The lingering sensation from that moment was full of dread and shrouded in darkness. Not a lack-of-light kind of darkness, but a lack-of-good kind of darkness.

The other part of the problem was who she'd have to face to get to the bottom of the matter. She wasn't so sure she was prepared for that yet. Yesterday, she had been holding Stephen's photo when something in the hall caught her eye, she looked up and got the shock of her life. That's what had caused her to drop the photo, almost breaking it.

She'd have to face it sooner or later. Try to connect again. They had something important to tell her, she just couldn't shake the dread deep in her gut.

Just as time ticks on and gravity holds us to the earth, she knew this unresolved issue would linger unimpeded and unaffected. It would continue to haunt her if she didn't deal with it now. She wanted her house back and this was one of the last hurdles. She hoped.

Aggie weighed her options and decided to do nothing wasn't a valid one. She couldn't live like that, wary of every shadow and every bump in the night. This was her house now and that was that.

Aggie chose the living room to try to connect. It was comfortable and familiar, maybe that would help. She picked the two items on the kitchen table that she'd been ignoring up to now: Stephen's box of letters and his framed photo. She held her breath as she picked up the photo, just in case. *Whew.* Nothing, yet.

She moved into the living room with the box and photo, looking to the stairwell as she crossed the opening to the hallway. Still no one. Immediately, she scolded herself for being jumpy. You'd think she'd be used to it by now. *There's nothing to be afraid of, you were just caught off guard yesterday.* Again, it was more of a pep talk than a declaration.

The couch would be fine. It faced the lake, and the TV. It's where she used to sit. Before.

Aggie began to prepare. No sense in putting it off. *Keep marching forward, girl.* The setting had changed and she now held different objects, but the process was the same as earlier in the day. It had worked before, logic dictated that it would work again.

She took slow, deep breaths. Imagined a white space in her mind's eye. Held the objects loosely and close to her heart. She cleared her thoughts and waited. She placed an image in her mind and spoke the name softly, "Judith." Slow breaths, white space.

"Judith."

It began the same way as before, a small headache behind her eyes. Then, goosebumps raised up on her arms and the familiar pain of grief lodged like a lump in her chest. She counted to ten in her mind, opening her eyes at nine. Judith was sitting beside her on the couch. Her old friend and mentor, her second mother. Like she'd never been gone.

Aggie tightened her grip on Stephen's things and shifted in her seat so she could see Judith clearly. She blinked hard against the tears that threatened to flow. She took one more deep breath, it would be OK. She watched Judith and waited for her to take the lead. Aggie had no idea what she wanted from her.

Judith looked at Aggie until she had caught her eye, once she did, their eyes locked. Aggie hesitated, but only briefly, then fully opened herself up to this once in a lifetime experience. At the very least, it was a second chance, a gift of more time with her friend. Minutes passed and Aggie took it all in. She could hear her old friend's voice once again, but in her mind. She guessed both new at this type of thing, there was some sort of learning curve. Just the same, it was comforting and reassuring. Tears spilled down her cheeks when she felt Judith's pride. Months of anxiety and fear of disappointing Judith, not having met her expectations, were washed away.

Once this had been conveyed, and Aggie had gotten a hold of

herself, Judith turned away and faced the television. Aggie did the same. A picture formed on the cold dark screen and began to play. There was no sound, but Aggie recognized it as their favorite program on the murder channel. Aggie nodded, she missed those times, too. Judith shook her head no and pointed at the screen. Aggie turned back to the screen and focused harder, what was she supposed to see? Judith waited patiently and then an FBI poster flashed on the screen - it was a missing persons/victims poster.

Suddenly, Aggie understood. It was *that* program. The one about the unsolved cold-case that had bothered Judith. The last one they had watched together before...

Judith nodded and the picture disappeared. She turned back to Aggie and pointed to the objects in her lap. Dread replaced the grief inside Aggie as she realized what Judith was saying. She shook her head in disbelief, Judith just nodded solemnly in response. Aggie's heart sank. She understood, realizing what Judith had suspected just before she passed. What she hadn't been able to share with her friend in life.

They continue to sit on the couch together and Aggie waited for the inevitable moment when her friend would be gone again. She had gotten the message and understood. Judith had trusted her with this information and she could trust her to take action, to resolve this issue. Was there more? What could it be?

As those thoughts appeared, Judith held her hand out. Aggie was scared to let go of the items she held, scared to lose the connection. Judith nodded, it would be OK. Aggie closed her eyes and remembered the invisible rope from before. She paused and searched for the same connection between her and Judith. As her fear diminished, she could feel it. Excitement replaced her fear at once. It was there. If she had faith, it would remain. With or without the photo and the letters.

Aggie set the photo and box of letters down and took Judith's hand. It was cool, but strangely solid. Judith stood and led Aggie into the kitchen, she took a right and they walked through the hallway and stopped in front of the stairs. Aggie's pulse began to race. She was anticipating a replay of the scene on the stairs, or something similar. She felt a tug on her hand and Judith smiled. That wasn't it.

Whew. Aggie let go a sigh of relief, mixed with a small chuckle. She looked to her friend again, expectantly. Judith was pointing to the window below the stairs. Aggie strained to make out what Judith wanted her to see. A tree filled the whole of the small window's view.

"Is it something behind the tree?"

Judith shook her head no, and pointed again.

"Is it the tree itself?"

Judith put her hand out flat and waved it in a 'sort of' motion. Now they were playing charades.

"Something in the tree? On the tree?"

Judith smiled and gave her friend's hand a small squeeze. Aggie returned the squeeze, closing her fingers around Judith's until there was nothing left but air. Judith had gone.

CHAPTER SIXTY-TWO

THE COUCH AND THE COFFEE TABLE WERE COVERED WITH OPEN envelopes, letters and postcards. In the center of the coffee table sat a photograph Aggie had just printed from her cell phone. She had decided that there was no time like the present to attend to Judith's wishes. That way, selfishly, she could put off the process of dealing with all the emotions that were swirling around her at the moment. She would deal with them, but later. There would always be later. She had a To Do List to deal with. She had finally checked of number three, but another item had just been added to it.

Once Aggie recovered from Judith's visit, she grabbed her cell phone and headed right to the tree Judith indicated. Aggie was aware of the tree, it was old growth and had been there since well before she ever moved in. Probably had been there since well before she was born. She never really looked at it, though. It was just a tree. She couldn't imagine what Judith wanted her to see. All she knew was that she had to find something in or on the tree.

She approached the tree with a sense of anticipation, she had no doubt there would be something to find. She was sure of that. If there was any doubt, it was in her ability to locate it. Aggie circled the tree slowly looking for cracks or holes where something could have been hidden. She started low and kept circling the tree until her eyes reached higher than a man could reach. There were no holes or cracks. Not yet ready to throw in the towel, she circled the tree again, this time looking at the surface of the three. Halfway around the tree, on the side farthest from the house, Aggie spotted it. She knew immediately that this was what she had been directed to. Aggie was looking at a carving, it was about the size of her palm and was at about shoulder height to her on the tree. Time and weather had softened the lines, but the image was clear. She saw two curved lines facing each other. They didn't quite touch and were pointed at the bottom. It looked like a disconnected heart.

Since it was the first thing Judith had shown her, she wanted to rewatch the program about the cold case. Luckily, the 'murder channel' had begun streaming old shows on their website. It hadn't taken too long to locate the specific episode she needed and she rewatched it with a notebook handy. Aggie jotted down everything that was relevant and soon filled several pages with dreadful information.

In the early 1970's, over a period of a few years, five young women had been killed. They had all been found along a particular stretch of California beach and they'd all been strangled to death. The authorities had been able to connect the killings due to similarities of their attacks, but also because of one distinctive clue. All the women had been cut on the upper left breast, above their heart. Two crude parenthesis shapes, pointed at the bottom, had been carved into the victims' skin post mortem.

As with other serial killers, the news media was quick to sensation-alize his cruelty and nickname him all at once. News of the Broken Heart Killer had young women and their families in Southern Cali-fornia terrified for years. The show came to an end by saying that the Broker Heart Killer had never been found. The killings stopped in late 1975. It was still considered an open case. At the conclusion of the show, the producers had put an FBI poster of the five women on screen along with contact information for authorities in Southern California.

Aggie sat back on the couch and closed her eyes, but the black and white images of the five dead women were still there. One hand covered her mouth and one held her stomach. When she was able, she opened her eyes and scanned the items on the coffee table. She reached for the photograph she just printed. It wasn't a disconnected heart she was looking at, it was a broken heart.

When Aggie first found the box of letters and postcards, she had experienced a mix of emotions. She was excited because she felt the contents might help explain some of the questions she'd had. She was also feeling conflicted, curiosity didn't give her the right to invade anyone's privacy like that. Now, she felt a lot less conflicted about going through the contents of the box. Yesterday, Judith had pointed right at it, Aggie had taken that as instruction from her to go through it. To find out what was in there. Aggie had a vague idea that the box contained proof of something terrible, but she didn't know exactly what she would find. It was important enough for Judith to come to her for help.

Aggie, stomach in turmoil, pushed on; if only to finish the task. She was now working her way to the bottom of the shoebox. She had begun by trying to sort the contents on the coffee table by date and then by letter or postcard. The system started to fail after she'd run out of space within arm's reach, but she adapted by grouping the dates on the postmark into larger time spans. The earliest dates were from 1968, there was nothing else past the summer of 1975. They were all addressed to Judith.

There was a small, plain manila envelope at the bottom of the box and it stood out from the rest. The envelope was sealed, it was bulky and unaddressed. Aggie was saving it for last, and not in a 'save the best for last' kind of way, either. There was a very creepy feeling about the envelope and she was not looking forward to finding out its contents. Her ears prickled with pins and needles from the anxiety as she got closer to it.

When she got to the bottom of the box and the only thing left was the dreaded, bulky envelope, she pushed it aside and turned her attention back to the letters and postcards. The early letters and postcards were short and to the point, quick reports of Stephen's experience on the road and sights seen along the way to his destinations in California and Nevada. As time went by, the letters got a little longer as he discussed beautiful sunsets on a sandy beach, or some of the people he met along the way, such as a contact for a new account. Postcards were sent from interesting sights along the way and were marked with a quick 'Juju, Wish you were here, Love, Stephen.'

As time went by, she noticed that the letters and postcards became further apart and fewer in number. She also noticed that the tone changed. They were less chatty and lighthearted, instead he talked about feeling alone and out of place. He talked about how he stilled loved his job and meeting up with his accounts and talking business with them, but during his down time, everyone else seemed to be paired up but him. She sensed some bitterness in his words about being on the beach and watching all the couples, hand in hand, pass him by. He occasionally stated his desire to find a girl of his own, the right one.

And then it happened. She came across a letter that had Stephen had written in a scribbling hand, instead of his normal blocky script. It looked as if it had been written rapidly and with a lot of excitement. He talked about meeting a nice young woman, her name was Kate and she was beautiful. He described what he knew about her and how he had made up his mind to ask her out. Aggie looked up from the letter to the image on the laptop's screen. The name below the first woman on the poster was Katherine Baldwin, killed in May of 1971. Aggie turned back to the top of the letter dreading what she might see. It was dated May 3, 1971. Her heart sank into her stomach. *Surely, it's just coincidence.* She couldn't convince herself of it, though.

She took a deep breath and grabbed the remaining pile of letters and postcards. She fanned through the stack. The second to the last item she came across, chronologically, was a postcard to Judith. She turned it over to read its message: 'Juju, I've met a wonderful young woman who is going through a tough time. She needs help and a place to recuperate. I have invited her to stay with me. Her name is Freddie. You'll love her. Stephen."

The last, lonely item from the shoebox stood out clearly and had piqued her curiosity earlier. It was a different color from the rest, the only one with a light blue envelope. It was unopened. Her first pass through the stack had only been to sort them into date order. Now, she took the time to inspect it more closely and she was stunned. It was not addressed to Judith, it was addressed to W. Skylark at this very address. *Winnie. No. Freddie,* she reminded herself. Aggie looked at the name on the return address, Clara Bell, then at the postmark, September 20, 1975.

AGGIE TOUGHED HER WAY THROUGH THE REST OF THE LETTERS IN HER stack. Sadly, matching up the first names of four more young woman Stephen had described to Judith and intended to ask out, to photos and dates on the FBI poster. Her stomach turned as she looked at the last envelope in the letter box. The bulky manila one. She lifted it out and weighed it in her hand. Not too heavy, its contents slid back and forth smoothly as she tipped the envelope back and forth. Her thoughts swirled at what it could be, but she pushed those thoughts away for a moment. She would just have to do it quickly, the way you take off a Band-Aid.

But, Aggie and procrastination were old friends. She smiled to herself as she acknowledged this about herself. She grabbed the small, bulky envelope and brought it with her to the kitchen. Her mouth had gone dry two letters ago, she needed a drink before she could do anything more.

She walked into the kitchen and set the envelope on the table while she busied herself with a tumbler, ice cubes and a bottle of diet soda. *Too bad I don't drink bourbon.* She drank half of it down with no further thought, and then refilled her glass. She brought it around the table and sat down facing the envelope. Its plain wrapping mocked her. *It can't be that bad. Whatever you think it could be, it can't be that bad.*

It continued to mock her, she looked away. Her journal was still on the table, it had been open to her famous To Do List since yesterday.

She'd updated it this morning before watching the cold case program. As her eyes made their way down the list, she felt empowered by all the progress she had made. She'd come a long way in a short time and had accomplished things she never thought she could. Opening a small envelope was easy compared to what she'd been through in the last few days. Aggie reached for the envelope, resigned and determined to check one more item off her To Do List.

∾

A DEEP BREATH AND A QUICK TEAR OF MANILA PAPER AND THE envelope was open. Aggie turned it over in her hand and let the object inside slide out onto the table. It was a folded pocket knife.

Aggie slid back in her chair to put some distance between herself and the knife. Her heart was beating in her throat and her mouth had gone instantly cotton dry again. She pressed her hands against her thighs to still the trembling that had begun. For several seconds, all she could manage was a few 'oh my Gods'.

It took some time and a few of her decompression breaths, but she finally got a hold of herself. She took the pen from her nearby journal and poked the knife with it. She pulled it closer to her so she could really see it. It had cherry toned wooden inlay grips with stainless steel ends, there was a capital S on one side. *Stephen*. It looked old and well worn, the edges of the wooden inlay were rounded from, she guessed, years of handling.

Aggie was taking long, deep breaths and letting them out slowly. Her mind was swirling with images of the FBI poster, Stephen's letters, and her notes about the types of cuts the girls had. If she wasn't careful, she was going to throw up. It all pointed to one thing. But could it be true? Her stomach tried answering for her as it began to turn over on itself.

She thought at once of Judith and the look on her face that night watching the program. She'd already been connecting the dots and coming to terms with her conclusion. The same conclusion Aggie was coming to now. Stephen was the Broken Heart Killer. He had long since passed, but Aggie knew her friend well. She had always been steadfast in her sense of right and wrong. Justice might not be had, but at the very least, she would have wanted to give closure to the families of those women. Judith had just run out of time.

CHAPTER SIXTY-THREE

AGGIE JUMPED FROM HER CHAIR AND RAN TO THE KITCHEN SINK. SHE leaned over it, closed her eyes and waited. *Hang on, girl. Breathe.*

The lurching feeling in her stomach passed after a minute and she was grateful at being able to hold it back. She turned on the cold water and splashed her face with it. The cool water refreshed her and Aggie stayed there, bent over, cold damp hands on her cheeks. She focused on breathing in and out. Her heart beat slowed and her stomach calmed, at least enough to straighten up.

She grabbed a paper towel and dried her hands, then her face. An idea occurred to her as she held the paper towel and her stomach lurched once again. She closed her eyes, took one more deep breath and steeled herself, willing her stomach to settle.

"It has to be done," she told her stomach and herself, "I'm the only one here."

Aggie grabbed two fresh pieces of paper towel, one in each hand, and looked at the table. Once piece in each hand, she walked over to the table slowly and confronted the folded knife. It looked harmless, actually. It was just sitting there. It reminded her of a popular second amendment slogan, "Guns don't kill people, people kill people." She tried to convince herself it was like that with this knife.

She reached down for it, grasping it with the paper towel. Using the other hand, she positioned the paper towel gently over the closed blade, grasped it and pulled. Nothing happened and her hand slid off the blade. *Crap.* She held the knife up and looked at it more closely. She found the release mechanism on the side opposite the blade and positioned one paper-toweled hand there. The other paper-toweled hand grasped the blade as she pressed the release. The knife swung open in her hands.

Aggie held the blade up close so that she could see it better. She looked at the blade, at both sides, at base where it connected to its housing. To the untrained eye it looked relatively clean. But when she squinted, in her mind's eye and fresh from watching the murder channel's show, she imagined she could see the victims' blood seeping into the nooks and crannies of the hinge mechanism. Hiding in there for years, perhaps, and safe from regular attempts to clean the blade. *Maybe...*

BANG! BANG! BANG!

"Crap!"

Aggie jumped back, turned towards the noise and thrust the knife out in front of her. Her gut raced and filled with hornets. No measly butterflies this time. Something, someone was in the front hall. *How quickly self-preservation surfaces in a person*, she thought this as she brandished the knife.

Stephen. Her previous encounter replayed in her mind and played out in front of her simultaneously. The banging she'd heard was him falling down the stairs. The next sound she heard was the shuffle of him rising from the floor. Heavy footsteps ran down the hall towards the kitchen, towards her.

"Freddie!" Angry shouts bellowed towards her from the hall.

She held his knife out and tried to steady her shaking hand. She only had a second until he appeared in the kitchen, what should she do? Her mind swirled frantically for an answer. Her instinct was to run, again. But, then, she'd always be running. She squared her shoulders and steadied her outstretched hand. This was her home now, he had to go.

Stephen was in the kitchen doorway, large as life, dented head, sunken eyeball, bloody.

"Fred..." His cry was cut off as the moment he spotted Aggie. "Where's Freddie?"

As before, that was quickly followed by angry demands for her to get out of his house.

"Wait. Stop right there!" Aggie replied with a demand of her own. "Just stop!"

One still paper-toweled hand grasped his knife. The other hand was raised in the familiar 'stop' signal, fingers spread, palm facing Stephen.

"Where's F-freddie? Who are you? Wh-why are you in my house?"

"Freddie's gone, Stephen." His head tilted to one side at hearing his name, she was speaking calmly now. "She's been gone for a long time."

"N-no, she was just here."

"She's been gone for a long time, so have you." Aggie lowered her stop sign hand, but kept the knife at the ready. "Stephen," she used his name again and tried to steady her voice, "you can't keep chasing after her like this."

Aggie watched Stephen closely for his next move, he looked around, she assumed for Freddie.

"Yes, look around. Do you see that things have changed?" His one good eye swept the kitchen and the part of the living room he could see from the doorway. "This is my home now. I live here."

"No. This is my house," he argued and shook his head, but the anger was leaving his voice.

"It was. But then you had an accident. On the stairs. Do you remember your fall?" He tilted his head the other way. Aggie pointed to his head with the knife, "do you remember?"

Stephen raised a blood covered hand to his face, ran it over his injured skull and eye socket. Aggie's stomach lurched again and she took a breath and willed herself to hold on. Aggie felt safe enough to lower the knife to her side.

"You were sick for a little while, and then you were gone." She paused to let it sink in. "Judith," she remembered the postcards,

"Juju, lived here for a while after you were gone. She was my friend."

He turned his attention back to Aggie and the mention of his sister's name. "Juju's gone now, too. She gave this house to me." She repeated herself, "this is my house now."

Aggie and the Broken Heart Killer stared at each other from across the room. He wasn't going anywhere. *Crap.* He was listening but he wasn't getting it. She was trying desperately to say the right things. An instruction booklet would've come in handy, but she was going to have to keep winging it.

She tried again. "There's nothing here for you anymore. Freddie is gone. Juju is gone. Don't you want to rest? Aren't you tired?" Aggie let those questions sink in. "I will take good care of your house, I promise."

He was still there, but she thought that maybe he was finally hearing her. She gave it one last shot, she was just grasping at straws now and crossing her fingers, "Juju is waiting for you. It's OK to rest now. Don't you want to rest?"

Aggie held her breath and waited. She watched as Stephen straightened up. He looked her right in the eye. Several moments passed in silence and then his shoulders sagged. He finally nodded his head and Aggie exhaled. The blood on his face and clothing faded until it disappeared. Once the blood was gone, she could see that he no longer had a dent in his skull and he was able to look at her with two good, but sad, dark eyes.

He spoke just once more, "Juju," and then he, too, vanished right in front of her.

Aggie dropped the knife on the table as she felt her stomach lurch one final time. There was no stopping it this time. She just made it to the sink.

CHAPTER SIXTY-FOUR

AGGIE GROANED AT THE MESS SHE HAD JUST MADE IN THE SINK. SHE stood up, wrinkled her nose and held her stomach. She stepped back, away from the sink, to catch her breath and realized she actually felt better. Her stomach had finally succeeded in emptying itself, her hands had stopped shaking, and she was pretty sure that Stephen was gone. For good. She hoped. She hadn't been sure how she was going to get to this point, but she'd take it.

She stepped back to the sink to clean the mess. She ran the cold water and flipped the switch for the waste disposal until the mess had been washed away. She squirted a bit of lemon scented dish soap into the sink for good measure and soon it was smelling fresh again.

Aggie sat back down at the table. She felt hopeful, but didn't quite believe, that they were all gone. Billy, Freddie, Stephen and Judith. She had her house back. It's what she'd set out to do. In the process, she tried to help them out, as well as herself.

It was a win-win situation and certainly cause for celebration. No one could say it was inappropriate by any means. She had expected to feel victorious at this moment, but she just felt empty and sad. She felt their loss deeply and had trouble comprehending the entirety of all the connections she'd made in the last few days, lives she'd come in contact with that were now gone forever. She reminded herself that she had helped them to resolve their unfinished business and, hopefully, now they could rest in peace. That was no small feat and it gave her a measure of comfort and satisfaction.

Aggie looked across the table for her journal but Stephen's knife caught her eye first. It was still right where she dropped it. She left it there, for the time being. But, she knew what she was going to have to do with it, what Judith had wanted her to do, give closure to five families who'd been needing it for over four decades. She would put a box together with Stephen's knife, letters and postcards, and her notes along with the photo of her tree, and bring it all to the Arizona FBI office. It was one final thing she could do for Judith and for those families.

Still deep in thought, she pulled her journal closer and looked at her To Do List. There were only a few items left and initially she had saved the toughest for last. Now though, on this end of it, she felt prepared and more than ready to complete the final tasks. She felt empowered by her recent accomplishments. These last items would be easy. Well, they'd be easier than they would have been a few days ago.

Aggie smiled and enjoyed the peace and quiet her house was now filled with. It just felt better. No headaches, no goosebumps, no more banging and tapping. She looked back at her To Do List and then up at the clock. *Crap. Rider.*

She grabbed her phone and texted her friend. She told him she'd had a slight delay and was he still able to meet her at the diner, maybe in about an hour? She took the phone upstairs with her as she waited for Rider to respond. She needed a shower first. Rider's response chimed on her cell shortly after she'd begun lathering up.

AGGIE GOT TO THE DINER FIRST AND DECIDED TO WAIT FOR HER FRIEND in the parking lot. By this time, it was the slow period midway between lunch and supper so there was no reason to hurry in to save a table. As she waited, she took stock of her stomach and her appetite. She actually felt pretty good, and she was hungry enough to eat. The after effect seemed to be opposite of what you'd expect. Her stomach had settled and was actually growling. She was pretty sure she could handle more than chicken soup and crackers, which is what she'd thought she'd have to order.

Rider pulled into the lot and took the space next to hers. Aggie gathered her purse and met him at the entrance of the diner. She forced a hug on him, even though they had just seen each other a few days ago. He hugged her back after a moment, chuckling as he did so.

The two friends went into the diner, chose a table, and shared small talk until their orders had been taken.

"Guess what today is," Aggie said, trying to hold back a smirk.

"Umm, Sunday?" Rider raised his eyebrows at her as he answered.

"Well, yes. But you don't have any other guesses?" she couldn't contain her 'cat that swallowed the canary' smile any longer.

"You'd better just tell me, Ag." Her smile was contagious and he was smiling now, too.

"It's Someday," she raised her eyebrows at him and waited.

"Sunday? That's what I just said." He shook his head at her.

"No. Someday." Aggie said it slowly. "Someday."

"Ok, someday. What does that mean?"

Aggie took a breath and smiled, "Remember when you told me that Someday might never come? Well, you were wrong. Someday is today." Aggie slid a folded piece of paper across the table to him. "It's Someday."

Rider laughed and grabbed the paper, remembering their conversation, but not understanding. "What are you talking about?"

Rider opened the paper and looked it over. There were scenic photos from all over Europe and the British Isles. Some, like the Ponte Vecchio, in Florence, and the Eiffel Tower in Paris, were circled. Others had stars or question marks next to them.

"I'm taking your advice, and I'm taking you, too."

"What?' He shook his head, "I don't understand."

"Life is too short. I've found that out recently. The hard way. All we have is right here and right now. The only way we can be guaranteed a 'someday' is to make 'someday' today. I'm going to do exactly what you said. There are places I want to go and I have the money to do it."

"Aggie," he shook his head, "I lost the assignment. I told you. I'm not going to Italy anymore." He pushed the paper back to her.

"Yes, you are." She pushed the paper back, "you aren't working right now, so you can come with me. I'm not taking no for an answer, and I'm not going without you."

Rider sat in stunned silence, looking at the printout.

"I just picked these out quickly, but we can pick others if we want. If you want to go somewhere I haven't thought of, we can do that, too." The excitement had Aggie talking rapidly and pointing out locations on the paper.

"Aggie, I don't know what you're planning, but I can't afford all this."

She shook her head, "I can. That's the point." She glanced at the paper, then back at him, "we can."

"What about all your responsibilities with your new position? What about not wanting to let Judith down? What about the plans you had for your house?"

"I've changed my mind. And, I happen to have it on good authority that Judith would understand." Aggie looked Rider in the eye so that he could see how serious she was, "I'm going into the office tomorrow and quit."

"What?"

"They don't need me there, anyway." Aggie continued, "Judith was preparing to retire when she passed away, everything was almost in place to have her directors take over for her. I'm going to put her plan into action and save myself from the stress and pressure. Plus, I don't need the salary. I've got plenty."

The waitress stopped at their table to check on them, "how are you guys doing? Need anything else right now?"

Aggie nodded, "yes, please. I'd like a hot fudge sundae for dessert. No nuts." She turned to Rider, "you?"

Rider chuckled, looked up at the waitress and shook his head no.

"Aggie, you're not yourself," he reached across the table and felt her forehead, laughing, "are you feeling ok?"

"I'm actually feeling great and I've got so much to catch you up on." She pointed to the printout and smiled, "what do you think?"

"Oh no." Rider just shook his head and laughed, "what have I done?"

"We can go wherever we want. While we're gone, I'm going to have a bit of work done on the house. When I get back I'll open it up as a small B&B."

Aggie took a light blue envelope out of her purse and showed it to him, raising her eyebrows, "I just want to make one detour first."

ACKNOWLEDGMENTS

Thank you to all my friends and family for all of your support while writing this book. You'll never know how truly precious it was.

To my father, Roland, for all the great stories growing up.

To my mom, Martha, for giving me that first book to read, introducing me to Agatha Christie, and for your help from the other side. I miss you terribly.

VISIT MY WEBSITE

Visit my website to find out what else is happening and to sign up for my newsletter. You will receive information on upcoming books, giveaways, behind the scenes, events and other exclusive tidbits. It is completely free to sign up, your information is kept private, and you can unsubscribe at any time.

Visit my website: www.MichelleBaillargeon.com